PRAISE FOR ANDREW HUGHES' NOVELS

'Filled with twists and turns … a fantastic read'
Patricia Gibney

'The kind of writing that pushes you gently into a different
world then holds you there until the last sentence'
Donal Ryan

'*Emma, Disappeared* is compelling, unsettling and very creepy'
Catherine Kirwan

'A vivid piece of writing'
Irish Times

'Skilfully planned, elegantly written … a riveting read'
Sunday Independent

'A bracing, lurid tale that is as engrossing as it is chilling'
Irish Independent

'Compelling and eerily authentic'
Robert Goddard

'A beautifully crafted novel that is also gripping and powerful'
William Ryan

'So superbly written that it soars as a masterly
work of fiction. Utterly compelling'
Dermot Bolger

Born in County Wexford, Andrew Hughes is an author, archiv
and historian. His first book, *Lives Less Ordinary*, was a social histo
of Fitzwilliam Square, Dublin. His debut novel, *The Convictions o
John Delahunt*, was shortlisted for Crime Book of the Year at the
Irish Book Awards. His second novel, *The Coroner's Daughter*, was
the One Dublin One Book choice for 2023.

andrewhughesbooks.com
@And_Hughes

EMMA, DISAPPEARED

ANDREW HUGHES

HACHETTE
BOOKS
IRELAND

First published in Ireland in 2024 by
HACHETTE BOOKS IRELAND

1

Cataloguing in Publication Data is available from the British Library.

ISBN 9781399730938

Typeset in Arno Pro by Bookends Publishing Services, Dublin
Printed and bound in Great Britain by Clays Ltd, Elcograf S.p.A.

Hachette Books Ireland policy is to use papers that are natural, renewable
and recyclable products and made from wood grown in sustainable forests.
The logging and manufacturing processes are expected to conform to
the environmental regulations of the country of origin.

Hachette Books Ireland
8 Castlecourt Centre
Castleknock
Dublin 15, Ireland

A division of Hachette UK Ltd
Carmelite House, 50 Victoria Embankment, London EC4Y 0DZ

www.hachettebooksireland.ie

For my brothers
Conor, Neil and Kevin

PROLOGUE

9 DECEMBER

FOURTEEN DAYS AFTER SHE DISAPPEARED

In weather like this the first half mile is the hardest. Outside my place the footpaths are deserted. Traffic is heavy with an early rush hour. I run past the Botanic Gardens and the Tolka House, further up Glasnevin Hill to the high entrance gates of Addison Hall, a modern apartment complex. I follow a meandering road through the blocks, catching glimpses of people in the warm light of kitchens and living rooms. At the back of the complex the road ends with a pedestrian gateway to a communal park, just a wide grassy slope that runs down to the Tolka River. Away from the flats and the streetlights it barely feels like the city at all. The grass is speckled white, and for a while the wind blows right against me.

A footbridge crosses the river. Further on, the path skirts the tall grey wall of Glasnevin Cemetery, but to the left there's a railing almost swallowed by bushes and gorse. The other side is scrubland, an overgrown strip between the river and the graveyard and the rear wall of the Botanics.

I peer into the wilderness for more than a minute, then take a glance behind me. The park is empty except for one lone figure in the distance, her head bent against the biting wind. I grip the top of the railing, feel the cold seep through my gloves. Here in the park, I'm just a hardy jogger, out before the weather turns completely. I've no plausible excuse to venture beyond the railing.

Brambles scratch at my legs as I trudge through the undergrowth. I'm aware of the black flow of the Tolka somewhere on my left. My trainers leave tracks in the snow, but they won't last long. Up ahead a clearing is surrounded by stunted trees with bare limbs dusted white. I listen to the crunch of my own footsteps, watch the clouds of my breath. Beneath the trees is a sheet of corrugated iron, rusting and bent at the corners, with snow collecting in the grooves. I stand over it for a moment, reach down to grip one side, and pull it back.

In a rectangular patch of dark earth, the body lies swaddled in bedclothes and bin liners. A deep black stain has soaked into the ground. Woodlice scurry in the sudden exposure. Wind rustles through brambles like a whispering crowd. I don't move. I just watch flecks of pure white settle on the black plastic shroud.

PART ONE

CHAPTER 1

28 NOVEMBER
THREE DAYS AFTER SHE DISAPPEARED

We all have a 'missing person' photograph of ourselves – we just don't know it. Somewhere on our phones, or stored in the cloud, is that innocent sunlit moment that our friends and family will show the world should the worst ever happen.

Emma Harte is everywhere as I make my way to work. Her face appears again and again on lampposts and hoardings and shop windows. With the bus stuck in traffic, I wipe away some condensation for a better look. There's that ambiguous half-smile, that serene gaze at passers-by. She's on a night out, her skin pale in the camera flash, dark hair in a tight ponytail, a touch of red-eye. There are lines of text underneath: descriptive particulars and where she was last seen, contact details for anyone with information. And yet nobody is pausing to look at her. No one is paying any heed at all, except for me.

The bus moves off and passengers come upstairs for the last few seats. I move my bag and let it slither between my legs. A girl in an oversized scarf, bobble hat, and rucksack with a yoga mat slumps into the seat beside me. A strap from her bag falls onto my knee. She notices but doesn't move it.

From the bag she takes a slim laptop decorated with stickers of Studio Ghibli characters, opens the lid and presses the button, then stretches her neck one way then the other. A ticket inspector has followed her up. He's starting from the front, intruding into bubbles, making people glance up at harsh overhead lights.

Her Windows login screen is a personal photo, not one of those Alpine vistas or sun-kissed beaches. I didn't know you could do that. It looks like a selfie from her laptop camera. She's sitting on the floor of a living room, backlit by the grey-blue glare of a television screen, hair draped about her face like a headscarf, her tongue sticking out. Behind her, a man's bare foot is lounging on the carpet, cut off at the calf.

As she types, a string of asterisks sweep across the password box, but above that her name is shown for all to see: Libby Miller. I slip my hand into my pocket and take out my phone.

The ticket inspector has found a victim: a Roma woman who he says is using someone else's Leap card. He's demanding her ID, and she's pretending not to understand. She's right too, even if the card isn't hers. He has 'profiler' written all over him. I might say something, but another passenger gets up to squeeze by and afterwards the inspector moves on to someone else.

Libby Miller's desktop has a plain blue background with a neat array of folders. She opens a Word document and is scrolling past its title page: *A Postmodern Perspective on Merovingian Gaul*. She's not used to the touchpad and her elbow keeps rubbing my arm. I bring my phone close, tilt it away from her and google her name. Twitter and Instagram profiles are the first two results. I choose Twitter.

Her profile pic is No-Face from *Spirited Away*, the banner a sweep of misty hills, stone walls and fields from somewhere in the west. Her bio merely says, *Sometimes I write things*. She has 236 followers, including one I know: an independent bookshop in Phibsborough. Her photos are group shots of happy student types crowded around bar tables. In a recent one she's blowing out candles for her twenty-second birthday. I'm about to try Instagram when the screen shifts and *1 new tweet* appears at the top of the page.

I glance to my right. She had opened Twitter without me noticing.

As someone who writes essays literally at the last minute and doesn't proofread, I'm either an excellent writer or my professors don't give a shit #gradlife #priorities

She's swiping the touchpad to the top right, all set to minimise.

I press 'like', wait for the ripples in the electromagnetic field, see the tiny *1* appear on her notifications tab, watch the cursor pause, almost feel the endorphins released in her bloodstream.

She clicks, of course, and sees that James Lyster has 'liked' her tweet. She hovers over my name and a pop-up appears. My picture, a close-up of my face in black and white, fingers partially covering one eye. A *Repealed* twibbon at the bottom. My bio: *Curator of photographs at the National Library of Ireland; all opinions my own and probably wrong. He/Him.*

It seems rather trite looking at it now.

But I can sense her puzzlement. I don't follow her, and she doesn't follow me. How could I possibly have seen her tweet, unless I happened to be on her page?

'Tickets there now.'

The inspector stands above us, brandishing a handheld scanner. Libby Miller opens a Hello Kitty wallet to show her Leap card behind a plastic window. Naturally, he doesn't require her ID.

I place my phone screen-down on my lap. My paper ticket is in my side pocket. As I reach inside, I notice a corner of the pocket is torn, just a few threads, and a small smear of red runs along the seam. I'm not sure how I didn't notice before. I touch the stain, look at my fingertip. A tiny pinprick of glitter reflects the light.

'Before lunch hour if possible.'

I fish out the ticket and offer it to the inspector, move my hand at the last second so his thumb and forefinger pinches the air. He examines it like a guard on Checkpoint Charlie and hands it back.

'Your stop is coming up,' he says.

'Yes, I know. Same as always.'

He moves on. I gather my bag, turn to Libby Miller and say, 'Excuse me.'

She almost tuts but catches herself. Without a glance, she half-closes the lid of her laptop, not enough that it goes to sleep, and pivots her legs into the aisle. I brush her shoulder as I pass.

The bus makes a sharp turn into Kildare Street and I brace myself in the stairwell. I go to press the bell but hear it ting from somewhere else. Headlights sweep past the windows. I'm about to pocket the phone when I notice a notification of my own. Libby Miller is now following me. I could wish her luck with her essay but that might be pushing it. I notice something else. Emma Harte's name is trending in Dublin. So is the word 'Missing'. I close the app and put the phone away, follow a line of people as we trudge into the rain.

For a moment I think her face is displayed on the advertising screen in the bus stop shelter, but it's just a model, not unlike her, smiling broadly with *I'm Living Proof* printed in large letters. The screen flickers and scrolls and now she's winking. *Anyone Can Quit.* I cross the street in the wake of a truck, step over a puddle where small waves are breaking on the kerb. As I approach the library, I feel uneasy that I've forgotten my key card. I go to pat my pockets, but there's a homeless man bundled in a green-and-blue sleeping bag in an unused museum doorway, a sign above his head saying, *The Bog Bodies – A New Theory in Sacrifice.* I wait until I'm passed in case I get his hopes up.

I always like the library in the hour before it opens. The rotunda is hushed and dim, only the shuffled footsteps of staff as they go to their offices. I pass through the exhibition room displaying the love letters of Constance Markievicz, a blown-up picture of her by the door, and her quote to Irish women: *Leave your jewels and gold wands in the bank and buy a revolver.* I reach a side door, wave my card at the pad. A high-pitched beep and then a loud wooden creak.

The office that I share with two others is on the second floor. It's a wide space with old Georgian windows looking out over Leinster House, a marble fireplace with an electric fan heater in the hearth, three filing cabinets, framed prints from Audubon's *Birds of America*. Helena, Bridget and I have a large work table each, all facing different walls so we have our backs to each other. On my desk is a box of calotype photographs from the 1860s left out from before the weekend. Beside that, some sharpened pencils sitting upright in a grubby cup, three erasers of different coarseness, acid-free folders, a hardback copybook, my work laptop, a *Thom's Dublin Directory* for 1865. I turn on the computer and then go into the small kitchenette to make tea.

Helena comes in just as the water boils. I see her from the doorway unwrapping a long scarf. She's young, only a few years out of the library course. She likes vintage clothes, floral dresses and bright-coloured tights. She's smart and funny, but strangely lacking in confidence, affecting a kind of babyish voice when speaking on the phone, which grates after a while, and laughing loudly whenever she's nervous.

I call out 'Tea?' to her and she says, 'Please.'

Her mug has a picture of Betty Boop blowing a kiss. I rinse it out, re-use my own teabag because she prefers hers weak.

She's sitting by her desk when I come in, donning white cotton gloves, her computer whirring to life. I put the tea beside her. She smiles and says thanks and asks about my weekend.

'Quiet enough,' I say. 'You?'

'I was smothered with a cold.'

'Wonderful, now we'll all get it.'

'Did you see the news?'

I go to the fireplace, flick the switch on the heater with my foot. 'About what?'

'Storm Lauren is coming. Snowmageddon. The Beast from the East. The whole city will be shut down.'

'Oh,' I say, taking my seat. 'Something to look forward to.'

I remove the lid on the box and take out the picture on top. The collection comes from a studio in Dame Street, one that took after-death photos of families posing with loved ones who are propped up and dressed as though they are still alive – a child leaning against her deceased mother, or a father cradling his stillborn, or a sleeping toddler surrounded by toy soldiers. Often the poses are so natural that it's hard to say which one is the corpse. But there's always a tell. The long exposures of early photographs meant the tiniest movements of people resulted in a slight blurring of their image. The dead are always crystal clear.

In this picture, a middle-aged couple sit on either side of a single bed, a young woman reclining between them, her hands clasped on top of the sheets, rosary beads laced in her fingers. Her head is tilted and her gaze is off to the left. One side of her mouth curls up in what looks like a half-smile. Her grieving parents are stony-faced.

With a scalpel, I carefully remove the mottled card frame and begin to brush dried glue from the edge. The studio often noted on the reverse a few details in pencil, and I have to identify the sitters from the clues, match names to addresses, trawl through death records to confirm the date. People shudder when I tell them about the collection, and I've stopped trying to explain that the images are poignant and beautiful, that people needed something to blunt their grief, and what could be a better *memento mori* than this, literally to remember death.

No writing on the back of this one. I look at the young woman again, her tranquil gaze and crooked smile. Likely to remain unnamed forever. I rehouse her in a clear envelope of uncoated cellulose triacetate, place her in an acid-free folder, assign her a number, and lay her to rest in a fresh archival box.

The brass doorknob scrapes and turns and Bridget comes in saying, 'Fucking weather.' She shakes water from her umbrella – a stray drop blots one of my folders – and hangs it on the coatrack. She flicks her blue fringe away from her eyes and puts a Costa cup on her desk. A wisp of steam escapes the lid. 'The queue was mental, that's why I'm late.'

Bridget and I did the UCD archives course together three years ago, were part of a fairly tight clique that would go drinking and dancing. We even kissed once at the end of a night out, but agreed the next day not to speak of it again. After graduation, we began working in the library at the same time and have always shared an office. Six months ago, I was promoted ahead of her, and ever since she has made a point of reporting every slip and small transgression, as if daring me to reprimand her.

'Yeah, that's fine.'

She sits down and begins moving things on her desk. To Helena, she says, 'Did you see the posters?'

'Hard to miss.'

'You'd be fucking sick of it all the same.'

'Maybe she'll turn up.'

'She won't. Not alive anyway.' Bridget pushes the button on her computer a few times. When nothing happens, she rummages under her desk to plug it in. 'It's time men were put under a curfew.

Home by eight to watch the football like good little boys, and leave the rest of us in peace.'

I can feel Helena glance over her shoulder. She adopts a lighter tone. 'Well, that would hardly be fair on James. I know you shouldn't say, "Not all men", but there's some truth to it.'

Should I be lending my voice to demonstrate empathy? Or is this a moment to listen and be educated? I remember a good line I saw this morning in a comment section and try it out: 'Bridget's right. If men had to worry about walking home the same way you do, we'd be living in a police state within a week.'

But I must have gotten the inflection wrong, or perhaps they sense a lack of sincerity, for my contribution brings the discussion to a close. For a hushed hour the only sounds are the whir of the heater, the rain on the window, the soft tap of computer keys, and a tinny strain of Julian Cope coming from Bridget's headphones.

I jump when my phone pings. Two missed calls. Reception is sketchy in older parts of the building, and calls often go to voicemail. The lady with the automated voice tells me I have two new messages, one left half an hour ago.

Jim, buddy. Any chance you can collect Lolo from Loreto tomorrow? Looks like I'll be stuck in Chancery. Just put her in a taxi, or come over if you like. There's Hop House in the fridge and I'm sure Danni will feed you. Let us know, will you? My brother Colin. He's talking to someone else as he's hanging up. *No not that one ...*

The Vodafone lady speaks again in her strange staccato rhythm. A message was left three nights ago, at 2.17.

A few seconds of rustling static like white noise on an old TV settles into footsteps and a guttering breeze. A siren sounds faintly in the distance. Just at the edge of hearing there's a person's voice, though it's hard to tell if it's a man or a woman. The message cuts out.

I wait in case there's more, but it's just the automated, *To return a call to this person, press six.*

Why hadn't I heard it before? I open the phone log, scroll back three nights. There's the call from Arthur early in the evening asking if I wanted to meet in Fagan's pub. After that another red arrow for a missed call: 26 Nov, 02.17. It's an 089 mobile number, one of those Tesco pay-as-you-go jobs. Definitely not a contact. I hit *Options. Save number? Return call? Delete?*

'James.'

I drop the phone and it skitters on the table. I grab it and look in case the number dialled by accident.

Bridget says, 'We're going for a smoke. Looks like you could do with one.' She has her John Players in hand. Helena is holding a vape cartridge.

'No, I'm fine. You go ahead.'

They file out and I wait for the door to click shut. I swipe out of the phone log. No point in deleting it now. It'll stay in the records forever. I make more tea, return to my desk and try in vain to concentrate on work. I type 089 into Google and then stop myself. Assume that every keystroke and search can be retrieved and pieced together. I open a new private window to be met with the message: *Remember, private browsing doesn't make you anonymous on the internet! Your employer or Internet Service Provider can still know what page you visit.* I close it quickly and am left with the original Google white screen, the cursor blinking in the search box.

I move to Helena's desk and open the lid of her laptop. She'd been composing a message to a friend in her personal Gmail. It's littered with exclamation points. In a private window I search for the 089 number in quotation marks and get two returns. One looks like a malware site that's listing dozens of numbers. The other is a pdf from Irish Revenue, a list of tax defaulters, the mobile number attached to a company name – re:Thread Limited.

In the corridor outside I hear Bridget's voice, her broad Dublin accent like a Sean O'Casey heroine. I close the private tab, try to remember if Helena's Gmail was minimised or not. The door opens as I close the lid.

Helena is first through, and she pauses when she sees me at her chair.

'Everything okay?'

'I've lost my staple remover. Any chance I could borrow yours?'

'Of course,' she says, coming closer. She moves a sheaf of papers and gives me the little fanged device. The fan in her laptop is still whirring. 'I think it's yours,' she says. 'I nicked it a few weeks ago. Sorry.'

She flashes a smile and I say that she's forgiven. Bridget goes into the kitchenette. I haven't moved and Helena is looking up at me, her eyes round, questioning.

'Actually,' I say, 'I might go for a smoke after all.'

CHAPTER 2

While preparing for her trip, Sarah had taken her few changes of clothes from the wardrobe, the books she claimed were hers from the shelves, but she'd left the bottom drawer of the bedside locker untouched. I never emptied it. Not much to look through really – a few hair-ties and pins, a can of Impulse True Love body spray. I pop the pink lid, hold the nozzle to my nose and feel a pang, but only briefly. There's an empty wrapper of a Galaxy bar, and the book she was reading, *Northanger Abbey*. An old, tattered copy, probably one she'd had for years. From the pages, a bookmark slips and tumbles to the carpet – the cinema stub from our third date, *Phantom Thread* at the Light House. I pick it up, look at the date and time, the barcode, the torn perforated edge, see her standing again in the bright lights of the foyer, the large popcorn she regretted buying. She thought the movie boring and didn't like Jonny Greenwood's score. That should have been the first warning.

I'm searching for some manner of heavy-duty make-up cleaner but all I can find is nail polish remover. Acetone-free, it says. Gentle on nails; kinder to skin. I read that again and try to fathom its meaning. Would that work? I'd ask Alexa but the problem is she never forgets.

In the kitchen, the Marks & Spencer beef bourguignon is simmering in the pot. Steam coats the dark sash windows above the sink. I fetch a bottle of Nero D'Avola from the rack. On the counter is an elaborate wine opener that Colin gave me last Christmas; at least, he paid for it, no doubt Danni picked it out. It grips the bottle by the neck. A large handle plunges the screw into the cork and whips it out in one smooth movement.

After dinner in the living room, the wine is already past the bottom of the label, a fire glows in the hearth, *Phantom Thread* is playing on Netflix, and my coat is spread over the coffee table, the sleeves hanging and brushing the tasselled rug.

I look again at the stain by the torn coat pocket, apply a mixture of nail polish remover and spray-on bleach, and carefully dab at it with round cotton pads. It seems to do the trick. At least it's no longer visible to the naked eye. The time may have come for a new winter coat.

On the TV, Day Lewis's character Reynolds is measuring – I don't know the actress's name – Alma in her shift at the end of their first date, while his spinster sister jots the girl's particulars with pursed lips and sharp strokes of her pencil. Alma squirms beneath the tape, and Reynolds scolds her to stand naturally. It's so wonderfully possessive, inappropriate, I remember laughing in the cinema. Sarah didn't like that part.

Perhaps she was right, though, that the third act drags. My iPad is half hidden beside me. I turn it on and begin to browse, read stories of populism and prejudice until my mood sours. Out of habit I type Instagram into the browser, and it autocompletes to Sarah's account: SarahSibthorpe_16. Her latest post is a bazaar in Istanbul, a close-up of a porcelain cup on a table, mounds of different-coloured tea leaves on a stall in the background. The caption: I was recommended the Love Tea! Organic chamomile, elderflower, lavender, and liquorice ... can't hurt to try I guess! and then a wink emoji.

She only has a dozen followers, and only one has deigned to like this post – her oldest friend Polly. But Sarah was never in it for the 'likes'. She looked at Instagram as her own digital photo album, something to remember in her old age. I scroll through stages of a round-the-world trip seen in reverse: a walled city in Montenegro, an Alpine lake in Switzerland, her browsing books outside Shakespeare & Company in Paris, and from a month ago, a close-up of the departures screen in Dublin Airport, the 18.42 to Charles de Gaulle circled.

The post before that shows the two of us together. It was during the summer, outside a small Italian restaurant on Capel Street. I remember squinting up at the waiter who took the picture, the low sun a glaring halo around his head. I'm never good in photos. Sarah would tell me I just have to smile with my eyes, but whenever I tried I ended up looking deranged.

I close her Instagram and open my own Twitter. A few notifications: some random followers, probably bots, a couple of 'likes' on some old tweets. Colin has tweeted a newspaper article about the fees barristers have to pay in their first year of devilling, and I retweet it out of loyalty.

Emma Harte's name is trending ninth in Dublin. I follow an *Irish Times* journalist after reading his article on Brexit, and a CERN physicist who I heard on the radio promoting his book, and then, because I like to keep my lists gender-balanced, I search for a woman. I scroll through the accounts Twitter recommends and spot a young Labour politician running for MEP in Dublin. She'll do nicely. The next account that Twitter suggests is Libby Miller, and I follow her as well.

The last of the wine fills my glass. The fire shifts and settles. Reynolds and Alma stare at each other over an omelette that he knows she's poisoned. Her eye never wavers as he places the fork in his mouth. I click the lid back onto the nail polish remover and place it beneath the table lamp. Emma Harte ticks up one place in the trending list.

There's no harm in taking a look. It might seem strange if I didn't. The 'top news' result is from the *Irish Independent*, the photo from the posters above the tweet. The family of a young entrepreneur missing from her Dublin home have issued an urgent appeal and say they are very concerned for her safety. Trinity College graduate Emma Harte (24) was last seen … Here the snippet of the article cuts off and the rest is behind a paywall. Twenty-four. Same age as me. The next few tweeters offer prayers for her safe return, and I imagine the Harte family picking through platitudes, desperate for news.

Store Street garda station is showing a GIF of some grainy security footage taken somewhere along Capel Street on the night of 25 November, the night she disappeared. Emma Harte is wearing a dark blouse with no coat despite the cold. She leans down to the passenger window of a car, speaks with the driver for a moment, and then stands up as the car drives away. Emma folds her arms and wanders out of shot. The in-camera text at the bottom shows the time at 1.09 a.m. The GIF reloads and the few seconds repeat on a loop.

The tweet below that is from well-known commentator David Flynn, a contrarian conservative, the type who complains about being cancelled while writing his weekly column. Another potential tragedy in our fair city. Is it too early to suggest that our girls take more responsibility for their safety? Stay halfway sober, don't wander the streets alone, and make a plan to get home!

The condemnation is swift and brutal, just as he'd hoped. Young women are lining up to suggest ever more intricate ways in which he can fuck himself. He has stirred the hearts as well of young men with football club crests for avatars. Two fellas shot in Crumlin yesterday and not a peep! Some posh bint gets lost on her way to the jacks and its all over the news #doublestandards.

I take the last long sip of wine. Without really thinking, I quote-retweet Flynn's message and add, He's not even sure she's a victim yet, and already he's victim-blaming. Disgusting.

My thumb hovers over the 'Tweet' button, but only for a second. Before I can close the app, I get two new notifications: *Libby Miller has retweeted your tweet; Libby Miller has liked your tweet.* Three new notifications follow quickly, then a fourth. I go to my own page. Ten retweets already. I refresh the page and it jumps to fifteen. Nearly as many 'likes', and now a reply. I tap on it and see Libby Miller's No-Face. She has written, Thank you for saying that, James.

I like the formality of her tone, the correct use of punctuation.

I'm wondering if I should reply, or delete the original tweet altogether, when the title sequence of *Phantom Thread* blinks and goes black, along with the lamp and the small LED on the internet

22

box. I'm left in the dim glow of the fire and the iPad screen. A yellow exclamation mark appears on the Wi-Fi logo. I lift myself from the sofa and go to see if Whiteside is still awake.

My flat takes up the whole basement of an old Georgian house – well, built in the reign of William IV, but in the Georgian style. I feel my way through the hall to the front door, let myself out into the narrow space below street level and climb the stone steps up to the driveway. The night is still, freezing cold, a slight glistening on the roadway and halos over the streetlamps. Across the road is Addison Lodge, an old coach house of a pub shuttered for the last ten months, its car park dark and silent. A little further down is the entrance to the Botanic Gardens, hulking granite walls and wrought-iron gates, panes from the glasshouses visible above, catching the moonlight. Other homes on the street still have electricity, so it's not a general outage.

Whiteside doesn't answer the front door, and I don't blame him. Good news never calls to the house, especially at this hour. I try the lion-head knocker again and wait another minute. Footsteps echo on the path. A passer-by looks up, perhaps wondering at a coatless man shivering in a dark doorway. But then he does a double-take, smiles as though he recognises me, and keeps his eyes on me until he passes.

I go back to my living room, fetch the iPad to use as a torch, and climb the narrow internal stairwell to the ground floor. The door at the top is locked with a simple slide-bolt. It's a fire escape more than anything. I've never used it to reach Whiteside's part of the house, and he's not able to come down. The bolt is cold and stiff and gives way with a sudden clunk. I let myself into his pitch-black hallway. The tablet casts a pale gleam on a mahogany table and thick patterned wallpaper. Dark floorboards creak underfoot. I pass an ornate oval mirror, see a ghost of myself, and continue on.

The door to his parlour is ajar. He's asleep in an armchair beside a Superser heater, a low purr from the gas, two glowing panels providing the only light. He's wearing the blue dressing gown that he never seems to go without yet is always clean. An open book is tented over one leg, too dark to see the title. His head is tilted back, wispy hair neatly combed, his mouth agape. I approach, treading quietly even though I intend to wake him. There's a soft silvery stubble on his cheeks. His grey slacks have sharp creases running down each leg. I reach out to nudge his shoulder, feel a brush of satin beneath my fingers, then change my mind and retreat from the room.

The fuse box is in the press beneath the stairs. A clutter of coats and umbrellas and ancient golf clubs, Wellington boots, a coal scuttle and shovel, three copies of the Yellow Pages still in their plastic wraps. One of the fuse switches is pointing left. It snaps back when I try to move it.

A timid 'Hello?' is spoken from the parlour, and when I duck out of the cupboard, Whiteside is standing in the hallway, a fanlight of starry sky above his head, a fire iron brandished in one hand.

'It's only me, Allen,' I say, and turn the iPad towards my face. 'The power's gone.'

He remains still for a moment, then slowly reaches towards a light switch and flicks it on and off to no effect.

'James?'

'Did you not hear me knocking?'

'Jesus, you put the heart across me.'

Under the stairs we peer and prod at the fuse box some more, but neither of us is particularly sure how it works. He says he'll call a proper man in the morning.

In the kitchen, he rummages for candles and saucers and a cigarette lighter. He pulls a bottle of Powers from the cupboard and two glass tumblers. 'To keep the nip at bay.' A sliced pan has been left open on the counter as well as a knife, its buttery blade touching the Formica.

He plonks a tumbler with a generous measure beside me. 'Sorry for all this,' he says. 'Whole house probably needs rewiring.'

I tell him it's fine. Allen is a good landlord. All year long we barely say a word to each other, except on Christmas Eve, when much like now he invites me up for a glass or two before I head to Griffith Avenue. He has lived in the house since he was a boy, and I'm genuinely interested in his tales of Christmases past. My mother is always sad to think of an old widower picking at a roast chicken and over-boiled Brussels sprouts alone, and has suggested more than once that I invite him round to Christmas lunch with our family. I assure her that he'd rather die.

'You weren't … entertaining, were you?' he says.

'No, not this evening.'

'Ah good, wouldn't make a great impression.' He swirls his whiskey and takes a sip. 'You had a late one the other night though.'

Candlelight flickers on his brow.

'I did?'

'Last Thursday, was it? Or Friday. I heard you battling with the bins. It got me out of bed.'

I recall now, the wheelie bin by the railings, a broken crust of ice when I lifted the lid. I took out the bags on top to put a full black bin liner underneath. While replacing the bags, a beer bottle slipped out and fell to the pavement. Somehow it didn't break, but it bounced and rang in the cold air, rolled over the pavement and clinked twice against the kerb. All the while, without me knowing, Whiteside was above, framed in a dark window, bearing witness.

'Thought it was foxes,' he says.

'Sorry for waking you.'

He waves a hand. 'Not at all. Night out, was it?'

'Christmas drinks after work.'

His lips purse a little. 'In November?'

'You can't book anything any later these days.'

'Of course, yes.'

'Will you be all right here tonight? Can I do anything?'

'Oh, I know my way around this house. Even in the dark.'

We finish the whiskey and head back to the hall. The iPad battery is dead. Whiteside gives me the saucer and candle. My hands are full, so he opens the door to the basement stairs. He seems stooped and frail with the inky black stairwell beneath him. I thank him for the whiskey, brush past and go down a couple of steps. When he closes the door behind me, I don't slide the bolt, and for a moment we listen to each other until I hear his soft tread heading back towards the kitchen.

Down below, the radiators are electric, and all the rooms are cold except the living room, where the last of the embers still glow in the fireplace. I settle on the sofa and pull my coat over me. Outside, the wind picks up. A draught from the flue extinguishes the candle. I could rise and fetch a lighter, add more smokeless coal to the fire, drag in the duvet from the bed. But I stay huddled and watch the glimmer dwindle to nothing. My subterranean room becomes black and cold as the earth.

I arrive at work with tablet and phone and a tangle of chargers. Bridget and Helena are in the kitchenette speaking over the sound of the kettle. I think I hear my name mentioned and then a laugh. I need the socket from the heater, but there's a chill in my fingers, and a needle in my temple that hasn't come from drink alone. Helena has hand sanitiser on her desk and I dispense a dollop, rub my hands like a miser, dab some on my mouth and nose. The sharp smell of ethanol clears my sinuses, wakes me a little.

'Here he is. The celebrity in our midst.' Helena has emerged with her fingers laced around her mug. She's smiling, almost beaming at me. Bridget tuts on her way to her desk.

'What's that?' I say.

'You're a viral sensation.'

I look at her for a few seconds before I realise what she means. The tweet before the blackout. I'd forgotten all about it. On my work laptop I open a browser.

'You must have been up all night reading responses. I thought it was so cool how you rose above the debate.'

Twitter eventually loads. 2.3k notifications. A few hundred extra followers. Emma Harte is trending No. 1 in Dublin. David Flynn is No. 6. I click on his name, see his tweet and my response, and another of his messages directed at me. Once again, I'm condemned by the Woke Stasi for thought crime. I know where I stand with women and young girls, and I'll fight tirelessly for their safety.

I glance through some other mentions. An avatar of Emmeline Pankhurst has quoted me and adds: Men, if you want to know what ally-ship is, look no further #raiseyourvoice.

A bearded Karl Marx is more cynical. Another white knight looking to get laid. Trust me, ladies, if he tells you he's a male feminist, run a mile.

From Newstalk, a researcher asks if I'd be prepared to debate with Flynn live on air. A girl with pink hair and limpid eyes responds to that: Um, have we forgotten that a person, oh I don't know, is missing and hasn't been found yet.

@RationalApe says it's chilling that an employee of the National Library should be so quick to censor. Why not remove Milton, Paine and Locke from the shelves. RIP free speech.

Libby Miller answers that one. Flynn had his free speech, now we're having ours. Nobody's been put in jail. That's how it works.

In fact, for all the tweets that are most critical, Libby Miller has some response. She is curating the thread, drawing the ire of the most rabid but dismissing them coolly, goading them into ever more frothing and spluttering nonsense.

Helena is scrolling through my mentions on her computer, pausing occasionally to take a sip of tea. 'The most retweets I ever had was twelve when I posted a photo of that sign that said, "No signs allowed."' Bridget makes a point of taking out her phone. She tilts her hair away from her ears to put in headphones.

I open the 'direct message' tab, type in Libby Miller's handle. *Thanks for fighting my corner, Libby. I don't know how you have the patience. If ever I need a public defender, I'll drop you a line.*

I read it over. Perhaps using her name is too familiar. I take it out and then put it back again. Does the line about patience have the right tone? Could it be misread as, Don't you have anything better to do? No, it's fine. I click 'Send'.

I take out the photograph I was looking at last evening. Elderly twin sisters sit in rocking chairs in a Victorian parlour. Both are dead. Someone has made their fingers clutch the armrests. It's interesting because the fireplace in the background has a family crest beneath the mantel. I was going to speak to the herald of arms to see if he can identify it.

On my screen a *1* appears on the envelope icon. Libby Miller says, *Any time, James. It was unfair for you to bear the brunt.*

Not much to say in response, but she follows up with another message. *I see you're in D7. I'm in the same neck of the woods.*

I know, we get the same bus into town. *Yeah, I'm in Botanic Road. You follow Breen's Books as well. Lovely little place.*

My favourite. Was in there just last week for the launch of Harry Branagan's new collection. Do you know of him? He had a great turn-out.

'No' is a bit of a conversation stopper, so I say, *Yes, I know him well.* I'm in the National Library. I can get my hands on his work in a moment. *Couldn't make it to the launch though.*

No reply for a few seconds. Ellipses appear beneath her name. She's typing something. Either it's lengthy or she's self-editing.

A JPEG is attached to her reply. *Here I am with the man himself,* she says. *He has regular readings in Breen's. You should keep an eye out for the posters.*

The picture shows Libby Miller and Harry Branagan in the bookshop. Harry is sheepishly holding a slim volume. Libby has linked his arm, is leaning slightly towards his shoulder. A table in the background bears piles of books, a few standing open in front, a dozen empty wine glasses and some unopened bottles of red and white. Merlot and Chardonnay. Chilean.

She sent it to me so I'd know what she looks like. It's a flattering photo as well.

Sorry I missed it, I say, running low on platitudes. *I'll be sure to make the next poetry night.*

Another pause. Perhaps she logged off, or turned away, or answered a call. I didn't give her much to work with that time.

No-Face appears again. *Do you know Gilead on Leinster Street? If you want to grab a coffee some time let me know.*

I do know it. Wooden benches like you'd find in a GAA dugout. Vintage clothes and vinyl for sale in one corner. They serve kombucha but not Coke, gluten-free pizza and paleo brownies.

Libby follows up before I can respond. *Don't worry, I'm not a serial killer.*

No smiley face, no exclamation point. Nice and dry.

I work in Kildare Street, I say. *If you're in town we could get a drink some evening. Neary's on Chatham Street maybe?*

The ellipses roll back and forth, and the screen shifts a little.

Yes, I'd like that.

CHAPTER 3

29 NOVEMBER

Two girls dash from the steps of Loreto, anoraks draped over their heads, their skirts twisting in a sudden squall. They shriek and giggle and are past in a moment. Sleet swirls beneath the streetlamps in St Stephen's Green. A bus trundles by, and a spray of muddy water scatters pedestrians. Usually I'd wait outside, but I duck into the hush and warmth of the main hall, stamp my feet on the mat and unwrap my scarf. A security guard sitting behind a lectern eyes me suspiciously.

'I'm here to collect Louise Lyster,' I say. 'She's in third year.'

He dabs his tongue with a finger and turns the page of his *Herald*.

The hall is dim, mostly deserted, a few stragglers from evening study slipping by to brave the weather. A crucifix is affixed to an arch above a long corridor. Framed photos line the walls, team portraits from years past, sunlit smiling girls with camogie and hockey sticks. There's a vending machine near the door selling Ballygowan and fruit. For a moment I think it's plugged out, but then I see a strip of paper stuck to the glass. 'The light inside me has gone out, but I still work.'

Lolo emerges from a classroom, spots me and gives a wan smile. Black hair covers half her face, the other side is swept over her ear. She wears fingerless gloves and a brown satchel is slung over one shoulder. She comes to stand in front of me.

'All right, Jimmy.'

'All right, Lolly. I presume your dad has filled you in.'

'Yeah, stupid that he won't let me take the bus.'

'I agree completely,' I say. 'Not my decision though. Are you ready?'

She nods, tugs on the satchel strap, then pauses and blinks. 'Ah, shit.'

'Lolo.'

'Sorry. I left a book in my desk. Won't be a minute.'

She turns on her heel and disappears down the corridor. Wind whistles through the hallway as another student leaves. I look again at the sports photos. Each one is labelled by year, and the girls' names are listed at the bottom. In college I went out with a girl from Loreto. Ann Wall. She was on the camogie team as well. An image of her, smiling up at me, arms wrapped up inside my coat, face half lit from the glow of a Burger King, waiting for the Nightlink back to her flat. I figure out the year she would have been here, find the photo, the team assembled in a goalmouth, and scan the faces. There she is, middle row, far left. She and the girl beside her are sharing a joke, their faces creased with laughter. I really should look her up.

'Mr Lyster?'

A woman on the cusp of middle age is standing beside me, white blouse and navy cardigan, an anxious air about her.

'Yes.'

'I'm Miss Rafter. I've been filling in for Mr Sachs, Louise's economics teacher.'

She pauses to allow for comment but nothing springs to mind.

'We had an unfortunate incident today with Louise and two other girls during lunch hour.'

'Oh, well, I'm not—'

'I'm afraid I had to report it to the principal and further action may be necessary.'

'Why, what happened?'

'First, I should tell you that the school has a zero-tolerance approach to any form of suicide ideation. I'm afraid to say that Louise encouraged another girl to kill herself.'

I look down the corridor. Lolo has returned with her book, but she has stopped to watch from afar.

'That doesn't sound right.'

'I assure you, I overheard it myself.'

'What did she say?'

'She told Marie Dobbs that she should "uninstall her life".'

I regard her for a moment in silence. She seems completely in earnest.

'I'm not sure that qualifies.'

'You don't seem to understand, Mr Lyster, the school has a zero-tolerance—'

'I do understand. It's not a difficult concept.'

I think of hushed conversations I've had with Colin and Danni. Cups of tea in the kitchen. Worried faces. Lolo is going through a rough patch. The other girls give her a hard time. Danni is looking around for new schools, but everything is full up. I think of Lolo over the last year, the waning of her spirit, a weariness in her step.

'These two girls,' I say, 'Marie and the other one. What had they done to her?'

'Why, nothing that I could discern.'

'Perhaps you should be more discerning.'

'Mr Lyster, I know it's a hard thing to hear about your child—'

'I'm her uncle. You're speaking to the wrong person. But I'll be sure to pass on the message.'

She frowns and her eyes search my face, believing somehow that she's been deceived. She arranges her cardigan about her shoulders and turns away.

Lolo and I step out into the cold. She folds her arms and bows her head. Taxis are lined up outside the Shelbourne and we climb into the first. The driver's fingers are stained yellow. He glances at Lolo while adjusting his mirror.

On the radio, a news lady is talking about a violent break-in on an elderly resident of Cabra. Gardaí have noted a string of such offences in the run-up to Christmas, and they caution vulnerable people to remain vigilant. She then says that there has been a report of a second missing person in connection with the disappearance of Emma Harte. Thomas Wickham, the boyfriend of the missing woman, was thought to be staying with family in County Longford, but his parents have now stated that this was not the case. He has not been seen since the evening of Friday, 25 November, and gardaí have appealed for him to make contact.

The taxi driver tuts and changes the channel to a phone-in debate on immigration. He nudges up the volume. Icy sleet skitters on the windows as we inch through the traffic.

I half-turn my head towards Lolo. '"Uninstall your life?"' I say, idly. 'I'll have to remember that one.'

Lolo stays still for a moment. She wipes away some condensation with her forearm.

'Don't worry, I'm not going to tell your dad.'

'Tell him,' she says, 'I don't care.'

'Where did they get Miss Rafter from?'

'I don't know. She's new.'

'Hopefully she gets home soon. Her cats must be starving.'

I glance across but Lolo doesn't smile. The driver cuts into another lane, revs the engine, only goes a dozen yards before getting stuck again.

I could tell her that she's not in any trouble. In years to come she'll wonder how she let herself feel slighted or wounded by these girls. But it would sound clumsy coming from me, condescending, for how on earth would I know what she's feeling?

So instead: 'What are you reading?'

She looks at the book still clutched in her arms. 'For school?'

'No, at home.'

'You wouldn't have heard of it.'

'Tenner says I have.'

'How is that a bet? All you have to say is, "Yes, I've heard of it."'

'I'm scrupulously honest.'

She tuts and looks outside again. We pass under the railway bridge on Pearse Street, near the back entrance of Trinity where students are filtering out. I look in case Libby Miller happens to pass. Then I picture Emma Harte, wrapped up against the cold, bag slung on her shoulder, glancing this way and that before dashing through traffic for the DART.

'*Crank* by Ellen Hopkins. It's about a straight-A student who becomes addicted to crystal meth.'

'How did she get hold of crystal meth?'

'A boy she liked gave it to her.'

'Typical.'

Lolo turns to me, and when I remain silent for a few seconds she holds out her hand.

'This cab will cost more than a tenner,' I say. 'So we're quits.'

Traffic eases a little once we're over the river. The snow is beginning to stick to the footpaths. Shopfronts and bars give way to terraced houses and tree-lined streets.

Lolo is still gazing out the window, but she seems more relaxed. She says, 'How's Sarah?'

'That I don't know.'

'How come?'

'Did you not hear? There's been a conscious uncoupling. At least Sarah was conscious of it.'

'When?'

'Oh, I don't know. A month or so.'

'Christ, Jimmy, you can't keep doing this.'

'What?'

'Expecting me to get to know these women who just disappear from my life.'

'Think of it as auditions for the part of your aunt.'

'I liked Sarah as well. She was almost normal.'

'Yeah, that was the problem.'

At Colin's house in Griffith Avenue, I spy Mam's silver Accord parked in the driveway. 'Mother is here?'

'I think she was helping to mind Senan today.'

I should call in, but I can picture the scene. Danni at work on the island in the open-plan kitchen/dining-room/conservatory/ TV nook, Mam perched awkwardly on one of the breakfast stools, Ultan and Senan playing video games in the corner.

'I'll see her again.'

'Nanny's not pleased with you.'

'Why?'

'She says she hasn't heard from you in a fortnight. She says you wouldn't know if she was alive or dead.'

'Tell her I keep an eye on the death notices.'

A brief smile. 'I will.' She thanks me for the lift and steps out into the snow. There's a blast of cold air until the door thumps shut. Colin's driveway has security gates, and she takes a moment to punch in the code.

The taxi driver says, 'Where to now?'

'Just a minute.'

The gates swing open ponderously. A motion sensor triggers and lights come on over the garage. Lolo has her own key. She's framed in the doorway for a moment, then slips inside and is gone.

The driver half turns his face by the headrest, a waxy sheen on his cheek. 'Better safe than sorry, wha'?'

He takes me into town, pretends that he has no change when we're settling up, but I wait with the door open while he searches in dashboard cubbies and the armrest box. The back tyres skid in the slush as he drives off.

A piercing wind whistles in from the bay. People hurry over the Ha'penny Bridge holding collars and hoods against their faces. I stand for a minute on the quay and watch flakes alight upon the Liffey like ash. Capel Street is more sheltered, though patches of ice are forming underfoot. The pubs are fuller than usual for a Tuesday night. A few students stumble out of PantiBar, all dressed in garish Christmas jumpers. One girl bumps into me, grips my arm to stop from falling and says, 'Fuck, sorry.' Her jumper says, *Santa's Naughty List*. She totters after her companions in the direction of Temple Bar.

I stop at the next corner. Mary Street. There's the AIB, the spherical streetlamps, the outside of Slattery's. Just here, Emma Harte stopped beside the car. I look up and to the right. Three buildings down, beneath a gable roof, is the security camera. It's pointed straight at me. A red light blinking in the darkness. I imagine myself in a grainy box, sleet swirling in the streetlights.

Slattery's feels uncomfortably crowded and warm. Liverpool are on the big screen. A swell of noise as Salah breaks free, and then curses when he puts it wide. I get a beer and take it upstairs to an empty table by the window. On my phone, I find a GIF of the security footage and let it play on a loop. I compare the scene below. There's the bollard on the pavement. The same square padlock on shuttered windows. Emma leans into the passenger side of the car, stands and watches as it drives off, then she turns in the direction of Mary Street, her hand brushing the top of the bollard. I look at the bollard in real time. A dusting of snow clings to one side.

The GIF loops. While she's leaning into the car, a man is walking on the opposite pavement. His head turns as though he's been called, though perhaps he's just noticed raised voices. The car sets off again. Just before it leaves the frame its right indicator comes on. Emma's hand grazes the bollard. The loop begins again.

A lounge girl comes by to throw down some beer mats. I scoop up the phone and sit back. In the bar below, the crowd cheers. She points at my glass and asks if I'd like another. I hadn't noticed that it was nearly drunk. I shake my head, tell her that I should brave the weather. She smiles, though I don't think she understood. Before I close the GIF I note the time again on the security footage: 1.09 a.m.

Everyone I pass on the way home is bundled up in hats and scarves, faces turned against the cold wind. I try to keep a normal pace and take the most direct route. Security cameras are everywhere. It's only when you're looking that you notice. Traffic cameras at busy junctions, CCTV pointed at bar doors and ATMs, lenses affixed to streetlamps. Once you're off the main road there's hardly any. Whiteside is closing the curtains of his sitting room just as I reach the house. The lights are on. He must have called someone to fix the power. In the well of the basement, snow is collecting. I check my phone once I'm back inside. Thirty-five minutes of a walk. That seems about right.

CHAPTER 4

2 DECEMBER

In Hodges Figgis bookshop, the corner for Irish poets is hushed and dim and empty as a church. There on a shelf beside Boland and Bolger is Branagan, a few copies of his recent collection, *Hinges*. The cover image is a Rorschach test inkblot, a symmetrical swirl of black and grey on white. 'Pelvic bone' is the first thing that springs to mind, but I wouldn't tell a psychologist that. A sticker on the front says, *Signed by the author,* and I open the title page: *Best wishes, Harry B.* I suppose even poets are sometimes stumped. When I peel the sticker it leaves a gummy disc, so I replace the book, take an unsigned copy, and bring it to the till.

Upstairs in a café on Grafton Street I find a seat by the window, order tea, and lay *Hinges* on the table. It's a good vantage point. Patches of snow linger on the rooftops opposite. Wet slush covers the pavement in front of Neary's. Still twenty minutes before I'm due to meet Libby Miller.

I leaf through some pages. Not as bad as I feared, though too many of the poems are anecdotal memories of Branagan's working-class childhood, of the 'My gran had a mangle in the scullery' variety. I make a mental note of some of the titles in case it comes up in conversation. The coffee machine clanks and sputters and I glance down. Libby Miller is approaching Neary's – four minutes early. She's wearing the same woollen bobble hat that I saw on the bus. Twenty yards from the pub she takes it off and pauses to stuff it into her bag. In the reflection of a shop window, she gathers her hair and sweeps it over her right shoulder.

At the pub she lifts her head to look through the windows of the bar, then goes another few steps to check the lounge. She turns and her gaze sweeps up and over the café I'm sitting in. A sudden movement now would make me conspicuous, so I stay still until I'm sure she hasn't seen me, then draw back from the window.

She's coming this way, weaving through pedestrians, searching her bag for her Hello Kitty wallet. She enters the door below. I pour the cold dregs from my teapot into an empty mug so it looks like I'm not sitting here with nothing. Colour it with a drop of milk. Should I put the book in my satchel? No, it gives me something to focus on, and it's charming in a way if she sees me with it. I plant my elbow on the table and rest my chin in my palm as Libby reaches the top of the stairs. There's only ten or so tables, half of them occupied. She doesn't look around as she approaches the counter, just greets the barista with a cheery hello, picks out chewing gum and a granola bar from baskets near the till and pays by tapping her card.

I could go to her now. Make a joke of it. 'Great minds think alike' or 'Libby Miller, I presume.' But it's too bright, too noisy and cluttered. Another moment's caution as she exits. I put *Hinges* away, take an unused napkin and fold it in my pocket. As I don my scarf, I see her emerge below, and I follow. When I reach the bottom of the stairs, she's already at the corner of Chatham Street. This time at the pub she doesn't pause. She pushes open the door and marches inside.

The bar in Neary's is a long Victorian affair, dark wooden panels and gas lamps, a curved marble top. Red leather seats line the wall, with a row of small round tables and bar stools. It's busy enough with the after-work crowd, though there are seats available. Libby is leaning on the counter trying to get the barman's attention. I wander past, make a show of scanning the tables. She spots me in the mirror behind the bar, turns and says, 'James.'

She's a head shorter than me. There's an amused slant to her eyes, a dusting of freckles around her nose. Her lips, curled up at one side, are full and a little dry. She has a slightly crooked chin, but it gives her face a determined set which is at once endearing.

'Yes, indeed. Libby?'

She nods, smiles more deeply, and holds out her hand. As I shake it, the clock above the bar clicks and whirs and begins to strike six. She grips my hand a little tighter, and says, 'Right on time.'

'Sure, I'm only down the road.'

'What are you having?'

I'm about to say, 'Not at all, it's on me,' but her gaze has become steady, and I sense that to quibble would count against me. 'A Hop House, thanks very much.'

'Pint or a bottle?'

'Oh, a pint I think. I'll find us a table.'

There's a spot at the back near the corner. One seat looks along the length of the bar and the other faces the jacks. I let Libby have the seat with a view. She arrives drinkless and says, 'He'll drop them over,' unwraps her scarf and folds her coat over the armrest. She's wearing a roll-neck sweater, peach-coloured with leather patches on the elbows. From skinny jeans she takes an iPhone and places it on the table, pushes her bag beneath her chair and sits down. The unlock screen has been activated, and the word *Emergency?* gleams beneath the number pad. Libby looks at it for a second, daintily dabs at *Cancel* and then turns the phone screen-side down.

The barman arrives, places a pint of Guinness in front of me and the Hop House in front of Libby before turning away. We smile at each other and swap the drinks over. I rotate the glass so that the Hop House logo faces towards me.

I say, 'I was a great disappointment to my father for never having a Guinness.'

'And I'm a disappointment to mine for being so unladylike.'

'I'm sure they'd have gotten on famously.' I raise my glass. She clinks it even though the stout hasn't fully settled. We take a drink. Unselfconsciously, she wipes foam from her lip.

'So,' she says, 'we might save some time if we admit to what we've gleaned from each other's social media.' Her eyebrow arches a little.

'Who goes first?'

'You do,' she says. 'Then I won't feel so bad for stalking.'

'Okay, let's see. You come from a small town in Mayo, Ballyhaunis maybe. You're doing an MA in medieval studies in Trinity. You procrastinate, at least that's what you want people to think. You like Studio Ghibli and local poets. You don't take shit from Twitter trolls. Oh, and you're a budding writer, but you haven't published anything yet, or posted stuff online. I checked.'

Libby has folded the corner of a beer mat and she smooths it out again. 'Quite the sleuth.'

'How did I do?'

'Claremorris.'

'Pardon?'

'I'm from Claremorris, not Ballyhaunis.'

'My condolences.'

Her phone rings silently, the screen glowing against the tabletop. She ignores it.

'You're a Dubliner,' she says. 'You've a brother who's a barrister. You went canvassing in the last two referendums. Both times for "Yes".'

'Of course.'

'You don't have an Instagram account, but that might be because you catalogue photos in work all day.'

I hadn't thought of that. Perhaps she's right.

'You were going out with someone called Sarah until fairly recently.' She pauses to gauge my reaction, so I frown and look to the side.

'Doesn't ring a bell.'

'And you're a feminist, or at least that's what you want people to think.' She smiles again to let me know that she's just repeating my line. 'Isn't it a relief to move past the normal getting-to-know-you chit-chat?'

We talk for a while about her master's, compare notes on old professors. Before I did the archives course in UCD I studied history and English at Trinity, and she points out that our time there overlapped. While I was a senior sophister she was a junior fresh. 'We might have passed each other in the library,' she says with a smile.

Libby is easy company. Her eyes focus when she listens. She knows when to be attentive or teasing or self-deprecating. She's observant as well, picking up on the fact that I referred to my dad in the past tense. She delicately asks about him, senses that I don't want to dwell, and fluently moves the conversation to another topic. I'll have to be careful around her.

I keep an eye on her glass so as not to outpace her, and when she's almost finished, I say, 'Same again?'

'Please.'

After I order I ask the guy if he can drop the drinks over, but he doesn't lift his head from the tap. 'Bit busy, bud.' I watch Libby in the mirror. She has her empty glass in one hand, phone in the other, her face pale in the screen light. When I return with the drinks, she seems a little disconcerted, and I ask if all's okay.

'Fine, yeah, sorry. It was just my friend, Miranda. There was something on this evening I forgot about.'

'Oh, if you—'

'No, no, she'll be grand.' She takes her pint and sets it on a mat. 'I don't want you to think … like, this wasn't a bailout call.'

'Yeah, I know.'

I hadn't thought of that, but she'd have hardly sent me for drinks if she wanted to escape.

'What's the thing?'

'Her first debate for DUGES. I was just meant to go for moral support.'

'DUGES?'

'The Dublin University Gender Equality Society.'

'Is that FemSoc?'

'In all but name. We're not allowed to say "feminist" because that would mean the society has taken a political stance, which is against the rules.'

'So feminism is a political stance but gender equality isn't?'

'According to the rules, yes.'

'Jesus.'

'I know.'

'What's the motion?'

She holds my eye for a moment. 'That this house supports a sex strike by women.'

'I see.'

'She's against it.'

'At least there's that.'

Libby picks up her phone. 'I'll just text her good luck.'

'Really, if you want we can scull these and go. Cheer her along. Hiss at her opponents.'

'You wouldn't mind?'

'I feel it's important that the motion is defeated.'

Libby smiles at me. She backspaces her text, puts the phone down and picks up her Guinness. 'All right, so,' she says. 'Drink up.'

Arthur Stokes sits at the end of the bar in Fagan's, right beneath the TV, where he guards a pile of newspapers and the remote control. He's young to be a barfly, but he's a natural. We were in secondary school together, where his fine grades and polished manners convinced my mother of his good influence. In Trinity, he studied law while I stayed in arts. He achieved a first as well without much effort, was headhunted by a firm in Merrion Square, but in his first year he blundered in a big case and never quite lived it down.

I take the stool beside him without a word, lift my finger to Kenny, who fetches a glass.

Arthur doesn't glance from the football pages. 'Thought you'd be in earlier.'

'I was on a date.'

He leans back to look over my shoulder, sees there's no one there and resumes reading. 'Dare I ask?'

I give him the short version, how the evening had started well enough, that even the trip to the debate wasn't too bad despite the atmosphere, the lighting, the smell giving me freshman flashbacks. Libby's friend Miranda had just begun her speech, railing against the notion that women should have to leverage sex for rights to which they were already entitled, when there was a kerfuffle outside. Members of the all-male Knights of the Campanile had set up a protest at the very idea of the debate, with bullhorns and chants and beating drums. The feminists went to confront them, leading to a noisy standoff in Library Square. College security wisely decided to remain in their cabins. I suggested to Libby that we slip away, but she couldn't leave her friends on the barricades, and so we called it a night.

Arthur listens to this with a pained expression. He says, 'These are the people that end up in government. It's no wonder we're fucked.'

A pint is set before me, and I draw a line in the condensation.

He says, 'Had a bit of good news today. About Mrs Featherstone.'

'Oh yes?'

'Her other kidney has given up the ghost. Won't be long now.'

Colin still sends business Arthur's way now that he's freelance. Probate work, in particular. In a poky office above the Centra in Drumcondra, Arthur has the wills of twenty or thirty rich boomers locked in his safe. For fees he can charge three per cent of the value of the estate, and one a year is enough to keep him in funds. He just needs them to die first.

Cold air swirls as the door opens, and two men come in. They look around as if they find the place quaint. One of them peers at the ad break playing on the TV and spots the remote by Arthur's elbow. 'Any chance you can turn it over to the match?'

Arthur frowns, runs a finger over the weekly fixture list. 'No one's playing tonight.'

'Sky Sports 1. Gloucester versus Toulouse.'

He tuts and turns his back. 'Would you ever fuck off.'

Kenny says, 'It's on in the lounge, lads,' and when they go through the dividing doors, he says to Arthur, 'I've told you to be nice.'

'If you give the rugby guys an inch the place is finished.'

The second half of the news comes on. Emma Harte's face is on the studio backdrop. The newsreader speaks over a clip, but the volume is too low to hear. Still-images scroll by of Emma in a college gown holding her degree, the close-up photo used on the missing posters, footage from the security camera in slow motion, the exterior of her parents' house – a semi-detached somewhere in Clontarf. Arthur turns up the TV at the tail end of the report. *Gardaí have renewed their appeal for information on a dark blue Volkswagen Passat. Anyone with information should contact Store Street garda station.*

Arthur takes a drink and says, 'Miss Harte, Miss Harte, you were up to no good.'

I glance at him. With a straight finger he pushes his glasses up the bridge of his nose.

'What makes you say that?'

'Kenny, there's a funny taste off this stout.'

'The lines were cleaned yesterday.'

'That must be it.'

Arthur does that sometimes, ignores a question to see if you'll ask it twice. I watch the news for a while until finally he says, 'The car in the CCTV. The guards say they're still looking for it, but they have the plates. If the car is off the grid, then the driver is dodgy. And the girl seemed pretty familiar with him.'

'Could have been someone looking for directions.'

'That's why God gave us Google Maps. Seems the boyfriend has vanished now.'

'I saw that.'

'I hope he has his story straight.'

'Maybe they ran off together.'

'And maybe she's at my place rustling up my favourite supper.' Abruptly he folds the paper, entrusts me with the remote and stands up. 'I'm going to head. I might visit Mrs F in the morning, see if she wants to add any codicils while she's still compos mentis.'

'Don't accidentally unhook her dialysis.'

'You know me. Terrible butter fingers.'

In the small take-out waiting area of the Chinese across the road, I fish out the half-beer mat with Libby Miller's number and add it to my contacts. Is it odd to text her on the same evening? When

I ask Google's advice I'm met with several articles along the lines of, *Are Young People Ruining Dating? Have you been breadcrumbed (strung along by your crush with random texts and 'likes' on your social media)? Or stashed (kept in reserve in case some other hook-up doesn't work out)? Or ghosted (completely ignored when you thought you'd had a fun time)? Welcome to the not-so-wonderful world of dating Generation Y.*

The hatch opens and a brown paper bag is thrust out. On the street, a police car passes by, lights flashing but no siren. A covered alleyway runs along the side of the restaurant, where a kitchen worker has slipped outside to have a smoke. She's leaning against the wall, framed by the arch of the tunnel, softly lit by some red and blue neon. One glove is half rolled over her thumb and the heel of her hand so she can swipe at her phone. When she takes a drag of her cigarette, she becomes wreathed in smoke, a pale, shifting swirl in the icy air.

Later, I start awake on my sofa, remnants of dinner on a plate beside me. The lights are dimmed, the TV on standby. My phone has pinged with a text from Libby Miller. I open it up. No written message, just a photo, a selfie in the half-light, her hair loose and hiding her face, the collar of the peach sweater she was wearing covering her chin.

It's gone midnight. I sit up and look at her, tap out of the picture and back in to ensure there's no hidden text. I scroll through my own messages in case I sent her something without realising. Is she drunk? Does she want me to reply in kind? I've never taken a selfie in my life and don't feel like starting now. I could ignore it – what did the article say? – ghost her, till the morning at least.

I tap on *Reply*, try to think of something pithy. So you got home okay?

The question mark disappears, then the k, the o, as I backspace it all away.

What harm to send a picture? Who knows where it might lead? I hold the phone at arm's length, tilt it slightly. The first few are too dark to see much. I leave the phone on the sofa, go to the dimmer and raise the light levels slightly, look at the room critically like a set designer. I open the top button on my shirt, then close it again.

My phone rings, vibrates itself over the cushion. Perhaps she grew tired waiting. I scoop it up, but Libby's name isn't shown. The strange 089 number shimmers in the black screen. I stop myself from hitting *Decline*, just let it ring. I could answer and not say anything, see if it's a man or a woman, if they know my name. Finally, the room becomes silent. I wait for the message that I have one new voicemail, but it never comes.

CHAPTER 5

3 DECEMBER

For a moment when I wake, I think everything's all right. There's a gleam of morning light at the edge of the blind, a stillness in the bedroom. I think of Sarah pottering in the kitchen, pulses from her Nutribullet while she fixes a Saturday smoothie. But there's no pillow on her side, just my phone with the *1 missed call* from last night still displayed.

The selfie that Libby Miller sent me is open as well. I never replied. Easy enough to pretend that I'm just seeing it now. When I check her social media to see if she's awake, I see that she posted the picture on Twitter about the same time she sent it to me, with a single-word caption: Mood.

One of her friends has responded – a couple of emojis with love hearts for eyes. I 'like' Libby's tweet and toss my phone aside.

She texts me soon after. You going to Tolka House later?

It's a pub not far from here. She hadn't mentioned it last night. For drinks?

Her response is just a link to RTÉ.

Gardaí have appealed for volunteers to help in the search for missing woman Emma Harte. It follows the discovery last evening of a mobile phone believed to belong to Ms Harte on the grounds of the Tolka House in Glasnevin.

Gardaí have described the discovery as 'significant'. Specialist diving teams will conduct searches in the Tolka River, while gardaí will draft in locals to help search the adjacent floodplain of the Tolka Valley. Volunteers are asked to assemble in the car park of the Tolka House at 1 p.m. on Saturday.

I call Libby, listen to the ringtone repeat, though I know she must have her phone to hand. At last, she answers, her voice so quiet that at first I'm not sure it's her.

'Libby, it's James.'

'Oh, hey.'

'Did I wake you?'

'No.'

Music is playing her end, Tame Impala. 'I had fun last night,' I say.

'Yeah, me too.'

She seems distant, distracted. Perhaps she's upset about the picture. 'Are you okay?'

I hear her rouse herself. She says, 'Yeah, fine. It's just weird,' and she giggles a little. 'No one calls anymore. It's all instant messaging.'

'Oh.'

'Good weird. You're an old-fashioned kind of guy.'

'We can continue by text if you like.'

'No, no, we'll have to finish what you've begun.'

She's walking now, and she turns down the music.

'So, Tolka House,' I say.

'Yeah, crazy that it's so close. A few of us from DUGES are going.'

'Was Emma Harte a member of the society?'

'I don't think so. She was a Trinity student though. It just feels like the right thing to do.'

'I suppose.'

'And James, you shouldn't talk about her in the past tense.'

Good advice.

Frost has lingered on the pavements. I keep to the grey perimeter wall of the Botanic Gardens, pass the pyramid roof of Our Lady of Dolours, Mother of Sorrows. Across the bridge, the Tolka House sits at the bottom of Glasnevin Hill. It's an old two-storey hostelry of a pub, double gates on one side leading to a car park.

Police vans have pulled in at the back. A dozen or so volunteers huddle in hi-vis vests. Next to a foldout table a woman is seated with clipboard and pen. She's wrapped up against the cold in a duffel coat, matching mittens and scarf, and a trapper's hat with fur-lined flaps covering her ears. She spots me as I pass and says, 'Volunteer?'

When I nod, she asks me to sign in. 'Just put your name and address there, and your time of entry. Good man.'

Libby's name is at the top of the page, her signature small and neat and slanted to the right. I make a note of her address: 4 Munster Street. Her friend Miranda is on the line below. They're housemates.

The woman sees me writing and says, 'Lots of locals here today.'

'I'm sure.'

'Are you all alone?'

In the bleak sunlight the question seems rather pointed. I gesture at the sheet. 'I'm friends with these two. I just have to find them.'

From a cardboard box she takes a hi-vis vest. 'Just make sure to sign out when you come back. We don't want to lose any of you.'

The car park is wide, bounded by the rear of the pub and a low stone wall, with the Tolka River flowing to one side. Near a slipway another police truck is parked, a motorised dinghy mounted on the back. The two girls are close by leaning against the wall. Libby Miller smiles at my approach. Miranda's look is more aloof, perhaps suspicious, but with a hint of forbearing, as if she's willing to give me the benefit of the doubt.

She says, 'You ducked away last evening just as things were getting interesting.'

'Yeah, sorry, it seemed you had the situation well in hand.' To Libby I say, 'Any more of your friends arrive?'

She makes a show of looking about. 'I don't think so. I was expecting one or two others.'

'It is freezing after all.'

Miranda wiggles a thermos flask. 'Would you like a sup?'

'I'm good.'

'Can you believe they charged six euros inside to fill that up? Gougers.'

She speaks with an odd air of excitement, as if she finds the occasion vaguely thrilling.

'Any word on what we're supposed to do?'

'Those guys will be talking to us soon,' Libby says, pointing to a pair of gardaí bent over a map on the bonnet of a squad car. A woman stands a little to the side, wearing a close-fitting burgundy coat, dark tights and brown shoes. Her face seems familiar.

Libby sees me watching and says, 'Emma Harte's sister, Clara.'

'How do you know?'

'I've seen her on the news with her mother. Appealing for information.'

Miranda says, 'Funny how none of Tom Wickham's family are ever on the news frantic with worry.'

Libby says, 'What do you mean?'

'Emma's boyfriend. He's supposed to be missing as well, and yet they don't seem nearly as worried.' She raises an eyebrow sceptically. 'I wonder why.'

Clara Harte is scanning the car park. Her gaze sweeps past me and doubles back, lingers for the briefest moment before she looks away.

I tell Libby and Miranda that I have to use the bathroom, skirt the crowd of volunteers and head to the rear door of the pub. A wave of warmth as I go inside, the smell of a carvery, the drone of a football match. To the left is a small corridor leading to the gents, with a noticeboard for the local pitch and putt, a window that looks over the car park, and a payphone.

Clara is speaking with the gardaí by the map. A breeze lifts one of the corners and it settles again. I pick up the receiver, drop a euro in the slot, find the 089 number on my own phone and dial it on the greasy blue buttons.

I keep my eye on Clara as the ringing begins. She becomes still, pats her pocket, pulls out a phone and looks at the screen. I take a breath and try to think of something to say.

A click as the phone is answered but no one says hello. I move the receiver away from my face, cover the mouthpiece. Outside, Clara taps out a brief text and puts her phone away. I listen to the earpiece. Only silence, except for the low jingle of a radio ad.

A whispered voice says, 'Is that you?' and I hang up. A tinny clatter as the coin drops. My hand is still on the receiver when the payphone rings. I lift it, hang up immediately, and leave it off the hook.

As I step back out into the yard one of the policemen yells out, 'Could you gather round, folks? Let's get going while the light is good.'

I fall in beside the girls. The debriefing is short, mostly common sense. Don't touch anything. Always be aware of your own safety. This is Dublin – there'll be a piece of litter for every square metre, so only mark something that looks recent and out of place. I look around for Clara Harte, but she hasn't joined the group. Instead she's near the entrance gate, speaking with the woman in the trapper's hat.

The police take us through a small gate in the back wall, where another garda is stationed, handing out wire markers to each volunteer like miniature pliable golf flags. He gives me half a dozen and then places his fingers on my shoulder.

'Is there a reason you're not wearing your vest?'

The fluorescent yellow bib is still stuffed in my pocket. He could have just told me to put it on, but they have to frame it as a question. Libby pauses for me to catch up. She tuts and says, 'Troublemaker.'

Scrubland stretches before us, a shallow slope of thick gorse, nettles and tall grass. The floodplain is surrounded by tall evergreens with apartment blocks peeking over the top. About twenty searchers have gathered, mostly young women, a few boyfriends dragged along, an older couple dressed in hiking gear. We form a line, are told to stretch our arms out either side and to keep that distance with our neighbours. Libby's fingertips brush mine. For a moment we look like an austere Pilates group, shuffling about in the wilderness until we get it right.

And then, without much fanfare, we set off. The pace is set by the gardaí dotted among us, slow, plodding strides, their lowered heads moving side to side in exaggerated diligence. The air is icy and still, the sun casting long shadows in the brambles. Across the river are the footpaths and high walls and manicured lawns of the Botanic Gardens, and further on, a sea of gravestones in Glasnevin Cemetery. One of the police has a dog on a long leash, an Irish red setter loping this way and that in the undergrowth, her tail wagging. A cadaver dog maybe. I wonder how she knows to ignore dead rats and ferrets and fallen fledglings. There must be something peculiar about humans. Back at the wall, a man is holding a TV camera on his shoulder, a woman beside him is pointing out things to film. He pans slowly across the line of volunteers. I look about. The rank has become ragged. I'm in the lead so I slow my pace. Already a few wire markers have been planted in the ground. We trudge on watchfully, like refugees in a minefield.

An hour passes. The sun dips below the trees, draining the landscape of colour. Cold is seeping through my boots and gloves. The only thing I find is a John Player's carton stuck in some thorns. It's too worn to deserve a flag, but I feel like I should mark something so as not to waste the afternoon. I wait for Libby to come alongside, and say to her, 'Anything?'

'A few beer bottles back there.' She shakes her head. 'They looked old though.'

Miranda is yards behind. She has left a trail of flags in her wake, leaving nothing to chance.

The dog barks, and everyone looks towards her. She's dancing around a small thicket of furze, scrabbling in the dirt and then nosing the legs of her handler. She barks again, begins to dig in earnest and is pulled away. The other policemen are marching towards her. Every volunteer has stopped dead as if afraid to move. The handler looks at his sergeant approaching, but already he's nodding his head gravely.

Libby puts her hand over her mouth and whispers, 'Oh, God.'

I put my arm around her shoulder and look across the river to the Gardens and Cemetery, and the patch of wasteland in between, quiet and undisturbed.

We're told to walk single file back to the car park, where we deposit our vests and wire markers in a cardboard box so they can be used again, like Christmas decorations. Behind us, in the distance, the police are gathered in the furze. I feel like they should be unrolling police tape, erecting cordons and white forensic tents, but they're standing about as if uncertain what to do.

A wind whips up. Icy sleet skitters on rooftops and bonnets. I suggest to the girls that we warm up inside the pub, hoping that Miranda will make her excuses, but she leads the way and holds the door open. We sit in the corner near the fireplace and front window. I order three hot whiskeys, ignore the barman's grumbles as he goes to put the kettle on.

Libby warms her hands on the glass. Her coat is draped on the armrest. She's wearing a navy sweater with the sleeves pulled up, a loose neckline so I can see the shadow of her collarbone.

'I don't know why I thought she'd still be alive,' she says.

'They never are.' Miranda is wiping a trace of old lipstick from the rim of her glass. '*We* never are.'

'I think most missing people turn up,' I say, and catch myself from saying 'actually', the favourite word of mansplainers everywhere. But Miranda has sensed it. Her eyes flick to me for a second and then back to her drink. I turn to Libby. 'You're right, though. I had a feeling it would turn out okay. Maybe because it was on our doorstep.'

'Maybe,' she says. 'Or because we all went to the same college. I mean, she graduated the same year as you.' She shakes her head slightly. 'I just don't know what we were hoping to find.'

I watch a tendril of steam rise from my glass. 'If I went missing, I'd want people to search for me. Perhaps that's all it is.'

For the next hour policemen come and go. Word filters among the punters about what's happening. A dozen mugs of tea are prepared and brought outside on a big tray. One garda rolls in a long extension lead. He searches about for a socket, accidentally unplugs the TV projector, to howls of protest. In the gents, I stand next to a whistling detective at one of the urinals, his white forensic jumpsuit unzipped at the front. On my way back to the bar I see the receiver of the payphone still off the hook. I listen to the dial tone for a moment and then place it back. The cadaver dog has been brought inside. She's sitting by the fireplace with a bowl of water and a bone of mutton.

Someone new is at the table. Miranda introduces him as Paschal, editor of the DUGES newsletter. He has floppy fair hair and a neatly trimmed beard. He's wearing navy corduroys turned up at the hems, what look like tan-coloured golf shoes, and pale lemon ankle socks. As I take my seat, Libby unconsciously leans towards me.

'Yeah, I tried to be here earlier for the search,' Paschal says while tapping on his Samsung. 'Couldn't get away. Just awful news.'

Miranda has her phone on the table and has been absentmindedly scrolling. She pauses, sits up and says, 'For fuck's sake, Paz. What are you at?'

She turns the phone to show us the latest tweet from the DUGES account: **Body found behind the Tolka House. On site now. RIP Emma Harte.**

He says, 'It's not as if it's a secret.'

'Could you not have used your own account?'

'That doesn't have as many followers. Anyway, it's good for the newsletter to get a scoop.'

'But her family mightn't even know yet.'

'Not our fault if the police can't do their job.'

I take out my own phone and look at the feed. It's plugging society events for the most part. A lecture on 'The Creep of White Liberal

Feminism'. A seminar on setting up your own OnlyFans account. Paschal's latest has a dozen retweets already.

Before him there's a nearly full bottle of India Pale Ale. Miranda has slowed down and is still on her second drink. Libby says to me, 'Do you want a Hop House?'

'Yeah, please.' I lean back as she squeezes by. Paschal watches as she goes to the bar. He lifts his chin a little when he looks at me. 'Postgrad?'

'No, I work in the National Library.'

'Ah, very nice. A cushy number in the civil service.' He flashes a smile that he probably thinks is disarming.

'Are you a medievalist like these two?'

'Christ, no, the very opposite. Engineering, with a focus on nanotechnology. My thesis is on plasmon-enhanced upconverting nanoparticles.'

You don't say. 'Final year?'

'Yeah, but the society demands a lot of my time so I might end up deferring.'

Miranda giggles to herself and says, 'Again.'

Paschal waits in silence until she glances at him. 'Second year was hardly my fault though, was it?'

Miranda's cheeks colour and she says, 'God, no, of course. I'm sorry.'

His gaze lingers, then he turns to me and smiles again. 'All ancient history.'

Libby returns, which is a pity as I was beginning to enjoy the tension. She has a Hop House for herself as well, and when she sits down she turns the pint glass so that the logo faces towards her.

Outside the window a white van pulls up. Four people climb out the back, dressed head to toe in white overalls, hoodies tied at the chin so that they encircle the face, blue surgical masks and latex gloves. They're walking unhurriedly, chatting to each other as they disappear through the side gates. A silver Mercedes parks beside the van, and an older man in whiskers and tweed emerges.

Libby is craning her neck to see. 'That's Matheson, the state pathologist. I've seen him on the news.'

Paschal traces a Z to unlock his phone. He opens Twitter. 'Hah, would you look? Garda HQ have quote-tweeted me. "Contrary to media reports, there has been no positive identification of the remains found this afternoon in Glasnevin. Speculation at this stage is unhelpful and may hamper the investigation."' He lifts his bottle by the neck. 'Nothing gives a story legs like official denial.'

Matheson has stopped to talk to a forensic technician near the gates. The latter holds a shovel over his shoulder, the blade slick with mud.

Libby rests her fingers on the rim of her glass. 'It must be so hard for that Clara girl. I mean, obviously losing your sister like that is awful, but for the boyfriend to be missing as well. She probably knew him, and liked him. And people are bound to say he did it.'

Paschal says, 'I can't see Wicker doing something like that.'

She looks across the table. 'You know him?'

'Not all that well. He was in Phys Soc when I started college, but I think he graduated the year after. Seemed like a sound enough fella. Not the murdering-your-girlfriend type.' He considers this for a moment and adds, 'Well, certainly not the burying-her-body-in-wasteland type.'

Miranda says, 'Well, who did it then?' and Paschal widens his eyes and says, 'I suppose it could have been anyone.'

Libby looks out at Matheson again. 'Usually I walk into town, go for a jog some evenings. I won't be doing that for a while.'

Paschal is shaking his head. 'That's the wrong attitude, Lib. If we keep teaching girls to inhibit themselves, instead of teaching boys not to attack women, it'll never change.'

'Well, it's a bit late for our generation.'

'But isn't that the same as victim blaming?' he says. '"Don't go out alone because you might be harmed, be conscious of what you wear, don't drink too much." We all piled on Flynn the other night for saying just that.'

Miranda fishes a clove from her glass with a teaspoon. 'The difference is that there could be a killer on the loose.'

'Oh, it was some randomer. An opportunist. Hardly a serial killer. I just think it would be an insult to Emma Harte's memory if her example was used to reinforce oppressive social structures.' He shrugs his shoulders almost wistfully, then gestures at me with the neck of his bottle. 'What do you think?'

'I think you should listen to these two.'

'I am listening. It's called having a discussion. I was wondering what your opinion is.'

Libby puts her hand on my arm. Paschal's eyes flick towards it. She nods at the window and says, 'Look.'

The cameraman and reporter from earlier are standing across the street. The reporter makes a frame with gloved hands and peers at the Tolka House, then points to where they should set up. Nearby, a garda in neatly pressed uniform has his cap tucked beneath his elbow. He's fixing his hair in the reflection of a car window.

The barman switches over to the news, and when a picture of Emma Harte appears in the montage of headlines he turns up the volume. There's a report on the discovery made behind the pub, and the newsreader hands over to their crime correspondent, Susan Mitchell.

A small cheer goes up among the drinkers when the front of the pub is shown live, its façade lit up in the gloaming. Mitchell is speaking earnestly to camera, and there's some hushing so we can hear what she says.

She introduces the garda spokesman, and the camera zooms out and pans to get him into shot. It's strange to glance outside and see the backs of their heads, the glare of the camera light, the silhouette of the microphone.

He confirms that human remains were discovered in the early afternoon, and that gardaí have begun a full investigation into the circumstances of that person's death.

Mitchell says, *It was widely shared on social media that this discovery is in some way related to the disappearance of Emma Harte.*

The garda has been nodding through the question. *Yes, we are aware of that. But we can categorically rule that out. For one thing, the deceased person found today is male.*

Miranda touches her face and says, 'Oh, thank God.'

CHAPTER 6

5 DECEMBER

I'm conscious of every call I make, every internet search, in case it can be cast in a suspicious light. It's perfectly fine for me to ring the office from home with my mobile, of course it is, but still I pause before I tap dial. I'm relieved when Helena answers rather than Bridget, then slightly frustrated waiting for her to get through her sing-song greeting.

'National Library of Ireland, Photographic Archive Digitisation Project, this is Helena speak—'

'It's only me, Helena.'

'Oh, hi, James. How're you doing?'

'Fine. Well, not so fine really. I got a terrible dose of something over the weekend. Don't think I can make it in today.'

'Oh no.'

'Should be okay tomorrow. Is Bridget in yet?'

She pauses, trying to think of a good way to put it. 'I don't think I've seen her.'

She's hardly behind the filing cabinets. It's almost 9.25. Bridget's starting to take the piss.

'You can hold the fort for the time being. I'll email later to let you know if I can come in tomorrow.'

She tells me to stay warm, to drink lots of orange juice. She's beginning to hum a tune as she hangs up.

The nearest public library is in Drumcondra, only a few minutes down the road and across Griffith Park. A lone jogger passes along the frosty path, her ponytail bobbing and clouds of breath rising in her wake. I cross the footbridge that spans the Tolka and leave the park by the eastern gates. The library looks like an old schoolhouse built in the 1930s, red and white brickwork and barred windows.

Inside, the reading room is mostly empty. A woman in a shabby mac is reading her newspaper beside Irish non-fiction. The small kids' area is empty except for some strewn picture books and an oversized abacus. On a table in the corner sits a bank of Dell computers facing the wall.

A man with cropped hair and round glasses is half hidden behind a stack of books on the front desk. I show him an old, lapsed library card and he says he can update it in a jiffy. He calls up my profile, reads my name and address from his screen in a voice louder than I'd like. 'You don't have some other ID on you by any chance?'

All I have is a work card which I fish from my wallet. He sees the National Library logo and says, 'Ah, straight from Central

Command. You won't find anything here that you can't get in there.'

'At least here you can bring the books home.'

'That's true.'

'The computers, do I have to book them in advance?'

'Usually, yeah, but if they're free you can just sit down.'

'I might use one now then if that's okay.'

'Take your pick.'

I choose the one in the very corner, shake the mouse to wake it up. The left-click button is polished and shiny. Some of the lettering on the keyboard has worn away. The computer clanks and whirs into life.

I could have gone to an internet café, but at the end of every hour-long stint on a library computer the temporary files, internet history and cookie caches are wiped clear. It's to stop sessions bleeding into each other, so that some young girl in uniform and pigtails researching her essay on Mary Robinson doesn't stumble across the previous guy's proclivities for adult nappies and frilly bonnets – though we're not allowed to kink-shame these days.

Also, the library computers have access to subscription websites: genealogy and academic journals, encyclopaedias and newspaper archives. I open up the ProQuest portal for the Irish papers, and search for 'Emma Harte'.

The most recent article from the *Independent* was published this morning, telling of the failed search on Saturday. The body discovered swallowed in the furze wasn't Tom Wickham, just a homeless man who had died in the scrubland during the summer and had lain unnoticed, unmissed ever since. Last Friday, the *Examiner* reported an appeal for information from Emma's family on their doorstep in Clontarf. There's a picture of her parents by the gates of a semi-detached. Her father in a navy overcoat and plaid scarf, his arm clasped tightly around the shoulder of his wife: peach puff jacket, hand half covering her eyes, grey roots in beige hair. And there's Clara, Emma's sister, lurking in the background, her arms folded, looking to the side as if someone has called her name.

Their home address isn't given, but the angle of the photo shows the footpath skirting the neighbouring houses, and in the distance a T-junction with the colourful edge of a Spar sign just about visible. I open a new tab, google *Spar Clontarf* and a map of the suburb is shown with three Spar shops marked. Only one sits at the top of a junction, and I zoom in to it.

The road it looks down is Victoria Avenue. I pluck the yellow ragdoll and drop him into the map, walk down the avenue in Street View, occasionally twist about to keep the Spar in sight. The pictures are from the summer, with the trees and gardens in full leaf, but I spot a gate that matches the one in the paper, black ball finials atop stone pillars, silver iron railings, a BMW saloon parked in the driveway. I click and pan about to get a good view of the house. The number is 56. I wonder if Emma Harte was indoors when the picture was taken. There's a ghost of a figure in an upstairs window. Probably just a trick of the light.

More library users have come in from the cold. The librarian is helping a young Polish guy make copies of his CV. A mother has deposited two toddlers at the kids' table. She has hushed their squabbling twice already but now seems to have given up. Her meander through the bookshelves has brought her to the DVD section.

Before last week the name 'Emma Harte' had hardly been mentioned in newspapers. There's one article from *The Irish Times* four years ago:

TCD Grant for Young Entrepreneurs

Recipients of the first annual Eoin MacNeill Award for emerging social entrepreneurship were announced yesterday.

The top grant of €100,000 went to re:Thread, a green company based in Dublin that aims to halt fashion industry waste by repurposing textiles destined for landfills.

Emma Harte, one half of re:Thread, said the money was a much-needed investment and a great boost for environmental businesses. Her partner, fellow Trinity third-year student Tom Wickham of Granard, County Longford, plans to expand to Galway and Cork over the coming year, with eyes ultimately on London and Paris. 'The future's green,' he said after the gala awards dinner. 'With this money behind us, some hard work, and a bit of luck, the sky's the limit.'

A picture of the couple is printed below the article. She's wearing a red evening gown, low cut with a simple gold-chain necklace. Her hair is straightened and tied back in a tight ponytail. Wickham has a slight sardonic edge to his smile, a square chin and dark eyebrows. He's the one clasping the Waterford glass award.

I google *re:Thread* and click on their site. It's just a dead link, nothing but a *This domain name is for sale* holding page. In the newspapers I search Tom Wickham's name. It's common enough, and it's tricky to sift through the local politicians, the GAA team sheets, the births, marriages and deaths returned in the results. I spot an article from the *Longford Leader* dated three years ago:

Suspended Sentence for Granard Man

In the District Court, Thomas Wickham (21) pled guilty to possession of 100 grams of cocaine with intent to supply. The drugs had a street value of €6,000, and Mr Wickham received a six-month sentence, suspended for two years.

When I google his name I stumble upon a new Reddit page from r/truecrimeireland. It's a little-used sub, with about half a dozen people discussing the Emma Harte case. Like Miranda the other day, Redditors are sceptical of Wickham's disappearance. The user WhiskeyJack1980 says there are still rumours in Longford that he's holed up in one of his parents' many properties. Why did they wait so long to report him missing? he asks. Four whole days is a long time to keep quiet. But plenty of time to plan someone's escape …

    I have a Reddit account, though I haven't used it in years. I try to remember the login details and get it on the third attempt. u/ArchiveJimmy – something more anonymous would be better, but it will have to do. I open a map of Granard and reply to WhiskeyJack's thread.

I can confirm those rumours, Jack. Friend of mine saw him in Gallid a few nights ago. Another friend delivered pizza to him in a house in Tromra. He's hiding up there, all right, and he's doing a shit job of it.

On the internet, all you need is cast-iron certainty and a sprinkle of local flavour. WhiskeyJack replies at once. I knew it. Keep us posted on other sightings, Jimmy. Same goes for everyone on this sub.

I reply with a quick, Will do. I link the *Longford Leader* article and add, Something to chew on.

In the library a voice says, 'James ... James Lyster. I thought it was you.'

The young mother, now holding a *Downton Abbey* box set, stands behind the computer desk. Up close I recognise Pauline, Sarah's old school friend, one of the few she kept in contact with over the years. I've met her four or five times when dragged out to get-togethers. A bit of a trial, maudlin after a few drinks, overly flirtatious, forever complaining about her useless gamer husband and nightmare kids. Sarah once said, 'She's my closest friend, but I never liked her.'

'Hello there, Polly.'

It would look bad if I started closing tabs so I stand up and come around to her. She seems slightly taken aback, then she smiles and comes half a step closer.

'I didn't mean to interrupt,' she says.

'Oh, it's nothing. Internet's on the blink at home, just catching up on some emails. Are those your kids?' I say, gesturing towards the children.

'Yeah, have to get out of the house for a few hours. We're all a bit stir-crazy.' She's flicking a tomato-based stain on her sleeve, realises that she's just drawing attention to it and stops. I wonder what tone she'll take when she brings up Sarah – berating? sympathetic? Instead, she just asks how she is. 'I never got a chance to see her before she headed off.'

'As far as I know she's fine.'

She frowns a little. 'Are the two of you not … ?'

'Oh, we're taking a little break while she's off on her adventures.'

Polly's eyes fill with concern. 'I'm sorry, James. God, she never tells me anything.'

'I'll be grand. Who knows what might happen when she's back.'

She nods and smiles sympathetically. 'Well, I'll leave you to your work.' She puts her hand on my forearm, lets it linger a second longer than she should, and turns away.

I hadn't planned on doing so, but the mention of Sarah prompts me to check her Instagram. The latest post, a selfie in the middle of a bridge spanning the Bosphorus, the wind sending her hair streaming across her face. The caption says, **Next step, Asia!** then a Turkish flag and a love heart. The post has more views than usual, and even a 'like'. From LibbyMill. When I click on the name I'm taken to Libby Miller's feed.

Why would she look up Sarah? And why would she engage? Did she just feel sorry for someone posting into the void? I think of Libby scrolling through Sarah's old photographs, judging her tastes, her dress sense, even finding pictures of me, and I feel a swell of irritation. Perhaps even resentment.

That afternoon I stay on the sofa and flick between *Judge Judy* and *Forensic Detectives*. I'm debating whether to open a bottle of something or abstain until later for a few drinks with Arthur, when there's a knock on the door. While walking down the hallway I hear the beep and static of a police walkie-talkie. I stop and stay still. Whoever's outside doesn't respond to the radio and after a moment the knocker bangs again. Above the door is a rectangular fanlight. No other way to see in except the Chubb keyhole and the letterbox. Would he peek through those? Beside me the door to the bathroom is open and I slip into the windowless darkness just in case, lightening my tread on the tiles.

A squeak, a small clatter and a papery flutter. He did open the letterbox but just to put something through. I hear him climb the stone steps and I approach cautiously in case he can see through the fanlight. A folded sheet of paper is on the doormat. Emma Harte's missing poster, but this one has a garda logo and the contact details are the local station.

> Emma Harte hasn't been seen since Friday 25th November. If you have any knowledge of her whereabouts, or noticed anything unusual on that date, please contact the gardaí.

From upstairs I hear the faint chime of Whiteside's doorbell, and after a few moments the click of a latch and the ponderous creak of his front door.

Over the guttering wind and hum of traffic I can just make out the voice that greets him – a woman's.

'Sorry to disturb you. We're just going door to door in connection with the missing person, Emma Harte. Have you heard about her case?'

Whiteside says, 'Yes, I read about it, the poor thing.'

A passing bus muffles her response at first. Then: 'Her phone was found not far from here so we're asking everyone locally if they noticed anything on the night of Friday 25th. You know, a couple having a row on the street, or a strange car parked somewhere, that kind of thing.'

'I can barely remember what I did this morning. Last Friday, was it?'

'No, the Friday before that.'

'Let me think.'

He'd hardly remember me struggling with the bins, would he? Hardly think of bringing it up now.

She grows tired waiting for an answer. 'Well, if you do recall something, be sure to ring the number on the sheet here.'

'Oh, I will.'

'We're also asking if we can check people's back yards, sheds and garages and so on. Sometimes a missing person goes in for shelter and can't get out again.'

'Heavens. Well, all we have is a bit of an old shed. The garden is accessed through the flat downstairs, but James would be at work.'

'Yes, I tried a few minutes ago. Are you the landlord, do you not have keys?'

'I wouldn't want to go in without his say-so. He should be home in an hour or two if you want to come back.'

'Sir, we have a lot of houses to check. It would be a great help to knock this one off the list. Our main concern is finding Emma, hopefully safe and well.'

He's going to agree. I look down the hallway. Should I climb into bed, pretend I'm at death's door? I could burrow back down on the sofa, turn up the volume and say I couldn't hear. But in both those scenarios I'd be on the back foot, so I open the door, step out into the stairwell and call out, 'Hello?'

The heads of Whiteside and the policewoman appear over the railing. She's in plainclothes, a long grey mac, mousy shoulder-length hair falling about her face as she's looking down.

Before she can speak, I say, 'Sorry I couldn't come to the door. I was in the jacks. Everything okay?'

Whiteside says, 'I thought you'd be at work, James.'

'Bit under the weather, Allen. Should I come up?'

'No,' the woman says, 'I'll come to you.' She thanks Whiteside for his help. He glances over the railing once more, steps back into his hallway and shuts the door behind him.

I'm reading the leaflet when she arrives on my threshold.

'Sorry to disturb you,' she says. 'I was just telling your landlord that we're going door to door in connection with …' She trails off, and when I glance at her she says, 'I know you.'

Her eyes search my face, wander over my shoulder into the hallway. I try to place her. She's in her thirties, slightly flushed. Her blouse is low-cut. No scarf despite the cold.

'James … Lynam, is it?'

'Lyster.'

'You never signed out.'

'Pardon?'

'At the Tolka House last Saturday. Three volunteers didn't sign out. You were one of them.'

I see her now, the woman in the trapper's hat with the clipboard. It never occurred to me that she was a detective.

'Oh, yes, apologies for that. The weather turned so a few of us warmed up in the pub. I hope you didn't send a search party.'

It's only as I say it that I remember we were part of a search party. Will she think it clumsy, crass, thick?

'Did you know Emma Harte? Is that why you volunteered?'

'No, but Libby and Miranda were keen to go.'

'Who are they?'

'Just ... friends. I was glad to lend a hand.'

'Hopefully it's not what made you sick,' she says, and after a beat she smiles.

She asks if I saw anything unusual on the twenty-fifth, and I flatly answer no. I wait for her request to check the back garden, and of course I'm happy to oblige.

The hallway is dim so I flick on the light. She follows me through the flat. The door to the bathroom is still open, and in the half-light it's clear that the sink is dry, the cistern is silent. I wonder if she'll notice. A glimpse of the TV as we pass the living room, detectives combing the undergrowth of some grey woods in the Midwest. The kitchen is fairly tidy except for several empty bottles by the bin. I bring her to the back door, fetch the key from on top of the lintel and struggle to turn the lock.

'It's always fairly stiff in this weather.'

She's standing beside me now. There's a faint smell of diesel from her coat, and vanilla from somewhere, her hair perhaps. The lock gives way with a clunk. 'There we go.'

A chill draught as the door opens. I lead her down the path in the middle of the garden. Tall redbrick walls on either side, trellises and a row of shrubbery. A rotary clothesline with yellow wire is listing, unused in years. It twists and creaks though there's hardly any wind. The shed sits at the end of the path. It could do with sanding and a varnish. No padlock, just an old-fashioned latch. It's tight quarters for two, so I open the door and step back for her.

'Can I look inside?'

She must need permission. I imagine her face if I said, *I'd really rather you didn't.*

'Absolutely.'

She stands in the doorway. The shed is mostly taken up with the reel mower, its green metal bars and rusting blades. There's a coil of hose in one corner, a yard brush and a wheelbarrow. A shelf of cubbyholes contains a hacksaw and pliers, loose screws and drill bits. The cubby for the hammer is empty and swept clear of cobwebs.

The garda says, 'Right, thanks,' steps out and looks at the narrow wicket gate in the rear wall. 'Is there a laneway behind the house?'

'No, we back on to the Botanic Gardens.'

'The grounds are just over here?'

'Yeah, well the car park anyway.'

She goes to the gate and takes hold of the rusted padlock.

'I think Allen has a key for that. I've never had to use it.'

She toes at the dirt and gravel at the base of the door, hunches down briefly and picks a flake of green paint from the stones. Her gaze wanders to scuff marks in the weathered old surround.

I say, 'Do you think you'll find Emma Harte?'

She regards me for a moment as if considering the question – did I mean her personally, did I mean found alive?

'Yes, I think we will.'

'I'm glad.'

Brushing the flake from her fingertips, she says. 'Thank you for your help, Mr Lyster. I'll let you get inside.'

She's the one who leads the way back towards the house. In the arched window of the first-floor landing, Whiteside is looking down at us. I think about raising my hand in greeting, but he turns away and is gone.

CHAPTER 7

6 DECEMBER

I wait beneath the portico of the library as a hail shower sweeps over Leinster House. The police take shelter in their little hut. A camera crew by the Dáil abandons an interview with a TD and they all duck inside. Libby Miller comes through the gate on Kildare Street, hurries up the steps and joins me beneath the pillars with a smile and a breathless hello. Her bobble-hat and coat are flecked with hailstones, which she begins to shake off.

I say, 'You look like a Christmas decoration.'

'Thanks.'

'Sorry for dragging you over.'

'It's fine. I have to be back at two though for a tutorial.'

'Let's hurry, so.'

I take her through the display room, but she keeps stopping to look at the Markievicz exhibits – black-and-white photos of the countess standing in the drawing room at Lissadell, or at the hustings on the back of a truck, or in military uniform during the rising.

'Did you choose these?'

'That was Helena. She has a better eye when it comes to exhibitions.'

Libby asks if she can see my office. I can just imagine Bridget's disdainful look, Helena's strained cheeriness. Besides, I prefer to keep these strands of my life un-entwined. Easier to pluck out that way.

'Next time, maybe, or you'll be late for your class. He's just up here.'

A narrow, wooden staircase leads to a smaller hallway, dimly lit and slightly shabby. I knock on the door, wait for the Picard-like 'Come.'

Inside is a wide office with two tall windows in a curved wall. The ceiling vaults above a wrought-iron mezzanine with packed bookcases and a spiral stairs. Douglas Tilley, the chief conservator, sits at a desk with a sheaf of folders. Not a computer in sight. Another table in the corner has a huge magnifying glass attached to a hinged arm, and an archival box beside a green table lamp.

Douglas – he doesn't answer to Doug – looks up and says, 'James, I was beginning to think you couldn't come. And this must be Libby.'

She sweeps off her hat and says hello.

'Is it Olivia? Elizabeth?'

She hesitates, glances at me, and says, 'Lilianna, but please don't call me that.'

'Oh, Lilianna is so much prettier. But as you wish.'

On the floor below, the library has a state-of-the-art conservation room – climate-controlled, stainless-steel racks and worktops, humidors and UV-examination lights, a locked cabinet of bleaches and chemicals. Douglas was rather out of place, and the younger technicians were forever aghast at his insistence on smoking a pipe. Still a few years from retirement, he couldn't be let go without ructions from the union, so he was banished to this office. It suited everyone. He much prefers it up here, working in peace on a few choice manuscripts. And his arcane knowledge of old methods comes in handy when one of the machines breaks down, or the internet is on the blink.

He gets up, beckons us to the table. 'James told me this might be of interest.'

He takes the lid from the box, removes a folder, and opens it beneath the lamp. It contains a manuscript of delicate linen paper. The script has the loops and flourishes of sixteenth-century secretary handwriting, and the text is in Latin.

Libby leans over and begins to read. Her hair falls from her shoulder, but she holds it so it doesn't brush the page.

"'I have taken on the task of setting out in its own separate volume the deeds of our own time and the sequence of events in this latest conquest of Ireland.'"

She looks beautiful in this light. There's a focus and stillness about her, except for the slight movement of her lips, and the ease with which she deciphers the text makes her seem timeless, a conduit to a writer five hundred years ago. I'm sorry when she stops and looks at Douglas.

'It's a version of Cambrensis,' she says.

'And as far as I know, one unpublished in any calendar.'

Libby had described to me the subject of her thesis: *The Book of Howth*, an Elizabethan manuscript copied and compiled from many texts, including *Expugnatio Hibernica* by Giraldus Cambrensis. I had asked Douglas if there was anything in the uncatalogued collections that might be of help. He said he'd have a rummage.

She says, 'But this is incredible. Is it available to the public?'

'Not as such, no. Not before it's properly preserved anyway. But I suppose while I'm working on it I can leave the box here. What harm if someone wishes to consult the manuscript at the same time?'

'God, I'd love to just sit down right now, but I have to ...' She pats her pockets looking for her phone to tell the time. I slip mine out.

One new text from the 089 number.

Libby says, 'Well?'

'Just five to,' I say and pocket the phone again.

'I have to run.' She arranges with Tilley to come back tomorrow afternoon, thanks him twice more, apologises for leaving in such a hurry.

Outside, the hail has cleared, but a cold wind still whistles in the portico. Libby turns to me before leaving. She takes my hand. 'James, this is so ... It could mean the difference between a merit and a distinction.' She stands on her tiptoes and kisses my cheek, draws back an inch or two and looks at me.

A gleam of white clouds reflects in her eyes. I wonder if the establishment of consent applies to kissing. 'Can I kiss you?' seems a little blunt in this fragile moment, but she removes any uncertainty by leaning closer.

When she backs away afterwards, she smiles, pulls her hat on with both hands, and says, 'I'll call you later.' I watch her turn and hurry down the steps. She glances back and waves as she moves through the gate and out of sight.

There's no message in the text, just a photograph, taken of me unawares. I'm sitting at a darkened table in a nightclub, head turned towards a crowded bar. Empty glasses in the foreground, the background a blur of coloured lights and shifting bodies. No timestamp, but I know where and when this was. The Biscuit Factory on the twenty-fifth of November. The Friday before last. Only Emma Harte could have taken the picture.

'It's hard to believe she's dead.'

Helena has paused beside me on her way to the kitchenette, empty mug in hand. She nudges the edge of a daguerreotype on my desk. Sky-blue nail polish. A half-healed papercut on her knuckle.

The photo shows a young woman in a Victorian gown seated in an armchair, an open book in one hand lying on her lap, her elbow propped on the armrest and her head reclining as though she's been caught in a moment's reverie. Her fair hair has been brushed straight and almost reaches her waist.

'It's so sad,' Helena says, and then asks if I'd like some tea.

The hum of the heater and the monotony of archival description soothes me slightly, lulls me perhaps. I think about the nightclub photo. Emma Harte snapped it, that's for sure, but this isn't her phone sending it. Her phone was found in the bushes of the Tolka House. She must have sent the picture to someone else that night. To her sister perhaps. But this isn't Clara's phone either, for when I dialled the 089 number someone else had answered. Perhaps the person ringing me doesn't even know my name. To them I might just be a random number and a blurry picture, a night-time shot that even my own family would be hard-pressed to recognise.

The door opens and Bridget comes in, takes her seat without a word, and nudges her computer awake. It's nearly half two. I check my email in case she sent a request for a long lunch, but no. She already has her earphones in.

I click *Compose*, type Hi Bridget, then delete the Hi.

If you keep coming in late, I'll have to report it to HR. It's not fair on Helena. If there's an issue outside of work, you know you can always tell me.

I check for typos, sign it James instead of Jim and hit *Send*. I glance over my shoulder. She has a Word document open, not a browser.

I google my own number. Odd perhaps, but not particularly suspicious. Only one result – a National Library link to an ad for a Culture Night event two years ago when I had to give guided tours of the library to members of the public. A wretched experience for everyone concerned. *Places are limited so book early. Contact James on ...* and then my number.

No surname at least. I email the link to the library's IT woman. Hi Grace, I've gotten a few enquiries about this event over the last few days – people obviously can't read the date!! Can you delete the page to avoid further confusion? Hope all's well ... Jim.

The exclamation points are a necessary evil. I search for 'James' and 'National Library of Ireland'. The first page of results are library collections: James Joyce manuscripts, James Galbraith photos. But on the second page there's a link to the library's staff chart. I'm listed under *Photographs: Curator, James Lyster*, together with email address and a thumbnail photo.

A creak in the corner as Bridget pushes back her chair. I keep my eyes on the screen as she approaches, but she passes my desk and goes to Helena.

'You coming for a smoke?'

A moment's hesitation. 'A bit early for me.'

Bridget doesn't reply at once, but I sense some silent communication, head-nods, meaningful glances. Finally, she says, 'Suit yourself,' and stalks from the room.

Helena begins to hum softly in the ensuing silence. My phone pings again, but it's Libby Miller. Mad busy in college this evening. Maybe we can grab a drink or a bite to eat tomorrow night?

At the same time, Grace replies with a single-word email: Done. I refresh the Culture Night ad and am met with the reassuring blankness of a '404 Error' page.

I say, 'Helena,' and wait for her to swivel around to face me. 'I was showing someone around the exhibition room earlier. She thought the Markievicz pictures you picked out were brilliant. She's right, too. You did a great job. Not sure I said so before.'

She smiles broadly and lowers her eyes, grips her armrest tighter. 'Oh, thanks. That's lovely to hear.' She becomes a little embarrassed and turns back to her work.

I text Libby. Sure. Let me know when you're done with Tilley and we'll figure something out.

And with those few tasks complete, I turn my attention to the dead girl.

That evening I clean the flat, change the bedclothes, scour the rooms for any hint of Sarah. Just a few strands of auburn hair under the sofa, the can of Impulse, some fabric softener in the press that I can pass off as my own. I go to the tall Ikea bookcase in the living room. Libby Miller is a head shorter than me, so this is the first shelf she'll see: McCarthy, Foster Wallace, Dostoyevsky. A bit heavy-handed. I promote some Atwood, Tartt and Winterson from the lower shelves. The *Oranges Are Not the Only Fruit* is untouched so I break its back a few times, leave some creases in the spine. *Wolf Hall* would have ticked all the boxes, but I lent it to Arthur. He's probably using it as a beer mat.

On the way home, in one of those poky electronic shops on Parnell Street, I bought a Huawei MediaPad on the cheap. I place it on the coffee table, unbox it carefully like one of those YouTuber shills, but only because I want to rewrap it later as a Christmas gift for Lolo. I plug it in, boot it up. The home screen shows pink and white clouds set against an evening sky. I tap on the default browser, ignore my own Wi-Fi, and connect to Whiteside's upstairs.

In Twitter I search for *Tom Wickham* and a long list of users are returned. I scroll down until I see an avatar that looks like him. His username, @DoubtingThomas13. A dozen namesakes had thought of that one already. Bio: *Founder and CEO of re:Thread, proud follower of @LeinsterRugby, copious drinker of bourbon.*

He used to be a prolific tweeter, but nothing in the last two months. Perhaps he deleted his most recent offerings. Nothing too controversial in what's left. Retweets of edgy comedians, right-of-centre journalists, the odd Fine Gael politician. Banal observations on sporting events and gigs. No mention of Emma Harte. The pictures in his feed tend to be memes or newspaper articles, the odd seascape taken from Dollymount Strand. He follows hundreds, but is only followed by fifty-two, and I open the list to have a browse.

Emma had no social media presence – I already checked – so I know she won't be there. It's the usual list of nobodies, most of the names completely unfamiliar, except one at the bottom that catches my eye: @PaschalsWager.

Equality and Nanotechnology and Such. Editor of the @DUGES newsletter.

My phone pings, or so I think, but it must have been a chime from somewhere else. The doorbell upstairs maybe. Still, I look at the screen, find myself disappointed that Libby hasn't texted, though I knew she'd be busy. I tap out a message: **Hope the work is going well. Remember to eat something!**

Do I want to be that person, bombarding a girl with texts after one kiss? Let her message me if she wants. I'm ready to delete, but in the end I replace the exclamation mark with more ambiguous ellipses and hit *Send.*

Paschal had mentioned that he knew Wickham, though they seem to have little in common. Paschal's feed is painfully earnest: organising a boycott of a canteen in the college over its appropriation of Vietnamese cuisine; no-platforming a visiting academic because of her problematic views on sex work. I open the advanced search tool and look for tweets sent from @PaschalsWager to @DoubtingThomas13.

A dozen or so are returned, all dating from the summer and autumn four years ago. I remember Miranda giggling in the Tolka House that Paschal had to repeat second year, and his frosty response: 'That was hardly my fault though, was it?'

One tweet says, Another washout at Electric Picnic saved by @DoubtingThomas13. You should have your own yelp page. Always five stars. After that they stop abruptly.

Libby responds with a picture of a half-eaten burrito and a can of Coke Zero under the garish lights of a canteen, and the message, Never fear.

Not much to reply to that except a thumbs up or a smiley face, and that's not going to happen. I leave the phone aside.

My doorbell rings. The blinds are pulled, so no one can see in, but it's obvious the lights are on. An image of that detective comes to mind, her long grey mac, her knowing glance. I approach the window, making sure my shadow doesn't cross the blind, but from the gap at the side I can't see anyone on the steps.

The doorbell chimes again, followed by a soft rapping on the window. I retreat to the kitchen, search in the medicine cabinet and drop two Solpadeine in a pint of water. I'm watching them swirl and fizz when my phone rings.

I look at the name and answer at once. 'Lolo?'

'Hey, Jim, are you at home?'

'Is everything okay?'

'Fine, yeah. I'm on your doorstep.'

She's wearing an anorak and a loose keffiyeh scarf. She has a bag slung on her back, fingerless gloves. Sleet is falling heavier now. I look over her head to street level where all is dark and silent.

'Where's your dad?'

'Can I stay here tonight?'

Her shoulders are hunched and she's shivering slightly. I tell her to get inside and warm up. As she goes through the hallway, I climb a few of the steps. A glimmer of light between Whiteside's curtains. No traffic on the street.

She's leaning over the radiator. I could ask her what happened, but it's not the first time she's fought with her parents. Instead, I just say, 'Tea?' and she nods once. In the kitchen I down the Solpadeine, put the kettle on, take my phone and text Colin. **Lolo is here**. When I bring in the two mugs she's sitting on the sofa, bag at her feet and coat on the armrest. She's reading the side of the Huawei box.

'That was going to be your Christmas present.'

'Oh, I was going to get a ... No, this is great, thanks.'

'I'll give it to Ultan.'

I sit in the armchair, blow some steam from my tea, and lean back. After a moment she says, 'I hate them.'

'You've had a row. It'll pass.'

'I don't remember not hating them anymore.'

'That can't be true.'

'You don't know what they're really like.'

Colin was twelve when I was born. He was big as a youth, broad-shouldered like our father, so for me he always seemed a generation apart, an uncle rather than a brother. He would disappear in the morning, off to a different school, hang out with friends in the evening. I was a nuisance more than anything. We've grown closer as I've gotten older, but perhaps Lolo is right. I don't really know him all that well. I don't know what he's capable of.

'What's the problem now? More school stuff?'

'I've started going out with someone. Let's just say father doesn't approve.'

'Give him time. I'm sure he'll be won over.'

'It's not just that. It's … everything.'

She sits there, quiet and dejected.

I say, 'So what's the plan? Are you staying on the sofa until you graduate? Because I'm afraid I can't afford the fees.'

'I'm going to move in with Aunt Gwen.'

Danni's sister in Oughterard. I've only met her at funerals and baptisms.

'And your new fella?'

A defensive shift in her shoulders. 'He'll come out when he's able.'

My phone rings, and I show Colin's name to Lolo.

She says, 'Don't answer it.'

'I must.'

'If you do, I'll leave.'

'Then I'll have to walk beside you till he finds us. And I won't have time to get my coat, so I'll probably die of pneumonia.' I swipe to answer. 'Col.'

'Put her on to me.'

'Maybe we should let things cool down a little first.'

'We were up the fucking walls. She snuck out of the house, do you know that? Danni only found her gone when she checked her room.'

'Well, she's safe and sound. She's grand here for the night. I can bring her to school in the morning.'

Lolo says she's not going anywhere.

Colin on the phone: 'Was that her? Tell her I'm coming to get her. I'll be there in ten.' He hangs up, and I place the phone on the armrest.

'He's on his way.'

Lolo stands, starts putting on her jacket.

'Where are you going?'

'I'll wait in Busáras if I have to. There's a bus to Galway at half-five.'

'Lolo, you'll have to start covering your tracks better if you don't want people to find you.'

She picks up her bag, but I reach over and hold one of the straps. She looks at me. 'Let go.'

'No.'

We stay like that for a few seconds, the bag held between us. Her eye never wavers, and I see a resentment there that I've never seen before. She lets the strap slip between her fingers. At first, I think she'll leave without it, but she slumps back down on the sofa and takes out her phone.

I tell her that I'm sorry, that I couldn't let her go, that it's not safe, but all she does is swipe and tap at the screen.

When the doorbell rings, Lolo picks up her bag and I follow her into the hallway. She answers the door to her father, walks past him without a word and begins to climb the steps. Colin is in his work clothes, loose tie and overcoat. I tell him not to do anything drastic tonight, wait until the morning to talk to her. He looks at me for a moment, his face a mixture of tiredness and regret. He shakes his head, says, 'You don't understand,' and then follows Lolo to the car.

CHAPTER 8

7 DECEMBER

'Human life is the most precious thing to be found within these walls, and safety must take precedence over any book or artefact, including national treasures.'

Malachi Moran, assistant keeper of manuscripts and safety officer for the entire library, is addressing us in a meeting room of wood-panelled walls and gilt-framed paintings. The tables we sit at are rickety foldouts, arranged in a square with an empty no-man's-land in the middle.

'Always obey the directives of emergency services and the police.' Malachi pauses to fix his spectacles. Did his eye flick towards me just then? 'For their authority is absolute in any crisis.'

With Storm Lauren tracking over the Azores, it was felt that a brush-up on the library's disaster strategy would be of benefit. Two people from every department were required to attend, and since Bridget didn't make it in because of icy roads, it fell to me and Helena. There are a dozen others: financial controllers, conservators, bored book porters in black shirts and slacks. Helena, being one of only two women, was asked to take the minutes.

As Malachi drones on I swipe at my phone beneath the table, notice Emma Harte's name in the *Irish Independent*. The article is buried low under 'Irish News'.

The family of missing person Emma Harte has made a fresh appeal for information on her disappearance twelve days ago. It comes soon after a possible sighting in Co. Louth proved unfounded. Miss Harte's sister, Clara (22), said that the family had not given up hope, and she appealed to her sister to make contact. 'Just let us know that you're safe and well.' Miss Harte has not been seen since the night of November 25th when she was captured on CCTV in Capel Street.

Not even a photo. Already the papers are beginning to forget.

'Remember, in case of fire, make sure all doors are closed. In case of flooding, make sure they're open.'

A message flashes silently on screen. From Danni: **Sorry for the Lolo drama last evening. You're a life-saver** and then a winky face. She never did get the hang of emojis.

Malachi has moved on to plans for the upcoming storm. We're not so worried about the blizzards and the snowdrifts, he says, but rather the thaw. Parts of the roof are like a sieve, and some of us will have to be on hand to check for leaks among the stacks. 'The question is how to coordinate such an effort.'

Helena suggests setting up a WhatsApp group for library staff. That way we could organise in real time who was available to come in. But Malachi dismisses the idea with a wave of his hand. 'Not everyone has a smartphone,' he says. He listens intently as Trevor, the senior porter, makes some irrelevant complaint about weight restrictions on book trolleys. Helena's cheeks colour, and she looks again at her notes.

I check Libby Miller's feeds just to see what she's up to. No recent additions on Instagram. She's tweeted a photo of the manuscript she's working on, a cat's inky paw print on the handwriting. Confirmed: cats were assholes in the sixteenth century as well. It has gained some traction, several retweets and responses. She might have tagged me in, but I get no credit. I see Miranda among the replies, go to her page, retweet a notice she posted for the next DUGES debate. She replies to me at once with, Thanks Flynn-slayer and a red love heart. I hover over the 'Like' button. That's the problem these days; we're forever obliged to like things we don't want to.

I become aware that people are looking at me. Malachi says, 'What do you think, James?'

I've lost the thread if ever there was one, but rather than admit that, I say, 'Helena, your idea sounded interesting. Would you like to finish your thought?'

She looks at me. Her shoulders straighten a little in her thin floral cardigan, and she says, 'Well, I just figured if we were in a WhatsApp group we'd know who'd be able to come in on a given day, which bus routes were open, and so on. We'd only need two or three, and maybe if you volunteer one day, you're exempt the next. Then everyone knows who's done what. Seems like a better idea than trying to phone or email everybody.'

The only other woman at the table, Vera from Accounts, says, 'That makes sense. We should do that.'

Malachi is frowning. 'But as I said, not everyone—'

'Who here doesn't have a smartphone?' I ask.

Only Trevor raises his hand. The chances of him volunteering to come in on a snow day were already non-existent.

'That's plenty to be getting on with. How about this: Helena will organise the group, and Malachi, you can keep the troglodytes informed as best you can.'

Helena smiles and nods, Malachi remains silent, and Trevor points out that it's lunch hour.

As we file through the lobby and go our separate ways, the security guard at the front desk beckons me over. His name is Tommy, a white-haired Dubliner who always chats about the football results. He lifts a large Brown Thomas shopping bag and plonks it on the desk.

'Someone left this in for you.'

The top of the bag is tied with a black ribbon, some pink felt paper visible through the gap. A name tag is attached to the handle, 'Mister Lyster' written in blue pen. The horizontal stroke of the L is overly long and underlines my name.

'Who was it?'

'He didn't say.'

'Young or old?'

'They all look young to me these days.'

I take the bag and head to the staff corridor, then pretend to change my mind and turn towards the public toilets. The men's room in the National Library happens to be the nicest in the city, a swirl of mosaic in Edwardian tiles, stained-glass partitions, a vaulted ceiling. There's an incongruous armchair that faces the urinals, though I've never been tempted to sit in it. I go into a cubicle and lock the door behind me, undo the ribbon and fish out the felt paper.

Folded up inside is a long Afghan coat – tan suede with white fur-lined collar and cuffs. I hold it up in the light of the cubicle window, allow the empty bag to tumble to the floor. No stains. No rips that I can see. There's a slight acrid smell in the fabric. Detergent and something else. Vinegar, perhaps. Hints of cigarette smoke. The pockets are empty, inside and out.

I ball it up and put it back in the bag, hurry through the lobby to the portico outside. The steps are wet with grit salt, everything else is dusted white. Usually, one or two people linger on the benches, but not today in the bitter cold. A figure stands at the pedestrian gate, a man in a dark green anorak with the hood pulled up. He's facing me, arms hanging by his sides. I'm about to walk towards him when a woman approaches and taps him on the shoulder. He turns to her. Their hoods couple and uncouple in a brief kiss. The two link arms and walk away.

'May I take the lady's jacket?'

A waiter with brown stubble and a soft voice enquires of Libby as she unburdens herself of laptop bag and scarf. The tables in Shouk are small, and I'm wedged in the corner at the end of a wooden bench with loose cushions. I'm glad to be stuck, so as not to navigate that slightly awkward greeting after a first kiss. We wave and say hi, and I wait for her to half-sit, half-collapse in the chair opposite. Her cheeks are flushed. Strands of hair float in the static from her bobble-hat.

I say, 'You made it.'

She smiles and says, 'You noticed. Did you get on okay with your brother?'

'Hmm? Oh yeah. He just needed something dropped in to him.'

Earlier I'd told Libby that I might be late for our date because of an errand I had to run for Col. In reality, I slipped away from work to bring the Afghan coat home. I thought of dumping it, but I would have looked conspicuous stuffing it into a city bin, and if I tossed it into some disused stairwell, someone else might find it. Best to keep it simple. The bins go out at dawn on Friday. The coat will go with them.

I glance at the back of a menu and then back at her. 'Fancy a drink?'

'God, yes.'

We order a bottle of white, a mixture of falafels, dips and pitta bread, and she tells me of her afternoon with the Tilley manuscript, discoveries made in the text, answers to problems that had troubled her for months. There's an enthusiasm in her voice that makes me glad I was able to help. She keeps trying to get me to taste the green tahini dip, but I refuse on the grounds that it looks like a prop from *The Exorcist*. She tuts, finishes her glass of wine, and tops us both up.

The last time I was here was with Sarah. Her hair was cut shorter than usual, and together with the blank way she looked at me, it was as if I was sitting with a stranger. Neither of us had spoken for several minutes until she took a breath, I thought to let out another sigh, but instead she said, 'Sometimes I think you don't even like me.' I had no response. She pressed her lips together. Her eyes glistened. She stood quietly and left with a poise that impressed me even then. One thing about Sarah, she had a knack for rising to the occasion.

Libby looks at me over the rim of her glass and says, 'You seem a little preoccupied.'

I berate myself for being legible, but I can hardly say now that I was thinking of my ex. So instead: 'You know Bridget who I work with? She didn't come in again today. It's tricky as we go back a bit, but I think I'll have to mention it to HR. Sorry, it's been playing on my mind.'

'No, it's understandable.' Her face has become solemn, focused, and I'm touched that she believes me.

I warm to the topic. 'It's unfair on Helena. She has to pick up the slack, and she's so eager to please. I'm sure she works on stuff at home. I get reports from her at all hours. But she deserves her down time as well. Next thing she'll become burnt out, and it'll be my fault for not handling it.'

'Well, it's Bridget's fault first and foremost.' Libby tears a piece of pitta but leaves it on her plate. 'Have you spoken to her?'

'I've emailed her about it.'

She raises an eyebrow, and I hold up my hands. 'I know, I know. I'm terrible at confrontation.'

'What did she say?'

'Not a thing.'

'Might be relationship trouble.'

There was talk of a fella a while ago, all right. A producer in RTÉ. Some pretentious name like Simeon.

'Or a health issue, or family problems.'

'She'd tell me if it was something like that.'

'People are private.'

'Yeah, but she'd be entitled to paid leave. She'd take it if she had to.'

I pour out the last of the wine, making sure Libby has a few millimetres more. 'Back in college Bridget would smoke a few joints, take some pills. Harmless stuff really. But I wonder if it's gotten the better of her.'

Libby shrugs. 'Could be. I've known people who've gone through rough patches.'

'Like Paschal?'

Her eyes fix on me. I expect her to ask, 'Why do you say that?' or 'How do you know?' but she remains silent, which I like. Her first instinct is to say nothing.

But the moment has to be smoothed over. 'Miranda mentioned something in the Tolka last week. How he deferred a year. He seemed pretty defensive about it as well.'

'Yeah, it was a bad time.'

'You were friends with him then?'

'We were going out.'

My turn to be slightly thrown. 'Oh, right.'

'Only for a few months. A college fling.'

'And you stayed friends.'

'We stayed in the same circle. It was three years ago.'

She's become uncomfortable, a little wary. Time to ease off. 'Sorry for going on. I'm sure Bridget will be okay. I feel better for having talked about it, though.'

Libby tilts her head and says, 'I'm glad.'

I move my hand towards hers, and when she doesn't draw back, I take hold of it. We stay like that as the waiter clears the plates. Libby rubs her thumb over my knuckles.

Snow is falling on Botanic Road and patches of ice have formed underfoot. Libby laughs and grips my arm whenever she slips. It's hard to see much beyond the pools of lamplight. We stop and kiss beneath a halo of swirling flakes, near a battered copy of Emma Harte's poster.

We turn into the driveway of the house. Whiteside is silhouetted in his parlour window as though he's been waiting for us. He closes his drapes, shutting out the light. The curtains twitch as Libby and I go down the basement steps.

I show her into the living room. I'd left the heat on low all day, and it feels cosy, a little too warm now that we're out of the weather. The dimmer switch on the upright lamp is on, and there's a welcoming glow picking out the gold lettering on the bookshelves. Libby looks around and says, 'It suits you.'

She goes to use the bathroom and I turn on the TV, cast Spotify from my phone and play some Tame Impala. In the kitchen I check on the Brown Thomas bag stashed beneath the sink, next to the bottle of bleach and Brillo pads. As the kettle boils, I glance through to the living room. Libby is taking off her coat, head tilted as she looks at the bookcase. When I bring in two mugs of coffee she's sitting on the sofa, reading the back of *The Secret History*.

'Miranda raves about this,' she says.

I put the mug on the table beside her. 'Borrow it if you like.'

'Can I?'

Borrow it, steal it, sell it. 'Of course.'

She opens the front cover, pauses and says, 'Oh.' There's an inscription from Sarah on the title page. A quote from the book: *Forgive me, for all the things I did but mostly for the things that I did not,* the date and two kisses.

Libby says, 'I shouldn't.'

'Really, I don't mind.'

'But maybe she would.'

I take the book from her and place it next to her untouched coffee. We kiss for a while, leaning back against the cushions. Her lip balm has a flavour, and for a while I try to place it. Pomegranate, maybe. Or passionfruit. Her hand grips the front of my shirt, slips down to my waist and the inside of my leg. From the armrest her coat slips and falls to the floor with a rustle, but she doesn't seem to notice. I think of the Afghan, and for a brief moment I wonder if I left the cabinet door open. I definitely shut it. Even if it's open and Libby goes in, she'd hardly have a rummage.

She draws back and says, 'Is it all right?'

'Pardon?'

'Is it okay for me to touch you there?'

'Ehm … yeah, sure.'

Her eyes close and we kiss again and lie back further. My hand is lost in the warm folds of her jumper. I think of her wearing the Afghan coat, smiling in a dark street with snow swirling overhead, holding the white fleece trim against her face, except it's not her face anymore.

I disengage and sit up straight. Libby is disconcerted. She half sits up herself. A strange tingling runs along my right arm, and I close and open my fist. I tell her I'll be back in a minute, keep my eyes on the floorboards and concentrate on walking steadily as I head towards the bathroom. I push open the door and lock myself in.

The hot water gurgles in the tap. I place my hands underneath until my skin is at the edge of scalding. I should tell her to go home, that it's not going to work. I'll apologise for leading her on. Or maybe not. Let her think I'm a piece of shit and that she's better off without me. When I try to look myself in the eye, the mirror is clouded with steam.

She's sitting cross-legged on the sofa, arms folded, her shoes on the floor beside her. She looks at me quizzically and says, 'What was that about?'

I try to make light. 'Sorry, must have been the hummus.'

Up above the doorbell rings just at the edge of hearing. Libby looks at the ceiling. She reaches for her coffee and takes a sip. She says, 'James, you'd tell me if this was just a rebound thing.'

I sit beside her and wait until she looks at me. 'Libby, listen—'

A loud bang upstairs, like the front door being slammed against a wall, and someone yells out. Footsteps on the landing. Another cry, more plaintive, is cut short mid-breath, followed by a thump like a dropped sack of potatoes.

Libby's eyes widen. She whispers, 'What the fuck is going on?'

I move to the window, peek past the blind at the basement steps. A faint light is cast on the railings above as if the front door is wide open. Otherwise, all is still.

Libby flinches at a sound like a smashed vase. Another clatter, this time with chimes, perhaps the mantel clock. I tell her to stay where she is.

'What are you doing?'

'I can't leave Whiteside like this.'

She follows me out to the hallway, pulls at my arm and whispers, 'Just call the police.'

Maybe she's right. What could I do by confronting anyone? Scare them off? I turn the Chubb on my front door as quietly as I can, and say to Libby, 'Phone the guards. We're at 196 Botanic Road. I'll make sure no one can come down the internal stairs.'

In the kitchen I search through the cutlery drawer. At the back of my mind I remember that serrated blades are most effective for cutting flesh, so I take out the carving knife. The bulb in the narrow stairwell has long since burned out. In the darkness I use the faint glow from my phone, which I turn to silent just in case. At the top, I check that the bolt is slid shut. It won't stop a determined barge, but it's better than nothing. There's a glimmer of hall light along the bottom sill. On the other side, the door is plain white with an old brass knob that could easily be mistaken for a hot press.

Footsteps sound on the staircase right over my head – a light, unhurried tread descending to the ground floor. Someone passes the door, a sweep of shadow. I listen for voices, or another's footfall, or a whimper from Whiteside, but there is nothing.

Perhaps I should return to Libby, see if the police are on their way, but I hear more movement in the hallway. This time footsteps pause on the other side. Two faint shadows linger on the sill. I pocket my phone, place my hand flat against the door. In the darkness I hear the knob scrape and turn. I feel pressure as it pushes inwards. I won't even let the door budge against the bolt. Make them think that it's locked fast. The pressure eases off, but I keep my hand in place. I realise that I've hardly taken a breath, and silently inhale through my mouth.

A crunching thud as they kick against the lock rail and the bolt almost gives way. I drop the knife, hear it skitter down the steps. Perhaps they hear it as well, for there's a long pause. I brace my shoulder against the door, push all my weight against it, feel the jolt as they kick again.

I stay braced, quickly touch the bolt, and find that it's come off its screws. I wait for the next blow, but all that comes is a gentle rap. Three knocks, followed by two more. In the distance there's a strain of police sirens. At once, the shadow moves away. I hear footsteps receding. Whiteside's front door closes with a soft rattle and then all is quiet.

When I go back down Libby is clutching the handle of the knife with both hands, the blade brandished. She drops it and comes to hug me. We creep upstairs, gingerly look into the hallway. Little sign of anything amiss, except the drawer in the hall table is pulled open, a tear in the wallpaper beside the front door. Blue lights are flashing in the fanlight overhead. The front parlour is bright, a Superser heater glowing beside Whiteside's leather armchair. The floor is strewn with broken glass and papers pulled from a writing desk. Whiteside is lying near the edge of the rug, his back to us, paisley dressing gown askew and half-draped on the floor. I kneel beside him, gently pull his shoulder back, and cradle his head. There's a gash in his brow. Blood seeps from the corner of his mouth. At first, I can't tell if he's breathing, but one of his eyes opens, swivels about until it focuses on me. His lips part. He licks at the blood on his mouth, and whispers, 'It's you, James.'

CHAPTER 9

Libby's place is a small two-up two-down in a terrace on Munster Street. She brings me inside, and we stamp snow from our shoes onto the welcome mat. There's a murmur from the TV in the living room, and Libby calls out, 'It's only me.'

She hangs her coat on the ball finial of the banister, already covered in jackets and scarves. The top of the stairs is dark. A faint smell of damp and burnt toast lingers in the narrow hallway.

Miranda's voice drifts from the front room: 'Wasn't expecting you back.'

Libby opens the door and says, 'You wouldn't believe what happened,' then she pauses and says, 'Oh, hey.'

Paschal is lounging on a brown leather armchair in the corner. His half-smile disappears when he sees me follow her in.

The room is lit only by the TV, a three-bar electric heater, and fairy lights strung over the mantelpiece. Kitschy framed pictures and a Sacred Heart of Jesus are dotted on the wall. A wide bookcase of metal shelving contains novels and Bettie Page postcards and a Barbie doll in bondage gear.

Miranda is curled up on the sofa working on her laptop with a history book open beside her. 'Paz dropped by and got snowed in.'

Libby says, 'Actually, it's not too bad out now.'

'What did you say happened?'

She gives an account of the break-in and its aftermath, how the guards called an ambulance for Whiteside and questioned us about what we saw, which wasn't much.

Miranda says, 'Did they tell you to clear out for the night?'

'No, but you couldn't stay after something like that. They were waiting for some guy with a forensics kit to show up.'

'Just for a robbery?'

'Well, it was assault.'

Paschal takes a pouch of tobacco and packet of Rizlas from a coat that's draped on the chair and begins to roll a cigarette. To me he says, 'Will they be swabbing your flat as well?'

'Nothing happened down there.'

'I'm sure they won't, so.'

Libby says, 'Paschal, if you're going to smoke that, do it outside.'

'It's freezing out.'

'I know.'

He holds her eye as he licks the edge of the roll-up, then pats down the loose tobacco and leaves the cigarette on the armrest.

Miranda closes the lid of her laptop. 'Assuming that college is open tomorrow, I'd better get to bed. I thought I'd be done wishing for snow days. Do you want a blanket for the sofa, Paz?'

Libby looks at her but doesn't say anything.

He says, 'Thanks, yeah. Sorry to intrude. Didn't know it would be a full house.' He smiles at me. 'I remember when I was the one being brought back from the pub, and look at me now.'

Libby remains quiet. She gets up and takes my hand by gripping my fingers, and leads me from the room without another word.

There's something uncanny about a strange room at first light. Everything is unfamiliar. Wooden buttons at the top of Libby's duvet. String bag hanging from the wardrobe. Green light blinking on a desktop in the corner. Libby has her back to me. She's almost in silhouette against the window, where a parting in the curtains reveals a dark grey sky. Her shoulder rises and falls. I say her name, and when she doesn't react, I get up quietly and put some clothes on.

The bathroom is freezing. Old-fashioned green tiles, a bath curtain with a giant goldfish on it. I wash my face in the sink. The hot tap makes pipes in the attic clank, so I use the cold instead.

Downstairs the door to the living room is ajar. Paschal's blanket is bundled up on the armrest. Perhaps he slipped out early, but his phone is there, peeking out from beneath a cushion. He's not in the kitchen either. A half-drunk mug of tea sits on the colourful polyester tablecloth. Still warm. Through the window I can see footprints in the snow and Paschal sitting miserably on a bench beneath an awning. He's wrapped up in his coat. A tendril of smoke rises from the end of his cigarette.

Back in the living room, I pick up his phone, trace a Z to unlock it and open *Contacts*. AAALibby is at the top. I search for *Tom* and *Thomas* but there are no results. I type *089*, and it auto-predicts three numbers. The one at the bottom I recognise immediately. The contact name is *The Wickerman*.

I hit *Dial* to see what happens. A creak sounds on the stairs. I pause to listen but then all is still. The number rings and rings with no response, and eventually ends in a dead tone. I'm about to dial again when the back door opens and clicks shut. I delete the call, lock the phone and slip it back beneath the cushion. When Paschal comes in, I'm fiddling with the button for the heater, and I pretend to start when I see him.

'Thought you were gone.'

'Just out for a smoke.' He goes to sit on the sofa. 'Sleep well?'

My coat is folded by the coffee table. I pick it up and say, 'I just had to get this.'

'I was using that as an extra blanket. Hope you don't mind.'

I head towards the door, then pause, and say, 'Paschal, I think we may have a mutual friend.'

'Really? Who's that?'

His phone is on silent, but it lights up and vibrates. He picks it up, frowns at the number for a long moment, and then answers with, 'Yeah?'

He listens and says, 'No, no, I crashed at Libby's. Come here, did your man get back to you about the lecture notes?'

He looks at me quizzically, the phone held between his shoulder and ear, and I realise that I've been staring at him. I nod and leave the room and head back upstairs.

From the outside the house looks pristine. Snow hides the cracks in the paving stones, the weeds on the steps, the flaking paint on the windowsills. Whiteside's front door appears undamaged. I climb the steps and push against it just in case. Nothing to see through the closed drapes of the sitting-room window. I go down to my own door, let myself in and listen to the silence.

Somehow the house feels less welcoming. In the living room two mugs of coffee are sitting on the table, a white film on the cold dregs. *The Secret History* lies discarded on the sofa. I pick it up, look again at Sarah's inscription and return the book to the shelf. A prickle in my neck makes me turn and scan the room, but all is still.

On the mantelpiece there are a few family photos: me holding Lolo when she was a baby; my parents flanking me in my graduation gown the year before Dad died; Colin and me in running gear in a rain-drenched Merrion Square at the end of the Dublin marathon. I always keep the frames leaning against the wall, but the last one is propped on its stand. Had Libby done that the night before? Maybe Lolo the last time she was here.

My phone rings, a local number that I don't recognise. I let it go to voicemail.

Mr Lyster, this is Garda Penny Collins of the Community Policing Unit in Santry. Just in relation to the break-in at your address last evening. We'll require you to make a formal witness statement as soon as possible, so if you ring me at this number, we can arrange an appointment. Also, there's a ... well, just give me a ring back. Okay, thanks, bye.

In the kitchen I check the press beneath the sink. The Brown Thomas bag is wedged under a bend in the pipe. Binmen are due tomorrow so it can keep till then. I rummage in a drawer for a screwdriver. The door at the top of the internal stairs is closed, the slide-bolt hanging loose. I take out the screws, reattach the lock a few inches higher. It won't stop anyone determined to kick it down, but it's better than nothing.

Jagged cracks show in the panels on the other side of the door, scuffed boot marks on white paint. Whiteside's front room is still a mess. For some reason I thought the guards might have tidied it up. It's cold and dark, a faint smell of natural gas from the Superser. I open the curtains to let in the light. Near the gate on the driveway there's another set of footprints beside my own. They only come towards the house a few paces, then whoever it was turned around again.

I've never been upstairs in Whiteside's house. The door to his bedroom creaks when I push it open. His clothes have been dragged from the wardrobe and lie in a heap on the floor, but otherwise the room is neat. The beige duvet is smoothed flat. Glass of water and a collection of McGahern's short stories on the bedside locker. A trilby and a grey woollen scarf hang from a hook. I go around the bed towards the window and see something leaning against the wall. The hammer that was missing from the shed.

From the window I look at the shed at the bottom of the garden, picturesque in the snow, the back wall and the Botanic Gardens beyond, bare trees and greenhouses in the distance. When Whiteside stands here, he can see everything.

Downstairs the front door opens. No movement for a few seconds, and then a woman's voice mutters, 'Christ.'

I call out hello and she answers tentatively. When I come onto the landing, she's looking up the stairs with her head tilted. It's

Whiteside's daughter, though I forget her name. She's pushing forty, wearing a navy quilted jacket, sandy hair in a ponytail. A small child stands beside her, age and gender hard to determine, just a face in a hooded anorak with mittens and Wellington boots.

I introduce myself, and she says, 'The tenant?'

'That's right.'

'Dad mentioned you last night.'

I say, 'Oh?' but she doesn't elaborate.

'What were you doing up there?'

'Just surveying the damage. I had to fix one of the doors.' I brandish the screwdriver as evidence. 'How's your dad?'

'No concussion or broken bones, but he's badly shook.' She stands at the threshold of the sitting room, looks around and shakes her head. 'Fucking scumbags.'

I glance at the child, who seems unperturbed. He or she has removed a mitten and is picking at the torn wallpaper.

'Guards said there's been a rash of these attacks targeting older people. Always is in the run-up to Christmas.' She looks at the paintings dotted about the hallway and front room. 'Nothing worth taking except the art, but they didn't seem to bother. Maybe they didn't realise.'

'We were able to ring the police from downstairs. It probably disturbed them.'

'We?'

'My ... girlfriend and I.'

Her eyes search my face, and then she turns to the child. 'Blair, stop doing that.'

No clues as to gender there. 'I can help with the clean-up if you like.'

'Oh, would you?' she says. 'I'm afraid I can't stay. We've got to get back to Wicklow and the roads will be a nightmare. Could you do me a favour and check on Dad over the next few days? Make sure he's warm enough, has a few groceries, that kind of thing.'

'They're not keeping him in?'

'He's adamant. He can't stand hospitals.'

'Perhaps he should stay with you.'

'No, that wouldn't work,' she says, as if it's self-evident. She bites the tip of her glove, withdraws a hand to rummage in a pocket and gives me a business card. Eliza Whiteside Design, Avoca, Wicklow. 'Call me if anything crops up.'

No magazines in the waiting area of the police station, just a row of fold-down seats like in a football ground, a glass booth where a bored garda leans at a desk, and a noticeboard that includes a poster of Emma Harte. Her face is half-covered by a leaflet warning people to pay their TV licence. There's little or no signal. I give up trying to browse the internet and text Libby instead, asking if she's made her appointment to come in yet. Only two other people wait with me. A mother and son, by the looks of things. He's gangly and surly, slouched with arms folded, wearing a school uniform though the schools are shut today. She looks bereft, like someone waiting for news in a hospital. They both glance at me when my seat creaks and I walk towards the noticeboard. I run my finger beneath Emma's poster so that it slides up and over the leaflet, and I let her come to rest again.

A crackle and hiss. 'James Lyster.'

The garda in his booth is standing, his finger on a button so that he can talk via speaker.

'You can go through now. Last room on the left.'

The interview room is windowless, brightly lit and bare except for a table with a beige covering, two wooden chairs, a wall clock and a black security camera high in one corner. Since the chairs are identical, I take the one with its back to the door.

As I go to put my phone on silent, Libby texts back. They never asked me to come in. Just as well as I'm swamped with work this evening. I'll see you tomorrow … xx.

Someone approaches. The detective who searched the back garden a few days ago enters the room, deftly kicks a doorstop away and waits for the door to swing closed.

'Sorry for keeping you, James.' She places a portfolio on the table, glances at the empty seat. 'Actually, I might get you to sit here. When people come knocking it's easier if I'm close to the door.'

'Oh, fine.'

I gather my coat and scarf and brush past her to take the other chair. Now I can't see the time. The camera is fixed on me. She places her phone on the table – a lock screen of three smiling children on a jungle gym goes black.

She says, 'I'm not sure I've introduced myself. My name is Detective Shaw. Shauna Shaw. Can you believe it? I almost turned my husband down when he popped the question, just because of the name.'

I'm not sure why she's adopting this lighter air, but I smile and nod and reach for a platitude. 'I can imagine.'

'Are you feeling better?'

'Pardon?'

'You were rather sick when I called to your house.'

'Oh, yes, much better thanks.'

'Strange that we keep bumping into each other.'

'Isn't it?'

From her portfolio she removes a pad of lined paper and begins to fill in the date and time. She's left-handed. A pale band on her finger marks where a wedding ring should be. Perhaps she can't wear it at work.

'Now, in your own words can you tell me what happened last night?'

'Where should I begin?'

'Wherever you want.'

I take it up from when Libby and I arrived back from the restaurant, how we were drinking coffee in the living room when we heard noises upstairs.

'Don't say "we", just what you saw and heard.'

She writes quickly, neatly, while gently biting the corner of her lip. Sometimes I have to wait for her pen to stop before I continue, but I take these moments to compose my thoughts. Occasionally she interjects with a question – what time a certain thing happened, what room I was in, whether I'd noticed anyone hanging around outside. Otherwise, she's a picture of concentration.

'The door you were holding shut, that's for the internal stairs?'

'That's right. It comes up into Whiteside's hallway.'

'And you have your own separate entrance for the downstairs flat and a back door to the garden?'

'Yes.'

'No one tried to gain entry via the back door?'

'No. You can't reach the back door from the street. You saw yourself.'

Her eyes drift to the side as if she's trying to remember. 'Have there been any other attempted break-ins recently?'

'No.'

'You're sure?'

She's no longer writing things down. I tell her that I'm sure. I ask her if she needs anything else, and she says, 'No, that about covers it.' She puts her name at the bottom of the sheet and then turns it to face me. 'Give this a read and if you're happy you can sign it up. I'll be back in a moment.'

She slips out the door. It shuts behind her and all of a sudden the room feels confined. I skim through the text, sign my name and place the pen next to her portfolio. A small sheaf of papers is tucked into the flap. The page on top has some handwritten notes, including *56 Victoria Avenue*. I lean forward to slip the page out but remember the camera just in time.

Shaw returns with a manila folder beneath her arm. She takes her seat again, pushes my witness statement aside.

'James, I believe you're a curator of photographs in the National Library.'

'That's right. How do you know?'

She smiles and says, 'Your Twitter profile.'

'Oh, right. Everyone's an open book.'

Her smile lingers, which makes it look a little strained. 'You haven't tweeted in a while.'

'No, I've been trying to cut back. You know what they say. Social media is where a good mood goes to die.'

'We're not allowed use it in the force. Probably for the best.'

'You could always create a fake account,' I say, and she glances at me.

She turns the folder around. 'I wonder if we could use your expert eye to help us with something.'

Two printouts of photographs are pinned to the inside covers so that they face each other. Black-and-white stills from security cameras. The one on the left is Emma Harte on Capel Street, from the footage used in all the news reports. She's looking at the car that has just driven away. In the corner is the date and time, 1.09 a.m.

The picture on the right I haven't seen before. A high-angle shot of a dark footpath and a shuttered Tesco on Dorset Street, the one I pass on the way to work every day. The time is 2.34 a.m. In a pool of streetlight, me and Emma Harte are walking together. Both our faces are a blur, like smears in a daguerreotype. She's wearing the Afghan coat with the white fur trim. The coat I'm wearing in the picture is currently on the armrest beside me.

I keep my face blank. Lean over to look closer. Shaw knows that I was on the search party in the Tolka House. The last thing I tweeted about was this very footage on Capel Street. I point to that picture and say Emma Harte's name.

She nods. 'The other photo just came to light. Though at the moment we can't be sure it's her.'

I point out the obvious. 'The girl on the right is wearing a coat.'

'Yes, but look at the heels of her shoes, the length of her hair.'

I should be eager, interested, keen to help. 'Very similar all right.' I want to pick holes or point out discrepancies, but there are none to find. So I say, 'Even the shade and style of the jeans are much the same.' Should I have said trousers and not jeans? No, they're obviously jeans. 'The timing seems plausible as well.'

'If you were to guess, would you say it's the same person?'

'I suppose you have to be wary of coincidence. But I'd say it's a distinct possibility.'

'I think so as well.'

'There's no other CCTV to fill in the gap?'

'Not as yet, no.'

'But then, who's the guy?'

Shaw closes the folder with the tips of her fingers and looks at me. 'That's the question.'

CHAPTER 10

8 DECEMBER

A light snow falls as I trudge home from the police station. In the flat, I peer into the hallway, shut the door behind me and switch on the central heating. The clank of pipes is unsettling in the silence. From under the sink, I fetch the Brown Thomas bag and remove the coat. I lay it on the floor, cross the sleeves to their opposite shoulders like a corpse, and roll the coat into a tight lozenge of tan and fleece, which I stuff at the bottom of my backpack.

I ring Colin and he answers with, 'Jim, bud.'

'Are you busy?'

'Yes. What's up?'

I tell him what happened the night before and he swears and asks if I'm all right.

'Fine. It's just ... I know this is stupid but I'm a bit spooked staying home this evening. Any chance I could crash at your place? Just for tonight.'

'Of course, yeah. I'll text Danni.'

In Griffith Avenue, Lolo answers the door in leggings and a dark hoodie, a phone held to her ear. She beckons me in without a smile, then climbs the stairs to a room that used to be mine. A cartoon is playing to an empty lounge. I go through to the kitchen – a wide extension at the back of the house with dining table and chairs, a separate sofa and TV, marble kitchen island, and a sliding door looking out to where Senan and Ultan are playing in the yard. Danni is stirring a pot at the stove, her hair loosely pinned. My mother is at the table, fingers wrapped around a mug of coffee.

I rap at the door as I come in, smile first at Danni and then say, 'Hello, Mother.'

'Hello yourself,' she says, 'when I'd practically given up on ever hearing from you again.'

'Have you not been getting my texts?'

'What? No.' She frowns and lifts her phone from the table, reaches for spectacles that hang around her neck, before she realises I'm pulling her leg. I lean over and kiss her cheek.

'Sorry, Mam. Just been a tad busy.'

Danni briefly hugs me with the ladle held to one side. She draws back and says, 'Col told us what happened. It's just awful.'

'Yeah, poor Whiteside bore the brunt.'

I go to the window and look outside as Mam bemoans the dangers facing the elderly. Ultan spots me and waves, just as his brother mashes a snowball on his head. Not much of a garden since the extension. We used to have goalposts in the corner. Colin would make me fetch the ball whenever he knocked it over the wall. Now there's a trampoline sagging under the snow.

Danni calls the boys in and they reluctantly traipse towards the house. They leave a trail of gloves and scarves on the kitchen floor. Danni picks them up while my mother purses her lips.

I say, 'Can I help with anything, Danni?'

She's herding the boys into the parlour. 'Could you just put the pasta on? Use a whole pack.' She takes my bag before I can say anything. 'I'll put this in the spare room.'

A pot of water is already on the boil. I fetch spaghetti from a press, use the trick of hammering the packet on the counter so the noodles burst through the top. Mam plucks some rolled-up tissue from her sleeve. She says, 'And how is Sarah getting on with her ... odyssey?'

'I don't know really. Fine, I suppose.'

'It's madness, going off on her own like that. If she was my daughter I'd be worried sick.'

I stir the water and allow the pasta to sink into the roil. 'Sarah can look after herself I'm sure.'

'I might give her a text, let her know that she can call if she's stuck anywhere.'

'Mam, we've broken up.'

'Yes, but that's only for the time being. Once she's home and she has this travel bug out of her system, then who knows?'

Mam had always been fond of Sarah, perhaps because we met in UCD, where Mam herself had gone to college. She'd say, 'We were so much more down to earth there.'

120

A commotion by the front door brings a welcome distraction. Colin is back from work. Some shouted greetings from the boys. A murmur between Colin and Danni, and then he yells out, 'Louise, come down for your dinner.'

He comes in with rumpled suit and loosened tie, but he seems in good form. He envelops Mam in a hug and asks how she got over.

'I walked. It's only a few inches.'

'Well, you're not walking back,' he says, and Danni offers to drop her home later.

Mam lives in the ground-floor apartment of a nearby block, redbrick and very plush. After Dad died, she couldn't bear to live in the house alone, so Colin suggested that he move the family in. He pays her rent every month. I've never asked what it is, but it's definitely not the going rate. Not these days.

Colin takes two Hop Houses from the fridge and opens them with the bottle-opener attached to the door. He hands me one just as Lolo wanders in, some gangly young fellow in tow, who she introduces as her new boyfriend, Specker.

Mam says to Danni, 'What did she say?'

'Specker.'

'What's that?'

'His name.'

'Oh.'

He has a fade cut, floppy blond fringe and prominent Adam's apple. He nods and says, 'Are yiz all right?'

Colin pauses with a beer halfway to his mouth. 'We are, Specker. Thanks for asking.'

On TV the news is mid-bulletin. A wide-angle shot of terraced Georgian houses on Mountjoy Square. It focuses on one, run-down with boarded-up windows, the door painted in rainbow colours, a banner hanging from the first floor saying, RECLAIM THE CITY.

A small crowd of people huddle on the snowy street, with gardaí standing to the side. Two vans pull up, the number plates removed, and a dozen men emerge in black jackets and balaclavas. Two carry a battering ram between them. They climb the steps, and with one well-timed swipe, the door is demolished.

Colin says, 'Turn it up.'

The masked men rush in as the volume marker creeps along the screen. We hear the yells of several squatters being escorted from the building. The gardaí turn a blind eye as they're steered into the unmarked vans and driven away.

Suddenly, Colin is on screen, a microphone hovering beneath his mouth, with the house in the background and a woman with crew cut and Doc Martens being manhandled down the steps.

Senan cries out, 'It's Daddy!' and Colin says, 'Shush, shush.'

Naturally, TV Colin says, *our clients are delighted with the ruling in the High Court today. It reaffirms a fundamental, constitutional right, that a landlord can do as he wishes with his own hard-earned asset, and that no one*, he glances at the camera here, *can usurp that right.*

It cuts again to the RTÉ reporter, who says that other Occupy movements in the city face similar evictions. The piece finishes with a panning shot of Mountjoy Square, picturesque in the snow, the vans driving off, one of the back wheels skidding, and then a close-up of the front door, its LGBT colours cracked and broken.

Kitchen Colin says, 'Did you ever think you'd see the day that a Lyster would be on the Six One News?'

Mam says that he was wonderful, so assured. On screen, the news has moved on to another story. Emma Harte and Tom Wickham are shown on the backdrop.

Lolo has stood and is staring at her father. 'I can't believe this. You're like a bailiff during the Famine.'

I slip the remote from Danni's hand, but she hardly notices. Colin says, 'You don't understand, Lolly.'

The newsreader mentions Wickham and I raise the volume.

'Your name was plastered on the screen,' Lolo says. 'How am I supposed to go to school now that everyone knows my dad shills for vulture funds?'

The news lady's voice becomes loud enough to dominate. *Mr Wickham had been declared missing in the days following the disappearance of Ms Harte, but now possible sightings of the man have been reported in his hometown of Granard, County Longford. Locals have suggested that he has been staying in the family homestead, and gardaí say they wish to speak with Mr Wickham as a matter of urgency.*

Everyone in the kitchen has turned to look at me. I frown at the remote and say, 'Sorry, pressed the wrong button.' I reduce the news to silence. 'What were you saying, Lolo?'

But Danni interrupts. 'Perhaps we should all sit down for dinner.'

Near the end of the meal, Colin tops up my glass from a bottle of red. 'You should have seen that house, Jim. Magnificent staircase and plasterwork all covered in mould. They were burning broken-up pallets in the fireplaces. Mattresses in every room, bongs and crack pipes scattered about.'

Danni says, 'Col,' and she glances at the boys.

I ask where the bailiffs came from, and he says they were private security. 'The ACA. Ex-guards, retired Special Branch, even a few old British Army guys. Not to be messed with. They'd find your burglar soon enough if the police can't be bothered. They have a website.' He pats a pocket, looks to the corner where his phone is charging and then gestures to me. 'Give us your phone.'

He'll make a fuss if I refuse, so I unlock the phone and slide it over.

Ultan is twirling spaghetti against a spoon. 'You always say no screens at the table.'

Colin sits back, begins tapping and swiping. Mam says to Lolo, 'Have you your Christmas tests soon, love?'

'In a few weeks. Should be okay.'

'And do you have exams coming up as well … young man?'

Specker says, 'No, I'm fourth year in St Canice's. I'm thinking of dropping out though, focus on my music.'

Colin says he didn't realise that was an option. He tuts. 'You got a message, Jim. From … no name. How do I get back to Google?' He begins pressing at the screen. 'Shit, I opened it, sorry.'

I want to reach over and grasp the phone, but I place my fork down and take a sip of wine.

With a frown Colin says, 'Weird,' and turns the screen to face me. 'Isn't that your front door?'

A photograph is looking down the basement stairwell at the front of Whiteside's, the snow on the steps stark in the camera flash. The curtains on the window are drawn, just as I'd left them. Otherwise, it's dark, so the picture may have been taken just now. Along the top of the screen, the sender's 089 number is displayed.

I say, 'Show me,' and take the phone back, quickly check for a message beneath the picture. There's none, but there hardly needs to be.

Colin says, 'Who'd send you that?'

'Whiteside's daughter. She said she was going to survey the damage today. Probably just letting me know my place is all right.'

He reaches for the phone again, but I slip it back into my pocket. 'ACA. I'll remember.'

I wake before dawn. A strange feeling of being home even though everything is different. The walls are smoothly plastered, the door is dark wood with a burnished chrome handle. On the carpet my phone is lying face-up, the screen reassuringly blank. I can't help but lift it, check messages, open news apps. Halfway down the RTÉ homepage I see the grainy picture of me and Emma Harte from the Tesco security camera. *New still released in hunt for missing woman.*

I tap the story, pinch-zoom the image. Emma's head is dipped down. Little of her face is visible. I'm glancing over my shoulder, which causes motion blur. The resolution is too low to make out anything of my clothes. Just a dark jacket, dark jeans.

I scan through the article. The same information about Emma and her disappearance. How the image just came to light. I see Shauna Shaw's name. She's quoted as saying that they can't be sure it's Ms Harte, though they did seek the opinion of an expert.

I place the screen on my chest. Was I the expert?

Gardaí are appealing for the man in the picture to come forward to assist with their inquiries. He's described as being about 5 foot 10 inches in height – I'm 6 feet – *short brown hair, and medium build.*

I get up to dress and make the bed, take my backpack, slip into the grey hall and creep to the kitchen. A display on the fridge says that it's downloading security updates. I open the door to pilfer a small carton of orange juice from a multipack.

'Can you get me one of those?'

Lolo is sitting at a counter near the window, doing homework in the meagre light.

'You'll go blind,' I say as I place the juice beside her. I tilt my head to look at her chemistry book. 'Do you have to get that done before school?'

'I'm not going. Not after Dad's performance on the news last night.'

'Your generation doesn't watch television.'

'Word will get around.'

'So why are you doing homework?'

'I'm just studying.'

Extricating the little straw from its plastic wrapper is proving difficult. I give up and put it in my pocket. 'I like Specker.'

'Yeah, me too.'

'Where'd you meet him?'

'A gig.'

'He was playing?'

'No, in the crowd.'

'What, he just came up to you?'

Her shrug is a little defensive. 'Yes. So?'

I ease back and nod, heft my rucksack with Emma Harte's coat on my shoulder. 'I have to head. Will you thank your mam for me?'

'For what?' she says, her eyes still on the page.

126

'Lolo, I'm sorry I had to call your dad when you came round last time. You know I'd no choice, right?'

She slowly blinks. 'I thought you had to head.'

I hold her eye and her cheeks colour a little. She looks back at her book.

'Yeah, you're right. Take it easy, Louise.'

The roads are dark and gleam with passing headlights. Grey slush collects in the gutters. I hail a cab. The taxi man tries to make conversation on the way into town but soon becomes sullen at my one-word replies. I'm dropped at the top of Gardiner Street and I make my way towards Mountjoy Square.

It's easy enough to find Colin's flophouse, with its boarded-up windows and graffiti. The front door has been replaced by a sheet of grey scuffed metal, bolted and padlocked. There's no sign of security on the street. Pedestrians wrapped against the cold pass by but pay me no heed.

I follow the road to the stable lane behind the terrace, count the houses till I come to the rear of the squat. The chain around the double gates is loose so the railings can be forced open by about a foot. I look both ways along the lane, up at the darkened windows of surrounding houses, then kneel and squeeze through the opening.

The back yard is narrow and long, a straight path in patchy snow and overgrown grass. Panes of glass lean against the wall to form makeshift greenhouses. I crunch along the path, conscious of my footprints. The back door doesn't budge when I press my shoulder against it. Beside it is a window opening secured by a sheet of opaque plastic with small metal studs along the edge.

Several give way with the first kick. The plastic bends and comes away, and I'm able to prise it off. I scramble over the sill. The room inside is bare and grey. Rubbish is strewn on the floor as though someone emptied a bin. The only door has a brass knob, freezing to the touch. If it's locked, I'm ready to retreat, but it turns and opens with barely a squeak.

I use the torch on my phone to find my way through the hallway until I can see the stained-glass fanlight above the front door, the mahogany staircase leading to the floors above. I push open a door to what was once the front parlour. It scrapes over warped floorboards. No light comes in through shuttered windows. My torch passes over a sullied mattress and bedding, a portable stove and gas cylinder, and the fireplace with Grecian urns and ivy carved in bas-relief. Somebody has swept up. There's a pile of lint and dust and a dead pigeon in the corner.

I climb the stairs. On the top floor is a small room with a square window looking out over the central garden, the terraced houses in the distance and Croke Park peeking over the rooftops. Like all the other rooms there's a mattress by the fireplace, but the bedding here is a bundle of clothes. I take Emma's coat from my bag and lay it on top.

It doesn't look right. I lift the clothes and separate them out. They're cold and damp and slightly greasy. I place Emma's coat between them, gather them together in a ball and drop them on the mattress.

My phone starts ringing. The police station number. A jaunty tone echoes in the squalid room. I let it ring out, go to voicemail, but instead of a notification, the phone rings again. She seems insistent.

'Hello James? It's Detective Shaw.'

'Oh, good morning.'

'I'm sorry if I woke you.'

It's just gone eight. 'No, I was up and about. Everything all right?'

'I'm calling to let you know that an arrest was made in relation to the attack on your landlord.'

'When?'

She pauses, as though that wasn't the response she was expecting. 'I believe in the early hours this morning. This is just for your own information and peace of mind. I've been trying to get in touch with Mr Whiteside or his daughter, but with no luck.'

From the window, I can see a van with ACA written on the side pull up on the street below. Two men get out.

'Has Mr Whiteside returned to the house, do you know?'

'No, I … actually, I'm sorry, Detective, I'm just getting another call.'

'If you see either of them, perhaps you can inform them.'

The men have climbed the stone steps. One is flicking through a heavy keychain.

'Of course, of course. I better take this.'

'Just quickly,' she says, 'if you're needed as a witness, we'll be in touch. The individual has many outstanding charges, so the assault on Mr Whiteside may not even be a priority.'

I hear the front door open, the strain of two voices and some heavy footsteps. I look at the phone, hear the tinny voice of Shaw say, 'Mr Lyster?' hang up, and silence the phone.

The men are speaking in short, gruff sentences that I can't make out. I creep from the room, look down through the hairpin turns of the banisters. The hallway below is flooded with light, a sweep of shadow as the men move about. One of them has gone into the front parlour. The other begins to climb the stairs, his gloved hand grazing the handrail. I take a step back, pause when a floorboard creaks. The man stops at the first floor and goes into one of the drawing rooms.

I slip down the stairs as quietly as I can, hear the man in the drawing room struggle to open a window shutter. On the return I can see the ground-floor hallway, the open front door and the snowy street beyond. I descend a few more steps, but I can tell the guy in the parlour is coming out. There's no way to pass without being seen. If I sprint, I could be on the street in a moment, but what if he grabbed me, or tripped me, or decided to give chase?

I turn around so it looks like I'm climbing the stairs, open the camera on my phone, point it at a broken baluster and call out, 'Hello.'

They each come out of their respective rooms, one guy above me, one below. I concentrate on my phone and snap a picture. The flash punctuates the silence.

The guy below, wielder of the keychain, says, 'Who the fuck are you?'

'You're the ACA guys, right?' I look critically at the photo on screen, bend down and take another.

'This is private property,' he says. 'How did you get in?'

A quick gesture. 'Door was wide open. Where is the door, by the way?'

'What?'

'I'm with the Office of Public Works. There's a conservation order on this building. What happened to the front door?'

Keychain looks at the temporary metal gate with some confusion. 'We had to knock it in.'

'It was two hundred and fifty years old.'

'Not our problem. We had a court order.'

'Let me see it.'

'I don't have it.'

I sigh, walk down the stairs, and make a show of examining the architraves and plasterwork. I stand next to him on the threshold of the parlour and take a picture of the room. It looks quite artistic, the fetid mattress and marble chimneypiece in cold, slanting light. Like something you'd see on Pinterest.

'Here, you can't be taking pictures.'

'Mr ... sorry, what's your name?'

'You don't need my name. What's yours?'

'I already told you. The fact of the matter is that nothing can be done with this house until a full conservation report is carried out. Until then, the ACA will be liable for any damage to the fabric of the building. Hold on there till I have a look at the front.'

I brush past him and out to the street. Traffic is light and I go onto the road, turn to take a portrait photo of the entire house. Keychain watches sullenly from the door, but perhaps conscious that he will be in the shot he ducks back inside.

I walk away. Quick strides to the nearest corner, and around it without looking back. The Church of St Francis Xavier fronts onto Gardiner Street. Giant pillars and triangular pediment hemmed in by Georgian houses. I take shelter in the portico and look towards Mountjoy Square to ensure that neither of the men has followed. Ice has formed over holy water in a wide stone font. I break through with my fingers and touch some water to my forehead.

Only a skeleton crew has made it to the library, Bridget, naturally, not among them. Helena is in the office when I arrive. She spends much of the morning following the progress of Storm Lauren on the Met Éireann map. A great swirl of green, yellow and red has made landfall at Dingle and is tracking towards Dublin. HR emails to say readers' services are cancelled for the afternoon and most staff will get a half day. Helena coos in delight and offers to make tea. She's in the kitchenette when Douglas Tilley phones.

He says, 'It seems snow will be general all over Ireland.'

'Did you make it in?'

'No, I've decided to hunker in Dalkey until the thaw. Lilianna let me know that she won't be stirring either. Could you nip upstairs to lock up the manuscript?'

Tilley's office is serene, just a creak in the mezzanine as icy wind rattles past the window. The archive box is on the worktable. I check on the manuscript beneath the lid, then take the box to the cabinet in the corner, lock it with a set of keys Tilley keeps hidden in his desk. A notebook is left on the worktable, deep red buckram with a black elastic strap. I open it up. Libby's lecture notes, quotes from history books with meticulous citations, snatches of Latin transcribed from the text. Her handwriting is forward-slanting and neat. Interspersed are small sketches, medieval characters from the margins of manuscripts, coats of arms, a rubbing from a round wax seal. Taken together the effect is beautiful, like the commonplace book of a Victorian scholar.

Flicking through the pages I spot my name, my phone number, and 'Neary's 6pm', and I see her again leaning over the bar, turning to greet me with that ambiguous half-smile. In her notes she misspelled

Lyster but that's okay. I close the notebook, take out my phone and snap a picture of the cover. I WhatsApp it to Libby with, Tidying up for Tilley. Do you need this?

She's online and replies quickly. Thought I'd lost it! How will I get it from you?

Fancy being snowed in at my place? I'll make dinner. I also have box sets and wine.

She takes longer to reply this time, perhaps thinking of excuses.

Box sets you say? I'm sold. I'll be over round seven … x

On the way home I stop into Tesco on Dorset Street, glance at the security camera that took the still of me and Emma Harte, pick out ingredients for a stew, two frozen pizzas and three bottles of wine. The flat is tidy, but I still give it the once-over. I light a fire, prep the veg. Mid-afternoon I check on Lauren's progress. Her eye is over the Shannon, tendrils in all four provinces now, and I feel an odd sense of comfort at her approach.

Headlights sweep over the top of the window. The engine of a car cuts out. One door opens and closes, and then another. I wait for footsteps to begin their descent, but they don't come. Instead, the faint voice of Whiteside's daughter, and a moment later, soft patters on the landing above me.

I climb the internal stairs to listen. A shadow passes the bottom of the door, and the daughter's voice again, clearer this time: 'Daddy, I'm just putting the messages in the kitchen.'

So, Whiteside is home. I thought he'd be kept in until the storm had passed. Perhaps I should call up to check on him, but they know where I am if they need help. A little later, while I'm looking at Twitter photos of snowfall in the midlands, the daughter's car backs up and drives away.

As the light is dwindling, I change into running gear and begin to stretch. I leave my hoodie draped on the radiator until the last minute, but when I step outside its warmth is quickly lost. An icy sleet skitters over the driveway. Clouds in the west are low and heavy with a strange yellow tinge. All of Whiteside's curtains are closed. The lights are on in the front parlour. I tie the string of my hoodie, pull the sleeves up over my gloves, and set off.

In weather like this the first half mile is the hardest. Outside my place the footpaths are deserted. Traffic is heavy with an early rush hour. I run past the Botanic Gardens and the Tolka House, further up Glasnevin Hill to the high entrance gates of Addison Hall, a modern apartment complex. I follow a meandering road through the blocks, catching glimpses of people in the warm light of kitchens and living rooms. At the back of the complex the road ends with a pedestrian gateway to a communal park, just a wide grassy slope that runs down to the Tolka River. Away from the flats and the streetlights it barely feels like the city at all. The grass is speckled white, and for a while the wind blows right against me.

A footbridge crosses the river. Further on the path skirts the tall grey wall of Glasnevin Cemetery, but to the left there's a railing almost swallowed by bushes and gorse. The other side is scrubland, an overgrown strip between the river and the graveyard and the rear wall of the Botanics.

I peer into the wilderness for more than a minute, then take a glance behind me. The park is empty except for one lone figure in the distance, her head bent against the biting wind. I grip the top of the railing, feel the cold seep through my gloves. Here in the park,

I'm just a hardy jogger, out before the weather turns completely. I've no plausible excuse to venture beyond the railing.

Brambles scratch at my legs as I trudge through the undergrowth. I'm aware of the black flow of the Tolka somewhere on my left. My trainers leave tracks in the snow, but they won't last long. Up ahead a clearing is surrounded by stunted trees with bare limbs dusted white. I listen to the crunch of my own footsteps, watch the clouds of my breath. Beneath the trees is a sheet of corrugated iron, rusting and bent at the corners, with snow collecting in the grooves. I stand over it for a moment, reach down to grip one side, and pull it back.

In a rectangular patch of dark earth, the body lies swaddled in bedclothes and bin liners. A deep black stain has soaked into the ground. Woodlice scurry in the sudden exposure. Wind rustles through brambles like a whispering crowd. I don't move. I just watch flecks of pure white settle on the black plastic shroud.

PART TWO

CHAPTER 11

25 NOVEMBER
THE NIGHT SHE DISAPPEARED

A Friday like any other, drab and drizzly, with a hum of heaters and fluorescent lights, and me, Helena and Bridget in our own quiet bubbles. Douglas Tilley had been working in the library for forty years, and drinks were organised in Davy Byrnes to mark the occasion. I almost declined, but then Helena said she could murder a pint, and Bridget agreed, and it seemed churlish to back out. We trooped over, like the old days when we'd grab a drink with Matthew from Manuscripts and Charlie from the Chief Herald's Office, a tradition that fell away once Matthew and Charlie became a couple and then broke up.

Turnout for Tilley was low. The younger crowd hardly knew him, the old-timers knew him too well. 'They only put on these dos to remind me to retire,' he said to me at the bar, and after a glass of Pinot Grigio, he slipped away.

One round led to another. Usually, numbers would dwindle as people headed home, or went to meet with real friends, but this evening felt different. We had a cosy corner to ourselves, about eight of us, Bridget sitting next to me, then Helena, who was being flirted with by one of the student interns. Cold rain drummed against the stained-glass dome in the ceiling, and when a platter of fries and cocktail sausages arrived, we knew we were in it for the long haul.

Bridget asked me if Sarah might come over, but then she checked herself and said, 'Or isn't she gone abroad or something?'

I reminded her, though it had been discussed often on previous nights out.

'How are you finding the long-distance thing?'

'We broke up last month. It was something she wanted to do on her own.'

Bridget didn't seem all that surprised, or bothered. 'So, what are you doing for the weekend?'

'Nothing, probably.'

She took a sip of cider and said, 'You've always been like that, James.'

'Like what?'

'You rely on a girlfriend for a circle of friends.'

I tried to laugh it off. What else could I do? 'Maybe I just want a few days to myself.'

She shrugged and put her pint down and said, 'I need a piss.'

I was left to stew for a minute. It wasn't like Sarah had that many close friends anyway. When I first met her in UCD she was sitting alone in a half-filled lecture theatre, straight fringe, short ponytail, a kind of loose muslin scarf tied about her neck. For the whole lecture I was thinking of ways to strike up a conversation. So it surprised me, when others were standing and chatting and gathering coats, that she turned to me without a hint of shyness and asked if I would like to get a coffee. She had always been comfortable in herself. Perhaps because she had grown up alone. Her mother died when she was in her teens, leaving her a nice flat on the outskirts of Stoneybatter. Her father, she hardly spoke to once she had the means to move away. No siblings. The friends she knew from school, and the ones she made in college, flitted in and out of her life. If anything, we spent more time with the people I knew. Family get-togethers, after-work drinks, the occasional lazy Sunday afternoon in the pub with Arthur.

In a cubicle in the jacks I checked her Instagram. Her latest post was a selfie under the arches of a colonnade in Bologna. She looked carefree and smiling. I pinch-zoomed to check the details of her face. No stray artefacts. No blurring. The same muslin scarf was peeking beneath the collar of her coat. I thought about leaving a comment. Something light-hearted and gracious. But how would that come across – a friendly ex letting bygones be bygones, or something more overbearing?

Just then Arthur rang, and I let it go to voicemail. He was wondering if I was heading to Fagan's for a few. I texted back: Out with the work crowd. Looks like it will be a late one ...

The club was on the quays, an old biscuit factory with a stage on the ground floor, a warren of bars and rooms upstairs, vintage furniture and tall windows looking over the Liffey. It was one of Sarah's favourites. A band had been playing earlier. Now a DJ had taken over. We got drinks in one of the quieter rooms, where a slightly older crowd was lounging on sofas or swaying to My Bloody Valentine.

Bridget was in good form. She dragged me to the floor when some Pixies played, and we danced and smiled at each other. I felt her shoulder brush against my chest. Her face came close, and almost too late I sensed her lips approach mine. I turned my face, half hugged her and said in her ear, 'I'm going to get another drink.' When I returned to the table with a full pint, her coat was gone.

I was the last of the group, sitting for a while alone at a small table beside a Victorian fireplace with a nest of white fairy lights and an old upright Steinway, the boards removed so you could see its innards. I was fishing in my coat for some cigarettes when a woman sat beside me. She had round eyes and a narrow mouth which put me in mind of a mantis. Her dark shirt was open at the neck, a swirl of tiny embroidered flowers on the collar. She placed a bag at her feet. At first, I thought she was commandeering the table, that she assumed I was leaving, and I thought, *Would you take my grave as quick?*

Silently, she put her wallet down, and then her phone. I waited to see if she would look at me and smile, or apologise for the intrusion, but she just kept staring at the black screen. I finished my pint and leaned towards her.

'Would you like a drink?' I said above the music.

She looked at me for the first time, a flicker on her face, perhaps amusement, but that soon passed. She opened her wallet and took out two fivers.

'No, it's fine,' I said, but she remained still until I took the money.

'A gin and tonic in a slim glass.'

At the bar I glanced back. Her phone was flashing. An incoming call. She dabbed at the screen to reject it. I brought the drinks over and placed hers down with a small stack of change. She had taken a sip before I could sit.

'What's your name?' I said with a smile, and she said, 'It's Emma. What's yours?'

'It's James.'

From her bag she took a small bookie's pen, slid the white napkin from under her glass, and asked, 'What's your number?'

Slightly on the back foot, I gestured to her phone. 'Would it not be easier to type it in directly?'

'That's not mine.'

'Oh.'

She remained looking at me with pen poised. I reeled off my number. She wrote it down, folded the napkin and placed it in the pocket of her jeans.

'Are you here with friends?' she asked.

'I was earlier. They called it a night a little while ago.'

'Why did you stay?'

'Just to finish my drink.'

'Now you have another drink to finish.'

The almost-full pint glistened on the table. 'Just one for the road.'

'So you're heading after this one?'

'Maybe. It depends.'

'On what?'

I looked to see if she was making fun of me. Her gaze was steady, completely sincere.

I said, 'Are you here with anyone?'

'Apart from you?'

'Yes, apart from me.'

'No. I'm waiting for someone.'

'It's getting late. Perhaps they're not coming.'

'If they weren't coming they'd have told me.'

She fished the lime slice from her glass and let it fall wetly on the table. For a moment her eye was drawn towards a doorway, and she became still. When I looked, the doorway was empty. Ice slid in her glass as she finished her drink. She placed it down and said, 'Can you get me another?'

I asked if she was all right. Was someone bothering her? If so, she could tell the bouncers and they'd get rid of him.

'It's not that simple.'

'Or the guards then.'

'Definitely not the guards.'

I waited to see if she would say more. When I stood to order the drink she placed her hand on my arm. 'Where do you live, James?'

'Glasnevin.'

'Can we go there?'

'This minute?'

'Yes.'

She was looking straight at me, her face blank, as if she didn't care one way or another how I might respond. Her fingers had gripped my sleeve slightly. I shrugged and said, 'Yeah, sure.'

She fetched her bag from the floor, placed the phone and the wallet inside. At the table next to us, some girls were huddled together in a group selfie. Emma stood, lifted one of their coats from the back of a chair without any of them noticing, a retro Afghan of tan suede and white fleece trim, and donned it in one movement. She said to me, 'Are we going?' and I said, 'Yes.'

She led me past shoe-gazing dancers and crowded bars to a stairwell. It was narrow and dark, a red hue from exposed lightbulbs. Her hair had gathered like a nest in the hood of the coat.

On the ground floor she started patting the pockets and withdrew a brown clutch purse. She looked at it quizzically as though someone had slipped it into her own coat.

She handed it to me. 'When we reach the door, tell the bouncers you found this here.'

The purse was heavy and clinked when I turned it over.

'Do you understand?'

I said, 'Yes,' and she nodded for me to go ahead.

The first bars of 'Pictures of You' had struck up, and there was a migration to the dance floor. I weaved my way towards the door. Two bouncers had their backs to me. The sharpness of the cold air made me pause, but when one of the men turned, I showed him the purse. 'This was lying at the bottom of the stairs back there.'

His eyes were wide-set, and I focused on the expanse at the bridge of his nose. He said, 'Do I look like fucking lost and found?'

Long ago I decided never to answer rhetorical questions, so I just stood there mutely.

The other guy took the purse, flicked the clasp and opened it up. Bank cards in their pouches, at least a couple of twenties in the wallet. Emma Harte skirted by and slipped out to the street.

The bouncer closed the purse and put it inside his bomber jacket. 'We'll take care of it.'

A small queue of stragglers was trying to get in before closing. Pale lamplight fell upon the Liffey. I looked both ways for her. At the corner of the bridge she was waiting, almost in silhouette, hands in pockets and hood raised, her breath rising in tendrils. When she saw me, she turned to cross the river and I hurried to catch up.

'Will I hail a taxi?' I said.

'No, I want to walk.'

I fell into step beside her. A smell of perfume on the cold air from the stolen Afghan. I'd had one-night-stands before, but usually the girl and I would have some mutual acquaintance. There'd be drinks and flirting, shouted conversations over loud music, fumbling in the cab ride home. She didn't seem drunk. Everything we had done so far had been at her suggestion. Was she on something? It didn't much matter to me, but if she woke up at my place not knowing who I was or how she got there, it would not bode well.

I stopped beneath the awning of a shuttered kebab shop, and after a few steps she did the same. I said, 'Are you stuck or something? I can lend you twenty quid if you want to get a cab home. It's no hassle.'

She seemed confused, perhaps annoyed. 'I thought we were going to your place.'

'It's just you've hardly said five words to me.'

'And that bothers you?'

'Well ... not particularly.'

'Then why have we stopped?'

'I thought you had to meet someone.'

'I changed my mind.'

A couple tottered past, a young guy giving a girl a piggyback ride, her bare feet wobbling in front, the straps of her high-heeled shoes wrapped in her fingers. She giggled and said, 'Coming through.' Emma watched after them benignly, as if they were friends of hers.

After a moment I said, 'Did you not have a coat of your own?'

She looked at me with the ghost of a smile and showed me a fleece cuff. 'This is my coat.'

Her gaze was steady, unblinking but gentle. She said, 'Anything else?'

I shook my head, and we resumed walking.

It was perfectly still, freezing cold, a faint halo of mist around each streetlamp. Emma turned down a narrow lane with cobblestones underfoot, the high bolted gates of warehouses, shuttered tattoo parlours and a taekwondo gym. She stopped at a building with a mural of a giant squirrel nibbling an acorn. Beside the door was an intercom, a keypad, and doorbells with nametags attached. Only the top one was filled in: re:Thread Ltd.

Emma punched in a code – diagonally from nine to one, the one tapped twice – and a bolt released. She pushed the door a little, put her hand on my chest and said, 'Wait here. I'll be back before you know it. I promise.'

She entered a pitch-black hallway, turned to close the door, but before she did she opened it to peer at me. 'If anyone comes, ring the bell.'

'Who's going to come?'

The door closed. I heard her footsteps retreat, and then silence. No glimmer of light except for the LEDs on the number pad. I placed my fingers on the cold metal door and pushed, but it held fast.

For a minute or two I leaned in the jamb and pulled my coat tight. My phone pinged. A WhatsApp from Helena to our small intra-office group, showing a photo from Davy Byrnes earlier in the night. Tilley was looking sheepish at the head of the table. The rest of us had our glasses raised. Bridget and me sat together in the background, her shoulder close to mine. I tapped on her name and saw she was online, which meant she could see that I was as well. Perhaps I needed to smooth things over. Make light of the near kiss. I typed out, That would have made for an awkward Monday ... and hit *Send*.

The little tick marks turned blue. She had seen the message. The word *typing* appeared next to her name as she composed a response. It was a long one. I watched the screen for a minute but nothing came. Bridget logged off. Next to her name it just said, *Last seen today at 02.11.*

I stamped my feet. The freezing night air was clearing my head. I looked again at the door and the windowless wall. The giant squirrel hunched over me. My finger hovered over the doorbell, brushing the cold chrome for a moment, before I stuffed my hands in my pockets and began walking towards Bachelor's Way.

I had gone a hundred yards when a dark saloon came slowly around a corner. Its wheels rumbled on the cobblestones. The car's full headlights shone briefly, as if the driver wanted to get a look at me, before they dipped again. I continued walking. When the car reached the door Emma had gone in it slowed to a stop and remained with its engine ticking over, a swirl of exhaust tinged red by the brake lights. I waited to see if anyone would emerge, or if Emma would come from the building and climb in, but the car stole away again and turned left onto Capel Street.

I went back to press the doorbell. All was silent for a minute. There was no buzzing noise, or static from the intercom, or flashing light. I pressed it twice more, then entered 9511 into the keypad and let myself in.

The faint glow of a fire-exit sign was enough to make out a corridor, a staircase leading up to the left, and beyond that a doorway, with a sliver of light along its sill. I considered going up the stairs but chose the doorway instead. It opened into a wide storage room with fluorescent lights. Laid out on the floor were giant bundles of clothes, each about six feet tall – jumbled-up shirts and trousers and dresses, like spoils from a war or a natural disaster. The bundles were arranged by colour. One was a hodgepodge in various shades of lavender, one had every shade of orange, another blue.

Along the far wall was a bank of washing machines; next to those, a large crate in metal brackets with a chute underneath. I looked inside and saw the interlocking tines of a shredder, a few stray threads stuck in its teeth. A large work table was strewn with scissors and measuring tapes, and a tightly wound bale of red cloth, about a metre in length. The bale had been scored lengthwise. Layers of fabric on either side of the cleft were puckered and frayed, leaving a large gap in the middle. Unrolled next to the bale was a leather holder for knives – a dozen or so blades in individual pouches. The middle knife was missing.

Everything went dark. I gripped the edge of the table to keep my bearings. Overhead faint streaks of orange lingered in the fluorescent tubes. The green fire-exit sign was partially obscured by a bundle of clothes. Otherwise all was black. I said Emma's name, and listened for footsteps or the opening of a door.

With the torch on my phone I looked about. The giant clothes piles, now drained of their colours, seemed vaguely sinister. I picked my way through them, shining the torch left and right. In the corridor I checked the stairwell but couldn't see a landing, so I went to the front door, pressed a red button on the latch, and heard the bolt release.

Emma Harte was standing across the street, the napkin on which she'd written my number held in one hand, her phone in the other. A faint siren sounded in the distance. When she saw me, she tossed the phone into her bag, and said, 'How did you get in there?' with a hint of accusation.

'I used the code.'

'Why didn't you just ring?'

'I did. You never answered.'

She brushed past me to make sure the door had closed tight. I told her about the car, how it had paused just here before it moved away.

'What kind of car?'

'I'm not sure. Dark blue, I think. Sort of medium-sized.'

Her round eyes held mine for a moment, and she said, 'You'd make a lousy witness.'

'Who was it?'

'Did he see you waiting here?'

I shook my head and gestured at the street. 'He passed me down there a bit.'

'What were you doing down there?'

No good answer came to mind. 'Walking home.'

She nodded thoughtfully. 'Do you want to go home now?'

'Yes.'

'Can I still come with you?'

The fleece on her hood ruffled in a breeze. Her lower lip was chapped. She bit it, perhaps self-consciously, when she saw me looking.

I said, 'If you like.'

We walked in silence. Dorset Street was deserted except for a couple kissing in the glow of an all-night Tesco, and the odd taxi on the prowl. We turned off the main road and passed between terraced houses. Sparse streetlamps in the darkness. A few windows lit behind closed curtains. It was so empty we walked along the broken white line in the middle of the road.

A faint noise made her stop and look back. Away in the distance the motion sensor of a driveway triggered, and we watched it blink out again. Nothing else stirred.

Emma said, 'How much further?'

'I'm just down the road.'

Whiteside's place was dark except for the porchlight that he often forgot to turn off. She paused when she saw the house.

'This you?'

'Just the basement flat.'

'Any roommates?'

'No, the landlord is upstairs but separate.'

Our shadows mingled on the concrete steps down to my door. In the living room, I put the dimmer on low while Emma took off the Afghan and draped it on the edge of the sofa. It slithered down the side and onto the floor, where she left it.

I went to the bookshelf that acted as drinks cabinet. 'I have some gin, I think,' moving bottles aside, 'but no tonic. There's orange juice.'

'Yeah, fine.'

I went into the kitchen. Earlier I'd left a bin bag tied up by the counter. It made the place look untidy, so I gathered it up, excused myself to Emma for a moment, and hurriedly brought it to the wheelie bins by the front gate. Ice had crusted over the lid. As I was making room, a beer bottle slipped and bounced on the pavement. I returned to the warmth of the flat, fetched the juice carton and ice tray and brought the drinks to Emma.

She was standing by my CD rack and had taken out a case. She said, 'You actually own physical media.'

'Yeah, I think it's the librarian in me.'

'The librarian?'

'It's what I do for work.'

'Oh.'

I said, 'That place you were in. Is that where you work?'

She showed me the album she was holding. 'I saw them last year in Whelan's.'

'Then we might have been at the same gig.' I pointed to a girl on the cover. 'I used to know the bass player.'

'Used to?'

'Friend of a girlfriend.'

Emma nodded. She ran her finger over the girl's face.

'Do you have a boyfriend?'

She slipped the case back into its empty slot. 'Yes.'

'Where is he?'

'Not here.'

'Was that who you were waiting for in the club?'

Instead of answering she sipped her drink. A lock of hair fell down over her shoulder. When I pushed it back, she stiffened, and I brought my hand away.

She looked at me then. Her eyes drifted to the side as if she was trying to recall something. She put her glass on the bookshelf, took my glass as well and set it alongside. She came closer and kissed me, pushing against me so much that I had to take a step back. Her hands snaked around my neck and gripped my hair. She bit down on my lip, just to the point of it stinging, then disengaged and stood back.

'Can I use your bathroom?'

'Ehm, yeah. It's just down—'

'I think I'll find it.'

Her bag was on the floor at the foot of the sofa. She took it and slipped into the hallway.

I touched my lip and looked at my finger. No blood at least. The bathroom door in the hall was a few slivers of light in the darkness. As I passed, one of the taps was running. Something clattered lightly on the tiles. I went to the bedroom, smoothed down the duvet, bundled dirty clothes into the basket and tossed some old trainers in the wardrobe. While drawing the curtains I saw a pale diamond of light on the lawn from Whiteside's bedroom window.

The bathroom door creaked open, and Emma made her way back to the living room. She'd left the light on. Small puddles of water had collected around the sink. The toilet lid was down as though she'd been sitting on it.

In the living room, she was standing beside the cold hearth. Her presence made the room seem unfamiliar. A basket of kindling and wrapped fire logs sat beside the fireplace, and she asked if we could light one. I told her I'd have to fetch matches, but she said, 'Wait.'

She felt in the pocket of the Afghan for a lighter, was about to hand it to me but changed her mind. She knelt down, placed a fire log on the grate and touched a flame to the wrapper. We watched the paper burn away and ignite the briquettes inside.

Emma got up and went to the drinks shelf to top up her gin. She looked at some book titles and ran a finger over smooth spines.

'You're like me,' she said. 'You buy more than you can read.'

'I'll get around to them eventually.'

'I just do it to fill the gaps.'

She pulled out the colourful cover of a fantasy novel. 'Bit out of place.'

'Belonged to a friend.'

'Girlfriend?'

'Ex.'

She thumbed through the first few pages. 'But it's brand new.'

'Recently ex.'

'What's her name?'

For some reason my first instinct was to lie, though the name would mean nothing to her. Emma looked over and smiled at my hesitation.

'Sarah.'

She nodded, as if that was what she was expecting, replaced the book, brought her drink over and knelt on the hearthrug.

'Show me a picture of her.'

'I don't have one.'

'Yes you do. On your phone.'

Her expression had changed. She seemed serious, almost stern, but then she tilted her head and smiled.

I swiped through the gallery, found one of Sarah sitting under cherry blossom in the Botanics. When I knelt beside Emma she took the phone from me, her knuckles brushing my palm.

'What if we rang her?'

'Don't.'

'She might like it. Make her believe you're still thinking about her. Though maybe she'd prefer it if you weren't thinking about her.'

Before I could take the phone back she began swiping.

'You have lots of her.' She paused and smiled and turned the screen to show me Sarah laughing in the dappled light of a rainforest, a baby macaque trying to take the sunglasses perched on top of her head. 'When was that taken?'

A while ago, I said. The first trip we took together. I reached out and Emma gave me the phone. I closed everything and locked the screen. 'Let me see a picture of your boyfriend.'

'No.'

'What, you don't have any?'

'I've loads, I just don't want to show you.' She took a sip of her gin, which at this stage was almost neat. 'How long were you going out?'

'Two and a half years.'

Emma looked around the room, the leather sofa and the framed prints of Malton's Dublin. 'She really left her mark on the place.'

'She had her own flat.'

'That makes sense.'

'What does your boyfriend do?'

'You like to keep things at arm's length. Don't you want to know what I do?'

'I asked earlier, and you wouldn't say.'

'He and I do the same thing.'

'You work for the same company?'

'We set it up. How did you and Sarah end things?'

'Why do you care?'

'I enjoy break-ups. Was it messy and melodramatic?'

'No.'

'Did she cry at least?'

'Yes.'

'You brute.'

'It was her idea.'

'That means it was your fault.'

'No.'

'So, what happened?'

The fire shifted, and a spark spirited up the chimney. 'She wanted us to move in together.'

Emma's nose wrinkled in distaste.

'She thought it was stupid paying two rents,' I said. 'But she didn't like it here, so it was either her place or a new place.'

'I like it here.'

'Thanks.'

'It's nice being underground. And it's important to have your own space. Do you ever just feel like walking somewhere wild and barren, just to be on your own?'

'I jog sometimes. Nowhere that remote.'

'I grew up near the North Bull Wall. Do you know it?'

I said I did. A sea wall that extends about a mile into Dublin Bay.

She said, 'Sometimes when it was stormy and the tide was in, and everyone was too scared to go out, I'd walk right to its very tip, out to the statue of Mary, so it was just me and her with the sea on all sides, like we were standing on the very water.'

'Sounds dangerous.'

'One or two hairy moments all right. But the feeling that no one could get at you. It was worth it.'

She studied my face for a moment. 'Do you have any wine?'

When I came back from the kitchen, Emma was lounging on the sofa looking at a framed photo of me and Lolo at her confirmation dinner. I had an urge to take it from her and return it to its place on the mantelpiece.

'Cute,' she said.

'My brother's daughter.'

'He must be a bit older than you.'

'A good bit, yeah. He married young.'

She nodded and placed the picture face down on a side table. 'A mistake you made sure not to repeat.'

'He wouldn't consider it a mistake.'

'Opting instead for a succession of Sarahs.'

She slouched back in the sofa holding a glass by its stem. With the toe of her shoe, she nudged an archival box on the shelf beneath the coffee table.

'Why have you taken a dislike to someone you've never met?'

'I have nothing but compassion for her,' she said. 'What's in the box?'

'Work stuff.'

'Can I see?'

'If you like.'

She placed the box on the tabletop and removed the lid. Inside were a number of folders with call numbers neatly written in pencil, and a stamp that said, *Not to be removed from reading room.*

Emma opened the first. A sepia-tone interior showed a young woman in a pale dress reclining on a chaise longue, her bridal veil pooling on the carpet before her. She appeared to be sleeping except one eyelid was half open. Beside her a groom, jilted by fate, wearing an ill-fitting suit and waxed moustache, stood glumly.

Emma said, 'I knew there was something about you.'

In the next folder, a black-haired woman sat on a wooden chair against a wall of cracked plaster. From her clasped hands a small crucifix protruded. Her lifeless eyes were open, gazing to the left.

'I just catalogue them.'

Emma reached for another folder. 'Did Sarah ever see them?'

'She wasn't much interested.'

'I bet.'

Twins in muslin gowns stared at each other across a table set for afternoon tea. Next, a girl lay propped up in bed, an open book cradled in her palms.

'Are they all women?'

'Not all of them.'

'Just the ones you took home.'

I reached over to close a folder and put it back in the box. 'They shouldn't be handled without gloves.'

Emma said, 'I'd frame them and put them on the walls.'

'They don't belong to me.'

'Has anyone noticed them missing?'

'They're not missing.'

She moved closer and touched my cheek. Her fingers smelled of gin and orange. I kissed her. We both tried to ease each other backwards, then settled on leaning sideways on the sofa. Whenever I opened my eyes, I found her looking at me. She lifted her leg over mine, kicked the archive box by accident, and folders and photos spilled across the wooden floor.

The door knocker banged. Emma gripped me tighter. Our faces were close together, and she drew back a little.

'Were you expecting someone?'

It was well past three o'clock. I shook my head.

The knocker banged again. I began to disengage but Emma kept hold of me.

'Don't,' she said.

'It'll wake my landlord.'

I stood up, torn for a moment between picking up the photographs and going to the door, but a third knocking, louder and more persistent, sent me into the hall.

Outside stood a man in a dark three-quarter-length coat. He was an inch taller than me, with a stubble beard and shrewd narrow eyes and hair carefully tousled. If I'd met him in a pub I'd have taken a dislike to him.

He held up his hands when he saw me. 'I'm sorry, man. I'd never usually do this. I hope I didn't wake you.'

I glanced down at my work clothes, and then back at him. 'Can I help?'

'It's just I'm trying to find …' He shook his head and ran fingers through his hair. 'I'm trying to find my girlfriend. Is she here?'

His eyes drifted over my shoulder, more focused than they were a second ago. He noticed my hesitation, and said, 'Look, I don't care how you know her or why she's here. I've no quarrel with you. I'm worried about her.'

His voice was steady, despite his seeming agitation. I nearly asked, *Worried about what?* but Emma could hear everything that was being said. If she had wanted to reveal herself she could have done so already.

I said, 'I'm sorry,' and began closing the door.

He held his hand against it. 'You don't understand. She has these … episodes, you see. Mostly harmless, but sometimes not.'

'You've got the wrong place. I'm the only one here.'

As if she'd been waiting for a moment to contradict me, Emma called from the living room, 'Is that you, Tom?'

His face lifted at the sound of her voice. 'Yeah, it's me. Can I come in?'

'Ask James.'

He glanced at me, took my stillness as an invitation, and brushed past. I closed the door and followed him inside. Dead girls stared at us from the floor of the living room. Emma Harte reclined on the sofa. She and Tom exchanged a look. I couldn't see his face, but hers seemed mostly indifferent.

I hurriedly picked up the photographs, returned them to their folders, returned those to the box. Tom didn't notice what they were, or if he did, he showed no interest.

He said to Emma, 'You weren't in the club.'

She said, 'I was. Just not while you were there.'

'You were supposed to wait.'

'I'd waited long enough.' She showed him her wine glass, still half full. 'This is nice if you want some.'

Tom unbuttoned his coat and hung it on the back of the armchair. His movements had become calm, unruffled. He came to stand in front of me and offered his hand. 'It's James, right? I'm Tom.'

His fingers were cold, dry to the touch.

'Sorry again for all this. I appreciate you looking after Emma.' He kept hold of my hand until I made a reply.

'It's fine.'

'No, it's not. Don't downplay what you've done.'

With that he walked over to the drinks shelf. The only remaining wine glass held a bunch of toothpicks, a yellow-handled paring knife for cutting lemons, and a couple of old corks. He emptied the contents onto the tray, wiped the inside of the glass with his hand, and poured himself some wine. He and Emma took a drink at the same time, as if they'd made some silent toast.

Quietly, she said, 'I don't need to be looked after,' and he said, 'I know.' He sat down in the armchair, closed his eyes, and took a long breath through his nose.

I looked at these two strangers and wondered how this fraught reunion had come to take place in my front room. A weariness came over me. I had an urge to turn away, to walk down the hall towards my bedroom and collapse on the covers. Let them resolve whatever they had to resolve, just away from here.

I said, 'It's getting late. It was nice to meet you both, but I'm heading to bed. I've a taxi app if you need a ride somewhere.'

Emma remained silent as she rolled the stem of her glass between thumb and forefinger. Tom continued to rest his eyes. In meditation, he said, 'James is right.' He roused himself and leaned forward. 'Time to get out of his hair.'

He lifted his arm towards Emma and beckoned with his fingers, as if inviting her to rise. Instead, without having to be told, she took her bag from the side of the sofa and handed it to him. He settled again comfortably, propped the bag on his lap, and moved the handles aside.

The first thing he removed was the phone, which he placed on the armrest, then the napkin with my number – a quick glance at me before he set that down too. He unzipped pockets, felt along the lining, even turned the bag upside-down at one point. When he was content that the bag was empty he gently tossed it back to Emma's feet.

'What were you doing in the factory?' he said.

She drew her legs up and leaned an elbow on the armrest. 'When?'

'An hour or so ago. And don't say you weren't there, because *he* was there when I drove by,' he said, gesturing to me. 'And so was this.' He picked up and waggled the mobile. 'How else do you think I found you?'

Slightly perturbed, I said, 'It has a tracking device?'

'That might be overstating it. It's a phone. It has a security app.'

Emma said, 'I don't think it's overstating it.'

'This is my work phone,' he said. 'I'm entitled to know where it is.'

'I'm not sure a burner counts as a work phone. Besides, you knew I had it.'

'But you're never where you're supposed to be.'

His gaze had become dark, more intense. Hers remained tranquil. I used the moment to place the archival box on the shelf under the coffee table, pushing it in so it was out of the way.

The movement seemed to distract him. He blinked twice, turned to me again, shook his head in a manner meant to appear rueful. 'Maybe you think I'm some overbearing creep.'

The thought had occurred.

'I do it because I worry about her. As I said, she gets these …'

'Episodes,' Emma said.

He sighed and said, 'Well, what would you call them?'

'I think there's a tendency to over-diagnose these days.'

'Yeah, you go ahead and make light of it again.'

'Well, let's ask an unbiased observer. Tell us, James, do you think I'm having what could be characterised as "an episode"?'

I said, 'I'm not sure what qualifies.'

'Oh, that's easy,' she said, and she began to count on her fingers. 'Delusions, hallucination, confusion, paranoia, and disturbing thoughts.'

The fact that she could reel off symptoms was not reassuring, but she followed up by saying, 'Tom likes to send me the literature.'

I said that she hadn't struck me as deluded, or confused, or as seeing things.

'That's so sweet of you.'

'Earlier, I might have said you were paranoid, but perhaps not now.'

'You see?'

'I'm not privy to your thoughts, though.'

She pursed her lips and nodded. 'Perhaps that's just as well,' she said. 'Still, four out of five's not bad.'

Tom stood abruptly, and for the first time I saw Emma flinch. She tried to play it off with a languid blink and a stretch of her neck. But Tom had seen it, and perhaps satisfied, he slinked to the corner to pour another drink.

Emma wouldn't meet my eye. She went to take a sip from her own glass, then changed her mind and placed it on the coffee table. She rose and fished the Afghan coat from the floor, but again she seemed to have second thoughts. She folded it on the sofa.

I said to her, 'Emma, if you want to stay here, you can.'

She turned her face towards me. Her narrow mouth curled up in a crooked smile. 'I'll be all right.'

At the bookcase, Tom drained his glass. He lifted the bottle to look at the label, and said, 'I'll have to look out for that.'

He slipped his coat from the back of the chair, donned it and came to stand in front of me. 'James, I really am sorry for the imposition. Maybe our paths will cross again. Back in the Biscuit Factory perhaps. We could have a proper chat.'

He smoothed the lapels of his coat and then held out a fist to be bumped.

I said, 'Why did you look in Emma's bag?'

His bunched fingers lingered in the space between us. 'Excuse me?'

'Her bag. Why did you check it?'

His hand dropped. 'No reason.'

'Did she take something that belongs to you?'

His glance became cold. He said, 'Well, that's not really your concern, is it?'

'I just want to make sure she's all—'

'Look, James. I understand. Every guy she meets wants to help. Everyone wants to save her. But it's just a game she's playing. Believe me, she doesn't need—'

Emma picked up the paring knife and stabbed it into the side of Tom's neck.

He looked at me in confusion. Blood spurted onto his collar. He frowned and touched the plastic hilt with his fingertips. His lips parted to speak but no words came. I felt a sickening shudder, as if my own blood was draining in sympathy, as if the ground had subsided. Everything seemed on the verge of unravelling. The lengths I had gone to. The care I had taken. It might have all come to nothing.

I said, 'Jesus, Emma.'

Tom collapsed to his knees. He hunched over. Blood trickled to the floorboards like deep-red sealing wax. He smudged the pool with his finger, leaned back and held up his hand to show me.

'Stay still, Tom,' I said. 'Stay calm.' But he rocked back on his haunches and got to his feet. He tottered and righted himself, took a step towards Emma and fell again. He tried crawling, but his foot kept slipping in the blood puddle, leaving long, curving streaks. He dragged himself to the armchair, climbed into the leather seat and slumped back with a long sigh, like air being let from a football.

The yellow plastic handle protruded from his neck. Blood wept from the wound, making the front of his shirt sodden and shiny.

I said, 'What did you do that for?' and she said, 'Why isn't he dying?'

'He is fucking dying.'

'Take the knife out.'

Tom's eyes swivelled back and forth to follow this exchange. His teeth were stained red. A pink air bubble expanded from his lips, popped and left a spatter of blood in the stubble of his beard.

I said, 'Can you speak, Tom?' and he nodded slightly, then shook his head.

'We'll get help.'

Emma said, 'If you take the knife out it will be quicker.'

Tom squinted at her like she was standing in a light. He lifted a bloodstained hand as though he wanted her to take it. But the effort was too great and he let it drop again.

Emma felt along her own neck. 'I mean, there's veins and arteries. What else?'

'We should call an ambulance.' But it struck me that if an ambulance arrived, so too would the guards, and I couldn't let that happen.

She said, 'There's the windpipe as well, though his breathing doesn't seem too bad.'

Tom rubbed his mouth with the back of his hand and blinked hard to keep his eyes open. There was a bloodstain on the armrest which he tried to wipe with his sleeve. He beckoned for me to come near.

When I stood over him, he became agitated and motioned me closer. As I leaned down, his eyes fluttered and closed. It seemed as though he would drift away, but he stirred himself, lifted his mouth close to my ear, and with barely a breath said, 'Don't try to save her.'

He pushed past me to his feet and staggered but remained upright. With his elbow extended, he gripped the hilt. His eyes lost focus. He looked at me and I shook my head no.

Tom pulled out the knife and blood burbled like a drinking fountain. His eyes rolled backwards and he collapsed face-down. The knife skittered to Emma's feet. She stepped over it and came closer, as if to better see what she'd done. She bent and pulled aside the hearthrug so blood couldn't lap at the tassels.

A long silence, as if the room itself exhaled. She said to me, 'You might want to find a towel.'

Tom was a dark, motionless form in the dim light, an unnatural cant to his arm. Streaks and smears covered the floor and the sides of the chair. For a moment I couldn't see the knife, and a thought flashed that perhaps Emma had picked it up again. But there it was lying by the hearthrug, small and innocuous, the yellow handle rippled with blood.

In the corner there was a gym bag with a World Cup 2018 beach towel. I went to get it while Emma fetched the wine and brought it to the sofa. I coiled the towel into a snake and used it to dam the puddle. Emma sat curled up with her legs folded beneath her, like Sarah used to sit when she was watching TV. Her eyes and fingers rested on the rim of her glass. She was breathing heavily, shoulders visibly rising, though she showed no other sign of distress.

For a minute I didn't say anything. I stood in the middle of the room, one side a picture of normality with Emma snug on the sofa, the other blood-smeared and appalling. It seemed somehow impossible, some dreadful mistake that would right itself or be undone. I could feel a sense of panic creep over me, but once I noticed, it dissipated, and I only thought of what to do. An ambulance was useless. Maybe if we'd staunched the flow. Maybe if he'd kept the knife in place. I looked at his nose squashed flat in the blood puddle.

No possible good could come from calling the police. Even if I could convince them that I wasn't involved, the process would hang over me for years. Not only that, my whole life would be picked apart, and every strand examined. I could call Colin, or Arthur, but what could they do? Why would I drag them into something like this? Emma had turned her eyes towards me. In them, all I could see was concern, uncertainty, and I realised that there was only one option left.

Sitting next to her, I poured myself the last of the wine. I said, 'Why did you do that?'

She stretched her neck, and leaned a little closer. 'I was just tired of him.'

In the hearth, the briquettes of the fire log had reduced to embers. I took a sip and watched the smouldering, struck for a moment by the cosiness of it all. A flicker played on Tom's dark curls.

'How are you planning to explain it?'

She said, 'There's no explaining it.'

'Had Tom ever hit you?'

She frowned as though she found the question silly. 'No.'

'Was he controlling? Coercive?'

'Not as much as he liked to think.'

'You need something, Emma. Some excuse.'

'I can't tell anyone anything.'

'You could say it was self-defence.'

'It doesn't matter what I say.' She shifted about to face me, and for a moment seemed conflicted about telling me something. Finally, she said, 'Years ago in college, Tom got himself tied up with some bad people. He'd sell drugs to classmates. Harmless stuff really. But he'd often get into debt with this … gang, and he was always being threatened. When we set up the business, they said he could clear his debts if we let them use the factory for deliveries. Clean some money with fake orders. He had no other choice really. *We* had no other choice.'

I held her eye for a moment and she didn't look away. I said, 'Are these people still after you?'

'No, it's not like that. But if the police started digging, it would all come out.'

'So what are you going to do?'

'We always had a backup plan to leave, in case things got out of hand. I'll just stick to it.'

The telling of this seemed to unburden her. She leaned back on the cushions and rested her eyes.

'Where will you go?' I said.

She didn't answer, though a slight crease furrowed her brow.

'Wouldn't your family be upset?'

'For fuck's sake, James, would you ask something useful?'

'What will we do with Tom?'

Here she raised her head to look at the body. She said, 'He'll have driven here. I'll take him with me. Dump him somewhere.'

It was a busy road. Even at this hour. There would be night owls. Taxis. 'We can't just carry him out the front door.'

'Would he fit in a suitcase?'

'None that I own.'

'How about carry-on? He might squeeze into two,' she said.

'And we cut him how, exactly? With a breadknife?'

'Keep him here so.'

A clanking sounded in the ceiling above, but it was just the timed immersion coming on. I told Emma that I knew of a spot. From the upstairs windows of the house, you could see the round tower of O'Connell's grave in Glasnevin Cemetery, the trees in the Botanics and the curve of the Tolka River. I said, 'There's an old wicket gate out the back that leads to the Botanic Gardens.'

'He'd be found in there.'

'We wouldn't leave him there. There's another place. Through the gardens and beyond the walls.'

'Beyond the walls?'

'It's scrubland. A patch of wilderness by the river.'

She considered this for a moment. 'Sounds like a lot of work.'

'Emma, I'm happy enough to take my chances with the guards. If you want me to play along, you need to help.'

She unfolded her legs, stretched her arms and stifled a yawn. She said, 'I know you won't go to the guards.'

For a moment I wondered if she had read my thoughts. If she had sensed a bluff.

But then she said, 'If it comes to it, I'll tell them that you stabbed Tom. That I tried to stop you. That I pleaded and begged, but you were unmoved.' She placed her hand on my forearm, rubbing her thumb back and forth. 'I'm sorry, James. Truly I am. You're a nice guy, and you don't deserve any of this. But they'd believe me. You know they would.'

I didn't say anything. Perhaps she thought I needed convincing. I was happy to let her think she had done so.

Gently, her fingers slipped down to take my hand. 'I like your idea,' she said. 'We'll hide Tom. I'll disappear. No one need ever know that I was here. In a short while it will all be forgotten, like you never even met me.'

Her gentle, soothing tone reminded me of Sarah, when she set out her reasons for wanting to break up. It was on this same sofa as well.

I nodded once.

Emma smiled and said, 'Thank you, James.'

We went to work. I searched the flat for cleaning gear – basins and bin liners, Fairy liquid and bleach, cloths and towels and an old green duvet cover. I'd bought a multi-pack of marigolds a few days before, and soon Emma and I looked like a couple embarking on a spring clean.

We laid the duvet cover flat on the ground. Before moving him, Emma checked Tom's coat for his car keys and wallet. I lifted Tom by the arms, Emma took the legs, and we held him aloft to allow the last few dribbles to drain from his neck. The skin on his wrist felt cool. Then again, his fingers had been cold earlier as well. It was easier to lay him face down on the duvet cover. I brought his arms into his side. We covered and rolled him to swaddle him up. Only his feet remained sticking out, his black suede Oxfords stained red. Two heavy-duty bin liners went over his top half, two over the bottom, and I duct-taped them together around his waist.

Occasionally while we were cleaning, my eye would flit to the plastic bundle, but I could trick myself into believing there wasn't a person there, especially not one I had spoken to minutes before. It was easier to think of it as a series of chores. An itemised checklist to tick off one by one.

The blood pool had turned viscous and sticky as car oil. The towels just seemed to move it around rather than absorb it, and we had to discard four of them completely sodden into bin bags, followed by a quick rinse of our gloves in a basin of warm soapy water.

I said, 'That's all my towels gone.'

'You only had four?'

'Five, with the beach towel. I had them on a strict cleaning cycle.'

'Maybe you can use tea towels,' she said. 'Or kitchen roll.'

For the stains, Emma took the armchair and I worked on the floor. Only bleach was any use for lifting the blood, and I hoped the peroxide wouldn't discolour the wood. I used a long-handled dish scrubber and then a fork to scrape congealment from knots and gaps in the floorboards. Several times I had to replenish the basin, pouring brown murky water into the bath, watching it swash against white enamel, then refilling the basin with hot water from the shower.

Tom's phone, the one that Emma had with her at the start of the night, the one she called a burner, had slipped down the side cushion of the chair. She retrieved it, examined it carefully for blood, powered it down, and then slipped it into the pocket of the Afghan coat.

An hour or so later, the room appeared as it was before except for the bagged body. I shone my phone torch over the floor, the chair, anything I could remember Tom touching.

I said, 'I wonder if it has a blacklight setting.'

'You're watching too much *Forensic Files*.'

'Perhaps there's an app in the Play Store.'

'What could be less suspicious than downloading a UV light in the dead of night?' She said for the moment the room only needed to pass a cursory glance. If I wanted, I could go over it again later. She pulled off the marigolds, leaving them inside-out. 'It smells like a swimming pool in here.'

'I can open a window. Burn some incense.'

'You have incense?'

'Sarah liked it. She left some behind.'

'And you burn it occasionally, play her favourite album, and pine for the old days.'

The sticks and holder were in the cabinet beneath the TV. Long octagonal boxes with names like Positive Vibes and Forest Rain. Emma said, 'Whatever happens, James, please don't ever be tempted to get back with this person.'

I was cleaning up in the bathroom when Emma joined me, wearing jeans and a sleeveless vest. She dispensed some Dove into her palm and ran her fingers under the tap, almost brushing mine. I looked at her in the mirror, waited for her to meet my eye. She had tied her hair back in a ponytail. In the harsh light I could see a dusting of freckles over her nose. I turned to her, pointed to a spot above her cheekbone, and said, 'You have blood there.'

She said, 'Where?' and I touched her face. She reached up and ran her fingers over the corner of my mouth. We kissed each other. She pushed her wet hands beneath my shirt, and her fingernails clawed at my skin. I put my arms around her, tried to take a half step towards the door when she bit down on my lower lip. I pulled away. We stood looking at one another. Her shoulders rose and fell in a deep breath, and she said, 'There's no time.'

She turned as if to leave the bathroom, then checked herself and went towards the toilet. She lifted the lid of the cistern and placed it on the toilet seat, then plunged a bare arm into the water and took out a small item tightly wrapped in clear plastic. She placed it on the ledge of the sink and dried her arm with a repurposed tea towel.

She didn't mind that I picked it up. Visible in the plastic was a black-and-silver flash drive, with the word *Ledger* printed on its side.

I thought of Emma using the bathroom earlier but leaving the toilet lid down. I said, 'Is this what Tom was looking for?'

'You'd have to ask him.'

'It's a memory stick.'

'I know.'

'What's on it?'

'I've always liked that term "memory stick". Like something a shaman would use.'

'Do you know what's on it?'

'Boot up your laptop and we'll have a look.'

'No.'

'Then forget about it.'

She plucked the drive from my fingers, placed it in her jeans and went back into the living room.

Tom was where we'd left him. We had filled three black bags with stained towels, gloves and cloths. I said I'd put them out in the wheelie bins.

She said, 'You're not serious.'

'What?'

'They could burst in the lorry. Smear blood on the compressor. I doubt things like that go unnoticed.'

'So, someone had a nosebleed.'

She said she'd take them in the car, toss them somewhere far away.

In the kitchen I searched for the padlock key to the wicket gate. I'd only used it once before, just to see where the gate led. Now I hoped the lock hadn't rusted over. We donned our coats and lifted the body. Tom had been spare, but he was tall and cumbersome, and the bags were slippery. I opened the kitchen door to the freezing dawn air. The barest light had painted everything in charcoal. It was difficult to see the wicket gate at the end of the garden, which I found encouraging.

We set off along the path, Tom's weight seeming to increase with each step. Twice we paused to secure our holds and get our strides in sync. I was in front, carrying the head end, my arms wrapped around his shoulders. The point of his chin jutted against my wrist. It made me picture his face, his stubble, his tousled hair. I moved my arm so I didn't have to feel it. We set him down at the gate, which was just a door in the wall made of wooden slats with peeling green paint. Already we were breathing heavily. Emma said, 'Exactly how long do we have to carry him?'

'A fair bit. Half a kilometre maybe.'

'It's too far.'

'We'll be fine.'

'He'd have been in the car by now if we went out the front.'

Possibly she was right, though I was loath to say so. 'Just wait here.'

I crossed the garden to open the shed and looked about with the glow from my lock screen. Everything seemed unreal, like a movie set hastily put together. At the back, tilted against the wall, was an old wheelbarrow, hemmed in by boxes and cans, and covered in cobwebs. I began to clear a path. Each scrape of wood or metal echoed in the low rafters. For a moment the barrow seemed stuck to the wall. It detached, and I sidled it out vertically, the wheel on the ground, the handles in the air.

Emma was leaning against the wall, waiting with her arms folded. At my approach she said, 'You couldn't have been any louder.'

'But look what I found.'

'Great. You hardly need me at all now.'

I unlocked the wicket gate and pulled it inwards, scraping slats over a build-up of dirt and gravel. When there was enough of a gap, we brought Tom through, and then the barrow.

We emerged onto a verge of shrubbery and bushes at the back of an empty car park. The main entrance to the gardens was across the tarmac, where a pair of security cameras were pointing at the automatic barriers. We didn't need to go near them, nor did we pass the visitor centre, where there may have been more cameras or some kind of night watchman. Instead, we carried Tom through a small thicket of trees to a little-used path. I went back to fetch the barrow, and we hoisted him onto the bed, his legs hanging over the yellow tyre and his shoulders and head lolling between the handles. After a few turns we emerged into the gardens proper.

Huge bare trees loomed in the gloaming. The lawns were covered in a perfect sparkling frost. We pushed Tom through the Yew Walk, the Peony Borders, the Annuals, past birch and hickory and hazel trees, until we caught sight of the long serpentine pond and its arching footbridge. We paused by a grassy knoll to look at the sculpture *?What Is Life?*, flowing ribbons of sheet metal culminating in a giant double helix.

Emma lifted the barrow to carry on. The front axle had begun to squeak. After a few moments she said, 'The wheelbarrow was a good idea.'

'Thanks.'

There was a high stone boundary wall between the gardens and Glasnevin Cemetery. We kept to the path that skirted the wall, once in a while catching a glimpse through railings of thousands of headstones stretching into the distance. As the path neared the Tolka it descended sharply. Warning signs were posted for parents with prams, carers with wheelchairs. None for killers with barrows. Emma briefly lost her footing. The front wheel skidded and wobbled, and Tom was almost pitched out to tumble down the hill. I grabbed one handle and Emma's elbow, and carefully we inched down the frosty decline.

The high boundary wall ended at the Tolka, meeting the bank almost perpendicular, with no other barrier to the wasteland on the other side. But the bank was steeper than I remembered, the river more swollen so that it almost lapped the base of the wall.

In the grey light, Emma said, 'This is your secret way out?'

'I know it looks tricky. But that's the point.'

'It looks impassable.'

'We might have to get our feet wet.'

'We?'

I scrambled down to scout ahead. If I hugged the wall I could have slipped across easily enough, but lugging a body would not be easy. Also, I hadn't considered how thick the brambles, furze and nettles were on the other side. Going barefoot for a few minutes wasn't an option.

Up on the path, Emma had shifted Tom's legs to one side and was sitting on the corner of the barrow. I told her there was nothing for it. We'd just have to take it slow, be extra careful. 'Falling into the river would be bad.'

'If I fall in the river, I'm going to murder you.' Her silhouette had become still, a wisp of breath coiling up like smoke. She said, 'Jesus, James. There's no need to look so worried.'

It was quicker to drag Tom down the bank rather than carry him, though the bags covering him became muddy and slick. Emma followed after, and we stood at the base of the wall, the edge of the water.

We lifted him. I took the top half again, arms enveloped around his shoulders. Emma carried the legs. I said, 'Tell me if your hold starts to slip. Don't chance anything.'

'Just fucking go.'

I leaned tight against the wall and backed towards the corner. I could feel mud subsiding underfoot. Water flowed over my boot and soaked through – a piercing, shocking cold. The wall was only half a metre wide, and I was past it in a moment, trying to find a foothold in the brambles. Emma and I were on opposite sides now, with Tom folded around the edge. I did my best to take his weight. My arms were screaming. She came around quite nimbly, and once she was clear of the bank, I dropped the body.

She said, 'Don't you think we should take him further?'

'Just give me a minute.'

'That wasn't so bad.'

'Did you step in the river?'

'No.'

'Well, I did.'

'Pity,' she said. 'And you've no towels either.'

Away from the river the brambles were less dense and the going a little easier. The scrubland stretched for hundreds of yards, bounded in the distance by the rear wall of the cemetery. Natural paths meandered through long grass and gorse and thickets of stunted, misshapen trees. At the edge of a small clearing someone had dumped a long sheet of corrugated iron, completely rusted now and flaking.

Emma said, 'Let's put him under there.'

The metal sheet had created its own hollow in the undergrowth. Tom fit snugly within it. We manoeuvred the corrugated iron back on top and pressed it down so no trace of him was visible. Emma stood silently for a moment. I looked about the clearing, wild and forlorn, but not without a certain uncultivated charm. I could think of worse resting places. The branches and leaves were dusted white. He would be preserved by the cold snap. But mild weather would soon return, and I thought of him decaying in the bags, decomposing and seeping into the black earth. What matter if that happened above ground or below?

Emma said, 'We should go before it's light out.'

We retraced our steps. My sodden shoe was horribly uncomfortable. The ground was so choked we had to go single file, and Emma invited me to go ahead. I felt a strange prickling in my neck at the thought of her so close behind. I fought the urge to glance back.

Getting past the wall was far easier without a body. The wheelbarrow was waiting for us on the path, and we made our way back to the wicket gate without speaking. Emma locked the bolt while I brought the barrow to the shed, and sidled it back into its corner.

Inside, the flat looked spotless, with a not unpleasant smell of bleach and incense. It was as if the night had begun again, and that I should offer Emma a drink, and put on music, and dim the lights. Instead I went to change my shoes and socks. We fetched the bin bags from the kitchen. I carried two, Emma took one, and we made our way through the front hall and out on to the street.

Emma saw Tom's car, a dark blue Passat, parked near the gates of the Tolka House. She popped the boot with the fob key and we placed the bags within. Emma gave a little gasp of pleasure as she pulled out a coat, presumably her own, a navy parka with a fur-lined hood. She swapped it for the Afghan, was about to place that coat in the boot, when she spotted some commercial wheelie bins by the gates of the pub. She opened the lid of one, and tossed the Afghan inside.

My eye had been drawn to a book sitting alone by the tyre irons, an old copy of *Anna Karenina*. The cover was well worn. It showed a dark-haired woman in a fur cossack hat, her face almost obscured by driven snow. Emma saw me holding it and said, 'Keep it, if you like. To remember me by.'

I was about to demur, but I'd never read it, and had always intended to, so I said, 'Thanks.'

She was patting her coat. She felt inside the breast pocket and pulled out another phone, a distinct pink-and-black zebra-skin case.

I said, 'Is that yours?'

She nodded. 'Don't worry, it's switched off.'

From her hair she took a bobby pin, used its point to release the sim-card holder, removed the sim and let it fall between the grates of a storm drain. The phone she tossed over the walls of the Tolka House, into the thick trees at the side of the car park. We heard it slither and tumble through branches into the undergrowth.

She closed the boot with both hands, and then came to stand next to me. An ambiguous half-smile. Her eyes round and searching. She stood on her tiptoes to kiss the corner of my mouth, lingered there for a few seconds, and then took a step back. Without a word, she climbed into the front seat of the car, turned the ignition, and drove away.

I looked at the book in my hands and flicked through some of it. There was an inscription in blue ink on the title page: *For Emma, 'Yes, there is something uncanny, demonic and fascinating in her ...' Love, Mum.*

The car moved around the bend of Glasnevin Hill and out of sight. I waited for the glow of its tail lights to disappear. Then I went home.

PART THREE

CHAPTER 12

9 DECEMBER

Storm Lauren doesn't disappoint. As darkness falls, gales and blizzards sweep across the city, and Libby barely makes it to my place before the whiteout. We cook frozen pizza and drink wine by the fireplace, start to kiss near the hearthstone, but that was where Tom bled out two weeks before, so I bring her to the sofa instead. In bed we keep the curtains open to watch snowflakes swirl against the window. We talk for hours, about where we grew up, our work, her friends, movies and books we like. She laughs at anecdotes about my family, so I laugh at anecdotes about hers. The next morning, we light a fire. She raids my bookshelves and we read for a while, then lie on the sofa, then venture into the drifts of the backyard. She builds a snowman and posts a picture on Instagram saying, **My new bloke.** You can see the green gate to the Botanics in the background.

As we prepare to head in, she raises her hand and waves over my shoulder, and I turn expecting to see Whiteside in a window, but he must have stepped away.

When my phone runs out of battery I don't plug it in, and it feels nice to be cut off from everyone. Libby texts a lot, mostly to her mother and Miranda, letting them know she's still alive. While we huddle under a blanket, I watch her tap out some replies. Messages to Miranda have a sardonic, playful edge. No abbreviated words. No emojis. Her tone with her mother is warmer, more sincere. For her, she signs off each text with: space, ellipsis, space, one kiss. I saw a documentary once on forensic linguistics – how killers used their victims' phones to send messages to loved ones, to allay fears or cover tracks. But too often they didn't structure the messages properly. They used the wrong punctuation, or misspelled words, or even spelled them correctly, and so were found out. One detective said, 'You have to be able to capture a dead girl's voice.' Seemed obvious really.

Libby is looking up at me, smiling. 'You're miles away.'

I kiss her forehead. 'Was just wondering if there'd be a chance to meet your folks over Christmas. We can talk about it again.'

She snuggles closer.

Later she wants to use the shower, so I show her the hot press and the switch for the immersion. The grey basin is propped against the wall, a slim streak of blood visible on its side, but Libby doesn't see it. She's running her fingers over a neat pile of identical towels and laughs to see a price tag still attached.

'Seems like you were expecting company.'

'Just wanted to make a good impression. The bedsheets are new as well, not that you noticed.'

While she's in the bathroom I take the basin to the kitchen. The taps would make the shower go wonky so I boil the water already in the kettle, use that to clean the basin, dry it off with kitchen towel and return it to the hot press.

On day three I brave the snow-packed streets to get more booze while Libby stays in to cook dinner. When I get back, her laptop is open on the sofa with the TV on standby. The kitchen table is half set, a pot of Bolognese simmering on the stove with a ladle submerged. Onion paper and garlic cloves litter the chopping board. The big knife rests on an empty tin of tomatoes.

I call her name as I move into the hallway, past the darkened bathroom to the bedroom at the end. The light is on. I gently rap as I push open the door. Libby's coat is draped over the back of a chair. The duvet is in a tangle, so I shake it out and lay it on the bed. I look out into the garden. No footprints in the snow. The shed and wicket gate at the end of the yard are lost in the gloom. Only when I'm going through the hall again do I see the door to the internal stairs ajar.

Up above, the door to Whiteside's hall stands open – a glowing rectangle of patterned wallpaper. I climb the steps and listen. Hushed voices drift from the front room, and when I get close, I can see Libby and Whiteside sitting together, speaking quietly.

I'm about to knock, but I've encroached too far uninvited, so I return to the top of the stairs and call Libby's name.

A pause, and then her voice: 'James, I'm in here.'

Whiteside's front room has been tidied since the attack. Warm light glows from a briquette fire and a lamp in the corner. He's in his usual armchair, red dressing gown, blanket over his knees, hair carefully combed. He would have looked normal but for the blue and purple blotches on his cheeks, the black stitching over his eye like a football lace. Libby sits adjacent on the sofa. Her head has turned towards me and she's smiling. Rather, she has begun to smile, and for a moment it strikes me as sudden and forced.

I say, 'Allen, it's good to see you home.'

He peers towards the door and says in a cracked voice, 'Hello, James.'

'God, they gave you a right going-over.'

'Yes.' He rubs his forehead with the tips of his fingers and then gestures to the sofa. 'Have you met Libby?'

She touches his arm. 'Mr Whiteside, I've come from downstairs.'

'That's right, that's right,' and he closes his eyes and nods and seems abashed.

'I'm sorry she got loose. I thought I had her locked up better than that.'

Libby tuts but looks at me warmly. Whiteside regards me without expression.

To Libby I say, 'Everything all right?'

'Fine, yeah. We bumped into each other on the drive, and I introduced myself. I promised I'd bring him up something from the pot,' and she points to one of the plastic containers that I save from the Chinese, filled to the brim with red ragù. I keep those containers at the back of the press. She would have had to rummage to find one.

'You should see the kitchen, Allen. It's like a bomb went off.'

'My kitchen?'

'No, downstairs.'

Libby stands and lightly says, 'All the thanks I get is abuse. I'll put this in your fridge, Mr Whiteside. It'll keep for a few days.'

She brushes past me and squeezes my hand, and I go to take her seat. On a little side table, inlaid with a picture of St Peter's Basilica, there's a plastic bottle of medication: oxycodone. One of the heavy-hitters.

I say, 'I'm sorry I haven't been up to check on you.'

Allen smooths the tartan blanket on his knees. 'I keep telling everyone not to make a fuss. At least I can count on you for that.'

'I got a call from the guards the other day. Don't know if they got through to you. They arrested someone.'

'About what?'

'About all this.'

'Oh, right. Yes, I think Eliza mentioned something.'

With an unsteady hand he pours water from a glass jug into a tumbler. He unscrews the top of the pill bottle, shakes out a tablet and keeps hold of it.

He nods towards the door. 'She's nice.'

'Yeah. Don't worry, she hasn't moved in or anything. We're just waiting for the thaw.'

'Why should I worry?'

'It's your house.'

'What goes on below I'm not too pushed about. As long as you're quiet.'

That's good to know.

'And if you're going to be snowed in you may as well have some company.' He attempts a knowing smile, but the movement seems to pain him. 'I saw you two the other day, out in the yard. You were ...'

After a pause, I fill in, 'Building a snowman,' but he says, 'Messing with the wheelbarrow,' and then he covers his mouth as if he's let slip a secret.

But he's just taking his tablet. He lifts the tumbler to sip some water. His eyes close as he swallows, and when he turns to me again he looks tranquil, contented. Libby bustles in. She sits beside me, tells Whiteside that the Bolognese is in the fridge, laments the lack of fresh food in his kitchen. She offers to buy in some groceries and I wait for him to say not at all, but instead he smiles at her.

'You're very good.'

The light outside is dimmed by a cloud and the room becomes gloomy. A small lamp with gold tassels is on a table by the sofa. I reach under the shade to push the switch with a loud click but nothing happens.

Back downstairs, Libby tends the pot and begins to tidy, sweeping up and wiping down the counter.

'I was only joking about the bomb going off,' I tell her.

'You were half joking, but that's okay.'

While pouring her a glass of wine, I say, 'Terrible to see Whiteside like that.'

She's squeezing a cloth over the sink, shaking suds from her hand. 'I thought he seemed quite well, considering.'

'Wasn't himself at all. Hopefully it's just the meds.'

She shrugs as she slips pasta nests into boiling water. 'Yeah, hopefully.'

I finish setting the table and ask what they were talking about.

'This and that.'

'He goes on a bit, doesn't he? If you let him.'

She doesn't answer, or perhaps she nods and I miss it. She stirs the pasta and turns the oven on low to warm some plates. Her back is to me when she says, 'He thought I was someone else.'

I'm polishing a dinner knife and make sure not to pause. 'Sarah, most likely.'

'No, not her.'

'Or Lolo.'

'Yeah, maybe.'

As she's plating up, I turn off all but one of the kitchen lights and play a three-hour YouTube video of a flickering candle on my phone, which I prop against the salt and pepper. When she brings the food she says, 'What's this?'

'Just setting the mood.'

I top up the wine and we clink glasses.

'*Buon appetito.*'

'*Altretanto.*'

The Bolognese is a tad bland, but it would be rude to move the phone now for the pepper grinder.

'It's delicious,' I say.

In the fake candlelight her eyes search my face, and she smiles.

Lauren's last gasp brings a few flurries and a keening, icy wind. Libby and I settle on the sofa, her head resting on my chest as we channel-hop. A fire is burning low. While passing RTÉ, the news is on, a picture of Emma Harte on the backdrop. I want to keep surfing, but Libby has shifted slightly, so I pause and raise the volume.

A montage of Emma Harte pictures and all the well-worn details of her disappearance. Then the picture of Emma and Tom Wickham from the Young Entrepreneur Awards four years ago, looking beautiful and happy in their formal dress. The reporter says that Thomas Wickham, himself missing for the past number of days, has been declared a person of interest after unconfirmed sightings of the man in County Longford. It had been suggested that Mr Wickham had subsequently fled the country via Northern Ireland.

I should say something, so I mutter, 'Jesus.' Libby doesn't respond at all.

The security photo of me and Emma Harte fills the screen. The last-known image of the missing woman, the reporter says, but the man in the still is not Thomas Wickham, and gardaí are urgently requesting that this individual make himself known.

I feel short of air, like the wind has caught my breath. I feign a yawn, concentrate on long, slow inhalations. In the grainy picture my face is turned but it seems so clearly, obviously me. The coat I was wearing then is draped on the armchair across the room. The same shoes are sitting next to Libby's at the foot of the sofa. Her ear is pressed against my chest like a human heartrate monitor. I can feel my pulse quicken. She must hear it. Even I think I can hear it. Should I push the blanket off, complain about the heat, excuse myself and go to the bathroom?

The news moves on. Libby still hasn't said anything, though her arm feels tense beneath my hand. She lets out a long sigh. I say her name, and when I glance down her eyes are closed.

I kiss her forehead. She stirs and looks up at me, smiles and says, 'Hey.'

'How about an early night?' I say.

She nods and burrows her head beneath my chin.

On the TV, the weather report confirms that a thaw is underway. I charge my phone and fret about turning it on, but there are only a few messages. My mother asking how I'm doing, the family WhatsApp group with pictures of the kids in the snow, except Lolo, and Helena telling all staff that the library will reopen on Wednesday. The respite is over.

Libby sits cross-legged on the sofa with a computer on her lap, surrounded by neatly written notes on index cards, a tablet displaying medieval manuscripts from the Bodleian, and a dog-eared Latin dictionary. Once in a while, she dabs at the tablet, pinch-zooms to a new line in the manuscript so that Gothic letters fill the screen. Her lips move slightly as she says the words to herself and then begins to type.

I focus on the movie, though I've already lost the thread. One of the problems with being an archivist of still and moving images is that you can't help but shot-list what you're watching in real time. EXT: *a Victorian country house surrounded by mature trees in autumn.* PAN L–R: *a small hatchback approaches and pulls up, the driver sits and waits and observes the house.* INT: *C/U an old woman at a window, lace curtains held aside by the tips of her fingers. Her face darkens as the headlights outside switch off.*

I turn it over, flick through the channels until I find the football. Champions League on a floodlit Spanish pitch. A goal has just gone in, and a co-commentator is eulogising in grating Liverpudlian. I lower the volume and Libby glances up.

'What are you doing?'

'Sorry, didn't want to disturb you.'

'I told you I don't mind.' She'd set herself up in the living room because the kitchen was too cold. There's a desk in the bedroom, but the Wi-Fi there is sketchy. Besides, she said, she'd done her Leaving in a house with five siblings, graduated college with three nursing student roommates. She was used to some background noise.

I raise the volume again, not as high as before. 'How are you doing?'

'Getting there.'

'Can I help?'

'How are your Latin declensions?'

'Not good.'

She smiles and says, 'Some tea, then?'

Another goal has gone in before I've settled again, and the commentator declares the game to be a classic, though he makes the word sound like a Welsh village. Arthur texts: You're missing everything.

Libby watches me tap out a reply and says, 'Who's that?'

'Only Arthur.'

'Is he down in Fagan's?'

'I'd say so, yeah.'

'Do you want to join him?'

I glance at her. 'What about you?'

'I'll be fine.'

'Come on down for a few.'

'No, looks like it'll be an all-nighter. You should go, though.'

'Well, if you're sure.'

I get my coat, lean over to kiss her. Index cards cascade and she says, 'Mind.'

At the door I glance back. She's bathed in warm light from the table lamp, a pale glow from the laptop. It feels odd to leave her alone. Before I go, a quick mental inventory of each room. Nothing I wouldn't want her to see. Still, I'm uneasy as I pull the door closed.

Fagan's is busy for the midweek match. Arthur has expertly kept a stool free with draped coat and hanging bag and some manspreading. I'd texted that I was on the way and a freshly poured Hop House glistens on the counter. He nods as I sit down, returns his attention to the screen, and says, 'You managed to escape.'

'It was her idea.'

'Suspicious.'

'Only to a mind like yours.'

'Sounds like she's moved in.'

'She was snowed in.'

'Well, I hope she's the one. You keep waiting for some Sally Rooney heroine to come along, but they don't exist in real life, thank fuck.' He lifts his pint and swirls the dregs. 'Actually, I'm doing a line myself.'

I wait for him to take a drink and return the glass to the bar. 'Do I know her?'

'She wandered into the office last week looking for advice on her mother's will. A house and half an acre in Howth. Very tasty.'

'And you've asked her out? Isn't that a conflict of interest?'

'Not for my interests,' he says. 'My interests are aligning nicely.'

A thumping header comes back off the post and grown men ooh like a pantomime crowd. At halftime, there's a tap on my shoulder. It's Colin, still in his work clothes, looking more harried than usual. Arthur glances back at the interruption, says, 'Ah, howya, Colin,' and offers his fingers over his shoulder to be gripped.

Colin says, 'Jim, I was trying to get you.'

My phone is on the bar. Three missed calls unheard in the din.

'Everything okay?'

'No, not particularly. Can we speak?'

Arthur looks between us and begins to rise from his stool. 'Take this, Colin. I'll leave you to it.'

'Actually, Arthur,' he says, 'it wouldn't be any harm to get your opinion as well. I mean, you can bill me your time, naturally.'

Arthur pauses, blinks. He does well not to lick his lips. 'Well, a bit of advice is free, of course.' He looks around. Behind him is the wood-panelled wall. The few lads next to me are old and half deaf. There's still a general hubbub in the bar. 'Stand in there,' he says. 'What are you having?'

Colin finishes a brandy in one gulp. He winces and keeps hold of the glass and then looks at me. 'Had an interview today. With the guards.'

'Oh?'

'You know that Mountjoy Square house? The big eviction case. They think that missing girl might have ended up there.'

'Emma Harte?' Arthur says at once, and Colin nods.

I rotate my glass on the bar. 'What has that got to do with you?'

'They asked me to come in, I thought to talk them through who the owners were, when the Occupy crowd moved in, who had keys to the place, all of that.' He goes to take another sip before he realises the glass is empty. 'Then they put a security photo of this girl and some guy on the table, say they have reason to believe it's me in the picture.'

'Based on what?'

'They start asking where I was on the night she disappeared.'

'Tell them you were home.'

'Do you remember Danni took the kids to see her mother in Sligo?'

'No.'

'Well, it fucking happened. And it was that weekend.'

Arthur catches Kenny's eye behind the bar and twirls his finger for another round.

'So, you don't have an alibi for one night,' I say. 'What's the worry? You're overthinking things as usual.'

'I told them I was with you.'

'What?'

'I panicked a bit.'

'For fuck's sake, Col.'

'I mean, they're hardly going to ask, but in case they do, say I was at your gaff. We watched the football, ordered pizza, shit like that.'

'But I was out that night. It's easily checked.'

'They're not going to check, and if they do, say you got mixed up with the dates.'

'Jim's right,' Arthur says. 'At the moment it sounds like a bit of a fishing expedition. Really, you should have clammed up as soon as they showed you the picture.'

'And how would that have looked? I'm not really worried about all that. The main problem is Danni.' He stops talking while Kenny sets out two pints and a brandy on the bar, then he looks at me again. 'I'm seeing someone else, Jim.'

He waits for me to ask who, but instead I take the empty glass from his hand and replace it with a full one.

'Delphine,' he says. 'Joined the firm over the summer. Slovenian. Incredible.' His eyes lose focus for a moment, and he takes a drink.

'You were with her that night.'

He nods, then shakes his head as if in disbelief.

'Would this Delphine not have backed you up?'

'Of course she would, but if it got back to Danni … She can't get an inkling of any of this. I'd hire a lawyer, but she'd sniff it out on the statements.'

Arthur says, 'If you need anything off the books.'

'Thanks, but I think it'll be okay. They said they had some DNA evidence, asked if I'd be willing to provide a sample. I said yes, just to get it over and done with.'

I feel my mouth go dry. 'Did you give the sample already?'

'No, I'm heading in again on Thursday.'

'Col, are you sure that's the way to go?'

'Of course. Proves it's not me at once. No more tricky questions.'

'But I mean, what if it's a false positive? What if there's a glitch? You've been in the house loads. Maybe you've left a trace without realising.'

'No, it's fibres from a coat or something. I didn't know what they were talking about.'

'Arthur, what do you think?'

'Yeah, normally, no way. People believe cops will plant drugs on someone, but somehow won't check a box on a computer that says, "This guy is guilty." But with the Danni situation …' He rubs his chin and says, 'There's a principle in chess. If you only have one legal move, don't waste any time thinking about it, just play it.'

I look at him. 'You've never played chess in your life.'

'Still, it's a good principle.'

Colin seems relieved to be backed up. 'You're right. Give the sample, get ruled out. If they ask you anything, Jim, you know what to say. And then all will be well.' He takes another long sip of brandy. 'Because if Danni finds out, I'm fucked.'

A voice behind him says, 'Hi,' and we all turn around.

Libby is standing there, bobble hat and scarf and uncertain smile. She glances between Arthur and Colin, and then focuses on me. 'I thought I could do with a break.'

On the TV, the ball ripples the net, and the bar erupts in cheers.

CHAPTER 13

14 DECEMBER

The Twitter trial of Tom Wickham began soon after his change in status from missing person to chief suspect, and by the time people are back at their desks following the thaw, the verdict is in: Guilty. A few self-proclaimed rational voices argue that there could be an innocent, even tragic, reason for a young man to go to ground in the weeks following the disappearance of his girlfriend. But then Tom's old tweets are dredged up, analysed, and cast in a sinister light – casual misogyny, problematic jokes, ambivalence in the referendums, support for Leinster rugby – the dossier is quickly compiled, widely shared, and it proves damning.

By break-time, *#justiceforemma* is trending in Dublin, and online wrath has turned on the gardaí. The murderer was hiding in plain sight. Sure, wasn't it always the partner? Now police incompetence had allowed Tom Wickham to slip away, and once again an Irish woman had been killed without consequence.

Libby is upstairs in Tilley's office. She forwards a newsletter from DUGES. Paschal has been quick to arrange a protest/vigil for this evening outside the gates of the Dáil, which is also just outside the library. *Irish Women: Reclaim the Night!,* with a picture of Emma Harte photoshopped and faded in the background.

Libby says, Are you going?

What could be better than standing in the cold for a performative and pointless gesture? Maybe she's asked because Paschal is involved, and she's looking for an excuse to avoid. Probably not.

Of course. I'll fetch you after work.

Word of the vigil spreads. While I'm getting tea, I see Helena reading the flyer on her computer. Some poor PR intern at @gardainfo attempts to mollify the crowd by tweeting, At present Thomas Wickham is still considered to be a missing person. Be assured, several lines of enquiry are being rigorously pursued. The tweet is ratioed into oblivion and deleted an hour later. The *Be assured* memes begin soon after.

In the kitchenette I ring Colin, keep my voice low beneath the rumble of the kettle.

He says, 'What's up?'

'Looks like the guards have their man with this Emma Harte thing. I'd say you could definitely give the DNA test a miss.'

'Already done.'

'What?'

'Went in first thing. Wasn't all bad. The young one who took the swab was a bit of a looker. She could stick her fingers in my mouth any time.'

'For fuck's sake, Col.'

'Sorry, should I have put a trigger warning before that, you fucking girl. Gotta go.'

I slip down to the main reading room, quiet for a Wednesday morning, a heavy, solemn silence broken only by the odd cough or creak of a chair. A few readers huddle by their desk lamps. Malachi mans the counter. He's dealing with a customer, so I get away with a brief nod as I pass. Under the high vaulted ceiling at the back of the room are the shelves that hold the Thom's Directories. I pull one down at random, thumb through the pages and study a paragraph. A few seconds is enough for the charade. I close the book and slip it back into place.

As I'm passing the bank of computers where the public can access the main catalogue, I pause as if considering something. I turn to one of the screens and click on the search box. The catalogue is on my own computer, of course, but it's natural to have a quick look here while I'm passing. No one is close by. I type in *DNA* and hit return.

Thirty-six results. Books on discovery of the double-helix, studies of genealogy and sociology like *The Blood of the Irish* or *Identity Politics and the New Genetics*. Several titles seem far too technical, but then I spot *Forensic DNA Testing – The Fundamentals*. It's stored on site as well. I take an order slip and pencil to note the call number.

The stacks are a warren of rooms made claustrophobic by tightly packed shelving, dimly lit by scratched yellow tiles in the ceiling. It's unusual for me to be here, though not forbidden. Still, I keep an ear out for porters on the prowl. I find the bay, the shelf, and the book, a slim volume produced by the US Department of Justice. In the contents two articles jump out. The first – 'Framed by your own genes' – tells of an old Wisconsinite who swabbed his cheek to discover exactly what shade of white he was, only for the results to closely match traces from a cold case campus murder. The old man was in the clear, but his son, who was a freshman at the time, was charged and convicted. The second is even closer to the mark: 'DNA profiles in a case where the defense is "It was my brother"; I.V Ewitt (1992)'.

At the end of the bay is a narrow window where some bare, natural light will make it easier to read. The window looks out over the rear of the library and a courtyard, still half-covered in slush, which acts as a staff smoking area. I skim the article, try to make sense of the jargon. Basically, one brother cannot be mistaken for another through DNA analysis as their profiles will be too distinct. However, if a tester was of a mind, she could easily prove that two samples came from siblings, because of certain matches in the Y chromosome.

Movement below. Bridget has come into the courtyard holding the front of her coat closed with one hand, a cigarette in the other. She's talking to someone hidden by the lip of a gable wall. She turns her face to blow some smoke, seems to peer straight at me, but her eyes drop again quickly. Shauna Shaw steps out from the wall and stands beside her. She appears different in the sunlight, more relaxed, wearing only a light jacket as if unperturbed by the cold, a cigarette dangling from the corner of her mouth. She and Bridget are about the same height. They are chatting lightly without making eye contact, as if just passing the time of day. They both exhale at the same time and smoke mingles in the icy air.

I hurry through the stacks and service corridors back to the office wing. Another window gives a view of the courtyard, closer now, but both Bridget and the detective are gone. I head back to the office. Helena is alone at her table with several photographs laid out, as well as the light box and loupe for viewing transparent slides. The kitchenette is silent.

She smiles at me over her shoulder, then remembers something and turns in her seat. 'James, I meant to say, that graphic design place let me down for the Markievicz flyer. Could you make the tweaks in Photoshop? You'll probably do a better job than them anyway.'

Just at that moment, Bridget comes in. I step aside to let her pass. She doesn't pause or glance at me. She doesn't say that someone is here looking for me. She just goes to her desk, tosses her lighter into a drawer, and shakes her mouse to wake the computer.

Helena is looking at me expectantly, and I say, 'Sure. Send on the files.'

As evening falls, crowds gather by the front gates for the vigil. I meet Libby under the arch. We take two candles from a box held by a marshal and light them with the help of obliging strangers. Photocopied prints of Emma Harte's smiling face are distributed. Libby looks at her in the candle glow and says, 'She was so pretty.'

She's starting to use the past tense. Nineteen days since Emma went missing, and now most people assume the worst.

Half the road is closed, with traffic at a standstill. Beeps of encouragement and irritation, teenaged girls shouting support from the top of a double-decker bus, a line of gardaí to stop people blocking the road completely. There's a squally breeze and spitting rain. The windows of Buswells Hotel are warm and inviting, and I almost say to Libby, *Could we not be just as vigilant in there?*

People continue to arrive, hemming us in. Some women hold homemade cardboard signs that say things like, *Sick Of It* or *She Was Just Walking Home* or the simple message, *Stop Killing Us*. Gardaí have to yell to keep protestors within the cordon. Libby spots Paschal at the gates of the Dáil. He's hard to miss with bullhorn and high-vis vest, talking earnestly with a female garda, shaking the wired speaker of the bullhorn close to her face. Miranda is standing nearby. Libby takes my hand, and we weave through the crowd towards her.

Miranda says to her, 'You're alive. I was all ready to sublet the room.' She has a pen and scrap of paper in her hand. 'I'm looking for speakers. Will I put your name down?'

'No, don't. My throat's not great.'

Miranda looks at me, 'What about you?'

'Well, I don't really think it's my place.'

A voice behind me says my name, and I turn to see a smiling Lolo – hooded coat, keffiyeh scarf, black fingerless gloves. I ask what she's doing here.

'It was all over school. A bunch of us came.'

'Did you tell your folks?'

She rolls her eyes and says, 'Of course.'

'I'm only asking.'

I introduce her to Libby, who says, 'I met your dad the other night. You must take after your mother.'

Lolo says, 'Oh, right.' She straightens her shoulders at Paschal's approach, pushes her hair behind an ear. Paschal greets Libby warmly. He just nods at me.

Miranda asks what the garda wanted, and he says, 'To get some people to disperse, for the rest to stay on this side of the street. Fat fucking chance.'

He notices Lolo, who notices that he notices, and offers his hand. 'Don't think we've met.'

'Lolo,' she says, shyly. 'Thanks for organising all this.'

'Least I could do.' He maintains his grip. 'What are you studying?'

'She's my niece,' I say, and he withdraws his hand.

'Ah, very good.' He flicks a button on the speaker, causing a static whine, and says, 'Well, let's get the show on the road.'

He turns to the crowd and raises the bullhorn. A hush descends, and he thanks people for coming, not only to remember a young woman lost in her prime, but also to decry the corrupt ineptitude of a garda force more interested in breaking picket lines and harassing peaceful protestors than actually protecting women and arresting murderers.

A smattering of applause. Already people are beginning to talk among themselves, and the general hubbub is returning.

I lean close to Libby. 'Would it not have been better for a woman to address the crowd?'

She shrugs and says, 'It's his bullhorn. He always insists on using it first.'

Away to our left a group of students begin banging on glass bottles – a steady double beat. One girl has a bodhrán. As she strikes it, she yells, 'Whose streets?' and is answered by the others: 'Our streets!'

They continue the chant. More in the crowd take it up, and soon the street resounds with hundreds of voices. Paschal, drowned out, turns to the rabble-rousers and spreads his arms. He yells, 'I wasn't finished,' but has the presence of mind not to do so on the loudspeaker, and after a long glare, he admits defeat.

I look for Lolo. She and a couple of friends have moved towards the chanters, and they're joining in, punching the air with each response. There's a ripple in the line of gardaí as they begin to shuffle towards the source of the noise. One young woman unwittingly backs into a garda and is shoved away, not so hard that she falls, but she turns on him with a shocked face. There's a swirl of anger from the protesters beside her. The police close ranks. But just as quickly the commotion dissipates, and both sides back off.

Miranda has taken up the chant with gusto, her passion causing her voice to crack. Libby is shouting as well, and I feel I should join in. It seems odd to say the 'Our streets' part. Should I say, 'Their streets'? That would make the chant a little muddled and rob some of its impact. It's even more awkward when the chant switches to a full-throated, 'Yes, All Men', accompanied by a football-like triple clap. The younger student lads looking to get laid have no problem shouting along, but this time I restrict myself to clapping.

The chanting has drawn in people from surrounding streets, swelling the crowd beyond the cordon. Kildare Street is completely blocked. Buses are stuck half-turned on the corner of St Stephen's Green. Motorists are leaning on their car horns like they've slumped over after a crash. One guy gets out of his BMW and screams at everyone to clear the way. 'Some of us have actual fucking jobs.'

Here and there lone men are observing from a distance, quiet scowls of resentment. Others are more overt, like the gang of young lads who are shouting that all the women here are too ugly to rape. One runs to the edge of the cordon and pulls his dick from the top of his tracksuit bottoms. The night is cold and all he can manage is an unimpressive wiggle, before he re-holsters and legs it. Disgusted women point him out to gardaí in the line, but they're unmoved. Libby has seen the whole thing and she remonstrates with a female garda.

'Why aren't you doing anything?'

D112 has sullen, dark eyes. She says, 'Step back.'

'This is exactly what we're fucking talking about. Why isn't anyone chasing him?'

'I said get back.'

Libby stares at her for a moment. The wind makes her bobble hat tremble. She leans closer and says, 'You know, you could be next. And all your male colleagues wouldn't give a shit.'

It sounds uncomfortably like a threat, so I pull on her elbow and say, 'Come on, Lib.'

Dozens of women scream at once with a noise like glass shattering. At the other side of the gates the gardaí have broken through the crowd and have encircled the original chanters. Bodhrán girl is pinioned by two police, her drum trampled underfoot. The others try to break free but are grabbed one by one. Protestors around them begin to chant 'Let them go' over and over, their pitch and anger rising each time. Suddenly Lolo is there. She approaches one of the men holding Bodhrán girl and begins to beat on the top of his arm. Another garda envelops her like he's picking up a child. He tosses her face-down, stoops and digs his knee into the small of her back. His arm snakes beneath her body and clutches the front of her face – black-gloved fingers clasping her mouth and her jaw. Lolo's eyes are wide with fright. Photographers surround her and lights flash.

I release Libby's arm and walk through the crowd. It's almost like they're parting for me. I look at the garda's face. Impassive beneath the low peak of his cap. Lolo is squirming beneath him. He licks his lips. The last few strides I begin to run. The garda looks up as I tackle him, wrap my arms around his head. He falls backwards and we roll. I keep my grip as he thrashes. He begins to punch and knee. I don't feel anything, except the pressure of his face between my elbow and chest. His cap has come loose. Black shiny plastic rubs against my jaw. The golden garda badge is flickering. He's strong. He pushes me about as he writhes, but I don't let go. There's a stampede of feet around us. Noise continues to swell – high shrieks of women, gruff shouts of gardaí. He's gotten hold of one of my arms and I can feel my strength ebb. This won't end well. I think of dick boy legging it down the street. The garda has his face free. He takes a gasping breath, says, 'You're fucking dead.'

Others have a hold of me now. Pincers in my arms, my side, a weight on my back. I'm turned over. Streetlights on Kildare Street shine with halos against the dark evening sky. Gardaí are standing over me in high-vis vests. People hurry past on all sides. I search for Lolo, but can't see past the legs of the police, their mud-spattered boots. I gaze at the sky and take a breath. Gloved hands reach towards me.

I'm put in a room with a table and three chairs, a security camera high in one corner, a clock, and a whiteboard with a thick black marker resting on the sill. The walls are cinderblocks painted light blue, like the corridors and classrooms in my primary school. I reach out and run my finger along a rough seam. My back aches from where the garda landed a few punches. I may have pulled a muscle in my shoulder keeping hold of his head. I don't know what happened to Lolo, or the others. At the station the police took my phone. They didn't ask for the code, but they may have ways of bypassing that. I vaguely wonder if they're allowed to answer it if someone rings.

It's warm in the room. I take off my coat to hang on the back of the chair, wander to the whiteboard and pick up the marker, pop the lid and smell the tip. Faint traces of writing remain on the board. Confessions perhaps. Maybe that's why it's there. Leave people alone until they crack and unburden themselves. I replace the marker on the sill with the lid off. In the corner I stand beneath the camera where I'm out of shot, wait to see if there's a reaction, but no one comes to check. Likely no one's watching.

I listen at the door. Silence, except for a faint, high-pitched laugh somewhere, the flush of a toilet. I take hold of the chrome handle, push down and pull back. The door opens a few inches and I immediately let go so it can click shut again.

I'm resting my head on the table when the door opens and Shauna Shaw enters. It's just gone eight o'clock. She has a phone and a manila folder and notebook in one hand, styrofoam cup in the other, with a swirl of steam escaping the lid. Blue jeans and black blouse open at the neck. She doesn't glance at me as she places her belongings on the table. She takes a seat, opens her notebook, and smooths down a page. She removes the lid from her cup and blows on her coffee. Her breath has a smell of chewing gum with a sour edge.

'Now, James,' she says, eyes flitting over me. 'Do you need anything? Glass of water, trip to the bathroom, medical attention?'

I'm not sure what station they brought me to – Pearse Street maybe, but it's definitely not Shauna Shaw's beat. I want to ask why she was in the library earlier, but instead I just shake my head.

She smiles and says, 'Good man.' She moves the folder from beneath her notebook but doesn't open it. 'Any questions before we begin?'

I almost mention Lolo. But then it strikes me: what if she slipped away in all the confusion? What if they just have her picture and are trying to put a name to a face? If I admit to being her uncle, would that be considered an aggravating or mitigating circumstance? Arthur has given me the talk often enough, usually after the fifth or sixth pint. Never tell the police anything. It cannot possibly help. You cannot talk your way out of a charge or conviction. Anything you say can only be used against you, no matter how innocent, no matter how seemingly exonerating.

'My solicitor's name is Arthur Stokes. He has an office in Drumcondra. I won't be speaking to you unless he's present.'

'Ah, dear Arthur. Will you get him at this hour?'

Her face is blank after she says this, and she waits for me to respond.

'Yes, I have his mobile number.'

'But there's a match on.'

'So?'

'So, will he hear his phone in Fagan's?'

'He keeps it where he can see it.'

She takes a sip of coffee, wrinkles her nose and says, 'Oh, that's putrid. Are you sure you don't want some?'

'I'm sure.'

'You're not a very popular man, James.' Again, she's expressionless, though this time she doesn't wait for me to say anything. 'Around here, I mean. The guy you tackled is well-liked. Not sure why. I've dealt with him a few times.'

'Can I ring my solicitor?'

She slides her phone towards me. The lock screen shows two young children, a boy and a girl, sweet smiles, skinny arms around small shoulders. 'Go ahead.'

'His number is on my mobile.'

'Your mobile ran out of battery.'

'I charged it this morning.'

'Do you think I'm lying?'

'Yes.'

'I'm not. I can show it to you.'

'Please do.'

She takes back her phone, looks contentedly at the children on screen and then makes it go black.

'Funny how life has these little twists and turns. There you were this morning, charging your phone, brushing your teeth, getting the bus with Libby into work. Someone organises an impromptu vigil for a poor missing girl, and you end up here, sniffing markers and talking to me.'

Perhaps she wants me to ask how she knows about Arthur and Libby. I remain still and she says, 'I think it's funny, anyhow.'

She goes to the whiteboard, puts the lid back on the marker and returns to her seat. 'You do know that you're in trouble, don't you? The courts don't look kindly on assaulting police officers, even the shit ones.'

She opens the folder, shuffles through foolscap pages of loose notes with neat, cursive handwriting, letters on garda stationery, empty forms. I glimpse a printout of the CCTV image of me and Emma Harte on Dorset Street.

Shaw looks at me again. 'I know you don't want to speak without Arthur, but he'd tell you the same. And then there's young Louise.' She tuts and shakes her head. 'I mean, youthful high spirits can only excuse so much. She's unlikely to end up in juvie, I grant you. But a criminal record, expulsion from Loreto, a millstone round her neck – all very much on the cards.' She folds her hands on the table, begins to twist a wedding ring over her finger. The last time we met she wasn't wearing it.

'I'm sorry, but my solicitor is Arthur Stokes. I won't say anything until I can speak to him.'

Shaw smiles and says, 'Why would you be sorry about a thing like that?' She rises again and pushes her chair under the table. As she leaves, the room seems to sigh, but it's just the pneumatic damper on the door. Her manila folder is open on the table.

The minutes pass slowly. High in the corner, the light on the camera continues to blink. There's a smudge of lipstick on the edge of the styrofoam. I need a piss. I watch the clock tick towards nine, and on the hour I get up to ask for the bathroom, but the door is locked. I rap at it gently, then knock and call, 'Hello.' No one comes.

At the table I look at Shaw's folder. The page on top is a printout of an email exchange with another garda discussing openings in the departmental crèche. But at the bottom is a paragraph with: DNA #31681351 – can you send me the results asap? and a Will do in reply.

Overleaf are photocopied pages from a garda notebook. The first is dated nine days ago with my address: Shaw's inspection of my flat, the afternoon I was pretending to be ill, when I led her through the house to show her the shed and the back yard. The words *Door to the Botanics* are underlined, but otherwise the description is dry and accurate. The other page comes from a few days ago. During the cold snap she called to the flat, but the door was answered by *a female who identified herself as Lilianna.* I must have been out, battling my way to the shops. What did she ask her? Why hadn't Libby mentioned it when I got back?

I leaf through the folder looking for the CCTV image of me and Emma, but instead I'm met with a mugshot of Tom. It's black and white. He's grimacing at the camera, his hair slightly longer than when I met him, his beard a little fuller, and for a second I imagine a yellow hilt sticking from his neck. I feel something, and wonder if it's guilt or sorrow.

I close the folder and retake my seat. I need to speak to Arthur. Or maybe I should aim higher, ask Colin if he knows someone good. An urge comes over me to just tell Shaw everything. But the story would crumble. *You'll never believe it, Detective, but the missing girl killed this man, and I helped her dispose of the body. Yeah, it happened at my place. No, I don't know where she went. Yeah, those are my towels that we used to wrap him up, my bin bags, my keys to the back gate. Dumping him by the Tolka was my idea. Like I told you, I don't know where she is, so stop asking.*

Arthur was right. Clam up. I'm sorry I doubted him. I badly need a piss.

Everything goes black and for a moment I doubt my own existence, but it's just the lights are off. I shout out, 'Hey,' and they come on again, together with a 'Sorry, sorry,' from a female voice outside.

'I need the bathroom.'

'I'm just the cleaner.'

'Well, get someone.'

'I'm just the cleaner,' and her footsteps shuffle away. I knock on the door again, bang on it three times, but all is silent.

Every so often I count along with the second hand to ensure it's not running slow. It's approaching ten. The pain in my bladder has become a dull throb. I wonder if there's some psychological trick. Keep you from the toilet so you can't focus on a cover story. I look around. Nowhere to pour the coffee to use the cup. I could drink the cold coffee to make room, but that might make things worse. Anyway, would a cup be enough to hold it all?

At a quarter past, the lock on the door turns with a clunk and Shauna Shaw glides in. She has my phone with her, which she plonks on the table beside me. The screen is dead. She sits down and straightens the folder, makes no mention of the fact that it's closed when earlier she'd left it open. She has a copy of the *Evening Herald* beneath her arm and she shows me the front page. Under a giant headline of GARDA SHAME, there's a large double photograph: Lolo on the ground outside the Dáil, the policeman kneeling on her back, gloved hand clamped over her mouth, her eyes wide and face pale in the camera flash; and beside that me with the garda in a headlock, his high-vis vest a blur, my face just about visible, people milling in the background.

Shaw looks at me and says, 'You're famous.'

'I need to use the—'

She holds up her hand. 'First things first, James,' and her voice changes as if she's speaking by rote. 'When a suspect is arrested after 5 p.m., he may be kept in a holding cell overnight, to be brought to the District Court before 12 p.m. the following day. The court has two options. Release you on bail to appear at a future date, though that outcome is unlikely for certain offences,' and here she lays her hand on the folder, 'or it can remand you in custody for a period of no more than seven days, during which time you may be charged. In Dublin, those on remand are sent to Cloverhill. It's not as nice as it sounds.'

'Did you contact my solicitor?'

'No.'

'Why not?'

'You don't need him yet.'

'Detective, I desperately have to go to the bathroom.'

'None of what I just said is going to happen to you, James. I'm releasing you without charge. You're free to piss wherever you like.'

She moves her hand from the folder, and I can't help but glance at it.

Shaw smiles at me. 'Are you pleased?'

'Why did you keep me here so long?'

'There's gratitude. You're worse than my son, and he's four. I had to pull some strings here. One of my colleagues may suffer as a result.'

'What happened to my niece?'

'Louise? She's probably at home.'

I get up and lift my coat from the chair. I half expect her to rise as well, but she remains seated. She says, 'James, try not to get arrested again. It will make things so much easier.'

'I don't intend to.'

'I know, but you're that type. You always seem to back into the limelight.' She folds the newspaper and hands it to me. 'Some light bedtime reading.'

CHAPTER 14

Paschal opens the door to Libby and Miranda's place and after a wide-eyed moment smiles and says, 'You mad fucker.' Libby comes into the hallway and rushes to hug me, standing on the cold pavement in thick woollen socks. She says, 'We thought you were locked up.'

For once, Paschal doesn't seem to mind the public display of affection. He ushers us inside saying, 'See? See, I told you they'd buckle.'

The living room looks like an impromptu communications hub. Computer and phone chargers criss-cross the hearthrug. Two laptops lie abandoned on the sofa; Miranda is sitting with a third. She beams at me and says, 'You've been sprung.'

I show Libby my phone and say, 'Do you have a charger?'

'Samsung? There might be an old one in the drawer.' She disappears into the kitchen for a minute. When I turn, Paschal has his phone pointed at me. The flash goes off. He looks at the screen and says, 'Perfect,' and begins to tap out a message.

'What are you doing?'

'Letting our supporters know we won.'

'Don't tweet my picture.'

'Why not?'

'I don't want you to.'

While holding my eye he dabs the screen and says, 'Oops.'

Miranda says, 'Paz, consent is a two-way street.'

He waves his hand and sits under his laptop. 'If it wasn't for us, he'd still be rotting in a holding cell.'

Libby comes back, untangling a white cord. 'The plug bit is missing but you can charge it from my computer.' She connects the phone through a USB port and I settle beside her. She sits cross-legged so one knee overlaps mine. I switch the phone on and wait for it to boot up.

'Were you guys all right, after?'

'No one was hurt. A lot of milling and jostling. The police closed ranks though so we couldn't get near you.'

'Did you see what happened to Lolo?'

'No, sorry.'

Paschal says, 'She was released. Same as you. Don't you understand what we did, James? We doxed the fuck out of that little fascist who grabbed her. The guards had no choice but to cave.'

Libby opens up the DUGES Twitter page. The last several tweets have had hundreds of responses, thousands of 'likes'. At the top is the picture Paschal took a moment ago. It's not bad. My hair is ruffled. I look tired but serious. Beneath it he wrote, This is what a feminist looks like. A hundred retweets already.

Libby scrolls past YouTube clips of the vigil and the scuffles. 'We were sent this a few hours ago. We amplified it and it took off.'

A tweet from an account with no profile. The message: Is this who we want policing women's bodies? And above that, a series of pictures. The first is the photo of the cop straddling Lolo, the one on the front page of the papers. Then a blurry close-up of the number on his shoulder, D106. Next, a screenshot of a newspaper article: a smiling D106 presenting a police cap and badge to a sick child in hospital, with the garda's name, Aiden Quirke, printed beneath, and some roughly photoshopped text saying, DIS YOU?? Finally, screenshots of Twitter and Facebook messages from an off-duty Aiden Quirke all collated together: calling a famous young actress a slag for being out on the town; ranking the Irish women's soccer team by fuckability; Facebook memes mocking women in burkas. Generally, him being an obnoxious, problematic bastard.

There are thousands of messages in response. Outraged women calling for Quirke's head and accusing the gardaí of institutional misogyny. Other sleuths have dived deeper into archived tweets, unearthing grubby gems. While I was in the holding cell, the story, online at least, had been changing. It was no longer about me or Lolo, or even Emma Harte. All energy had turned to the cancellation of Quirke.

Miranda says, 'Did they interview you in there?'

'Not really. I mean a few questions, I suppose, but mostly I was left on my own.'

'What did he ask?'

'She.'

Libby's head stirs, and I suddenly remember Shaw's notes in the file about her visit to the flat during the cold snap. Would she have identified herself when Libby opened the door? She must

217

have done. But then why hadn't Libby said anything? Perhaps she assumed it was all to do with Whiteside.

Paschal says, 'Was she hot?' and Miranda says, 'For fuck's sake.'

'She asked who organised the vigil, things like that. Don't worry, I wouldn't say a word without a lawyer.' I toss him the newspaper. 'You're mentioned in this though.'

My phone begins to ping with missed calls and messages. Several from Colin. A text from Lolo that simply says, Thanks. My mam asking if all is set for lunch on Sunday – she obviously hadn't seen the news.

While scanning the front page, Paschal says, 'Emma Harte is the best thing that's happened to DUGES in ages. We have to build on this. And we'll need you, Jim. You're the face of it now.' Suddenly he frowns and shakes the paper. 'Who the fuck is Pasquale O'Toole?'

Miranda laughs and reaches out to him. 'Show me.'

My phone can't connect to the Wi-Fi. I want to check work emails in case the news has caused a stir with HR. I ask Libby for the password. She plops her computer on my lap and says, 'Use this. I'll go make tea.'

Paschal calls after her, 'One sugar for me, Lib.'

I begin to type *National Library staff portal* but after the N and the *a* some of Libby's previous searches show up: *Nadal's left arm* – didn't think she was a tennis fan; *Nasty Gal* – a clothing line apparently; *baby names* – concerning.

Miranda says, 'I've never read an actual newspaper before.' She leafs through some pages and holds one open to Paschal. 'Look, a crossword!'

I backspace the letters and type *em* instead. Libby's previous searches: *Emma Harte Dublin*; *Emma Harte missing*; *Emma Harte*

CCTV. I click on that last one. The first link – coloured purple, so she's viewed it – is an *Examiner* article featuring the picture of me and Emma on Dorset Street. A click, and the picture fills the screen. How long had she looked at this? Just a glance, or had she pored over it for minutes, noting the buttons on my jacket, the stripe on my scarf, the shape of my chin?

She's clinking back in bearing a tray of mugs and milk and sugar bowl.

In moments like these it's important not to do anything quickly. Tap the keys softly. Don't frown or peer at the screen. Ctrl+H for *History*. Sort by date. The article and Google searches are at the top.

Paschal has reached for a mug, and Libby says, 'That's for James.'

'What's the difference?'

She nods to a slightly smaller mug. 'That one's yours.'

I right-click each page in turn. Hit *Delete*. Ctrl+H again to exit *History*. Navigate back to the DUGES Twitter page just as Libby is sitting beside me. I carefully swap her laptop for a mug filled to the brim.

'Thanks,' I say.

'Anything from work?'

'No. Either they didn't hear, or they don't care.'

She closes the lid and puts the computer aside, draws her legs up and sips at her own tea. 'Well, you weren't charged. If you haven't done anything wrong, you don't have anything to worry about.'

I look across at her, and when she smiles, I say, 'Exactly.'

At home the next morning I email Helena and Bridget to say I won't be in. It's true my back is killing me from the scuffle with the guards, though it would have held up if properly medicated. It's the questions, the comments, the sidelong glances I can do without.

Bridget is the first to reply with an ambiguous, 'I'm not surprised.'

Helena is more considerate. 'Well done on standing your ground. Look after yourself. If you're able, would you take a quick look at the flyer??'

I stay wrapped up on the sofa for a while and savour the silence. Libby went straight to college from her place first thing, and I'm surprised and slightly unsettled to find that it's a relief she's not here.

Flicking through old texts, I see the last message from the 089 number, received the night before the whiteout when I was at dinner at Colin's place. It's just a photo of the stairwell to my front door, to let me know that he or she had been there that evening, possibly while I was still inside.

But why? Why would they want to rattle me? I try to think who could have sent it. Emma Harte had put Tom's burner phone in the Afghan coat, which she then tossed into the bins outside the Tolka House. Had she come back to retrieve them? If she did, why would she taunt me with messages? She wasn't furtive or sly. It didn't seem like her at all.

Someone must have seen Emma ditch the coat. They must have retrieved it deliberately, knowing it would be evidence. Finding the phone was just a bonus. But who? The only name that comes to mind is Whiteside, which is absurd. If he truly suspected anything, his first call would be to the police. Besides, Allen would hardly know how to text a picture even if he wanted to.

I look at the ceiling and imagine him reclining in his armchair, his dressing gown pressed, his hair neatly combed, the bruises and stitches on his face.

On the other hand, he had witnessed me and Emma with the wheelbarrow that night. He had witnessed me battling with the bins. Just what else had he seen? Just what else might he be willing to tell?

I toss my phone aside and go to find some shoes. Perhaps it was time for Allen to receive a wellness check.

If I knocked on the front door he wouldn't answer, so I let myself up the internal staircase. I call out, 'Allen, it's James. I was heading to the shops and wondered if you needed anything.'

The hallway looks tidy. It feels warm. There's no answer.

I call his name again and venture to the sitting room. The door is ajar. With a gentle knock I push it open.

Whiteside is slumped in his armchair, a blanket half fallen from his knees, an open bottle of Powers and a vial of oxycodone on the table in front of him. At first I'm scared to move. But then I see his chest rise and fall, and when I approach I hear his gentle snores. A nudge of his shoulder elicits no response.

'Allen,' I say in a loud voice. Not a flicker.

I lift the oxycodone and read the label: *Take one tablet by mouth every 3 to 4 hours. Do not exceed stated dose.* I give the bottle a rattle. About a dozen left. The muscles below my shoulder blade are still throbbing. I pop the cap, let a tablet slither onto my palm. I look at the whiskey bottle and the empty tumbler. I look at Allen, with his shoulders slumped and his lip drooping.

I put the tablet back, replace the caps on the whiskey and the vial and move them both out of reach. There's a jug of water on a sideboard. I pour a glass and place it next to his armrest, then lift the blanket and lay it on his lap. A glaring sliver of sunlight falls on his face. At the window I close one of the shutters to leave him in shadow.

In his cold kitchen I check the fridge to see if he has enough to eat. The ragù that Libby made sits unopened on the top shelf. He's in no condition to heat it up. I look over at his cooker, the ceramic hobs speckled with grease.

In the cupboards I find a saucepan, place it on a hob, turn the heat to medium-high, and pour in the ragù. A quick stir with a wooden spoon, which I leave perched on the pot. I walk back through the hall and down the stairs to my own flat, leaving both doors open.

For the next twenty minutes I work on my laptop, taking care of the Photoshop files that Helena sent me – the reworked flyers for the Markievicz exhibition. She was right. The design crowd we got in to do the job produced shoddy PSDs. Uneven blends, terrible colour balance, the layers hadn't even been flattened. I touch up everything, while a delectable smell of Bolognese drifts from the rooms above.

As I'm ready to save the files I notice there's a large item stored on the clipboard. I'm not sure what it could be. I didn't adjust any of the pictures in the flyer. I open a blank document and hit *Paste*.

A photograph of Sarah appears. She's on Burrow beach, smiling broadly beneath the brim of a straw hat, her fringe partially covering her eyes. The background of the sea and the strand has been erased, so only the sharp outline of her summer dress remains. I look at the picture for a long moment. I type Ctrl+Z to make it disappear. Then I click on the *Edit* menu, select the clipboard cache, and hit *Purge*.

The smell coming from the stairwell has taken on a bitter, burnt quality. I go and look up through the open doors. In the hallway above I see a few faint wisps of smoke. In my own kitchen, I search in the drawer of old business cards until I find the one I want. I fetch my phone and dial the number.

After a moment: 'Hi Eliza, this is James Lyster here. Your dad's tenant. I'm afraid to say that I'm becoming concerned about Allen.'

As evening falls I'm walking through the quiet streets of Clontarf. A mizzling rain makes the pavements glisten under the streetlamps. Here and there, bare trees in front gardens are decked with fairy lights. Electric candles flicker on windowsills. In the fading light, the living rooms look warm and inviting as I pass with my collar raised against the cold. I turn down Victoria Avenue, count the houses until I reach No. 56. I recognise the ball finials and the silver railings from Google Street View. The old redbrick has a gable roof, protruding bay windows, an arched opening in the porch. There's no hint of Christmas decoration.

The gate squeaks as I push it open. A dry patch in the driveway suggests a car left only minutes before. Above the brass bell a small sign says, *No cold callers*. I ring it anyway.

A high-pitched yapping sounds from within. The porch light comes on, and a woman opens the door to peer out. She's about fifty, mousy hair with flecks of silver, a kindly face that seems anxious and careworn. Before I can introduce myself, she turns to hush the dog, then looks at me again and says, 'Yes?'

'Sorry for disturbing you. Are you Mrs Harte?'

A subtle shift in her mouth. Already on the defensive, she says, 'What is it?'

'I was hoping to speak to you about your daughter, Emma. You see, she and I were very close. I mean, are very close.'

She shakes her head. Her tone is apologetic as she says, 'No, no, this isn't a good time.'

'It would just be a few minutes.'

'I'm sorry,' and she moves to close the door.

'Mrs Harte, please.' From my pocket I take the old edition of Anna Karenina, inscribed to Emma from her mother.

She recognises it immediately. One hand grips the edge of the door a little tighter, the other briefly covers her mouth.

I say, 'Emma asked me to return this to you.'

Her eyes meet mine, and in them I think I see the question, 'Asked you when?'

She takes the book and runs her fingers over the cover. Tiny droplets of rain swirl in the porch. I pull my coat tighter, and ask, 'May I come in?'

The hall is softly lit. A staircase leads to a landing with stained-glass windows of acanthus leaves and songbirds. At my feet a small white terrier snuffles and wags his tail, satisfied that I no longer pose a threat. Mrs Harte leads me into a front room of leather furniture, bookcases and beanbags, an old record player with large headphones plugged into the jack. Strains of classical music echo in the ear cups. She lifts the dust cover and the tonearm, and the record coasts to a stop. Awkwardly, the dog clambers onto a beanbag. He rests his head on his paws and stares at me.

Still rather distracted and tense, Mrs Harte says, 'I have nothing to offer you,' and I say, 'That's fine.'

A family portrait in a Newgrange silver frame sits in the centre of the mantelpiece. Mr Harte and his wife and their two teenaged daughters, in descending height order, stand against a stark white background. Emma is the older sister. In the picture her hair is loose and hangs about her shoulders. Her head is tilted with a playful smile. The younger sibling has folded her arms by gripping her elbows, and she looks at the camera impassively.

At the far end of the mantelpiece there's another picture of Emma's sister, this time in a debs dress, her date a lanky fellow in an ill-fitting tux. The angle of the frame suggests that another photo once accompanied it. Emma and Tom Wickham perhaps? If so, how recently had Tom been removed? Immediately after she disappeared, or only in the past few days?

Mrs Harte settles in one of the armchairs. She has *Anna Karenina* in her lap, and she opens the title page. I take a seat in the leather sofa adjacent and look around. I like the room. There's no TV, but there are expensive-looking coffee-table books in large slipcases: *Andy Warhol Polaroids 1958–1987*; *Chanel – Collections and Creations*; *Pucci – The Archival Patterns*.

To break the silence I say, 'I can't imagine what you're going through.'

Which is true, but only to an extent. Before I came, I read all I could on 'ambiguous loss' and the psychology of hope, on the natural oscillation between optimism and despair when a person goes missing. I learned of prolonged grief disorder, and the peculiar heartbreak in which hope is an enemy. There are stages to go through. Eventually a clinician will say to Mrs Harte that her yearning must evolve. Instead of hoping that Emma is alive and well, she should hedge her bets, and pray for something more viable, that her daughter did not suffer, for instance. In the end, she must choose to say goodbye, even when she cannot know for sure what has happened, and learn to live with the sense that she has betrayed the person who counted on her the most.

Unless, of course, she knows that Emma is still alive and is helping to cover her tracks.

Instead of replying, Mrs Harte places the book on an armrest, and says, 'When did Emma give you this?'

'Months ago. I had mentioned in passing that I'd never read it. She said she could lend me her copy. Was it yours originally?'

She nods, and says, 'I bought it in Eason's during my first week of college. I gave it to Emma when she started in Trinity.'

The faint noise of a door closing can be heard in the floors above. I glance at the ceiling. A lot of room in this rambling Victorian house for a small family. If Emma wished to hide here, and if they were willing to maintain a charade, it would at least be possible.

I say, 'Maybe one day Emma will give it to her own daughter.'

Mrs Harte's brow creases. Perhaps she has become tired of false positivity and clumsy attempts at solace. Or perhaps I have aroused her suspicion.

But then she smiles. Years fall from her face, and I see a hint of Emma in her countenance. She says, 'Yes, I hope so.'

The tail of the terrier begins to patter in the beanbag, as if he has sensed a lifting of his mistress's mood.

She says, 'You're a friend of hers?'

'We met in second year. I was one of the finalists of the Young Entrepreneur competition. The year that Emma and Tom won.' I pause to gauge her reaction to his name, but she remains expressionless. 'We stayed in touch afterwards. In fact, we became quite close.'

'The three of you?' she asks.

I have to plump for an answer, so I say, 'Yes, the three of us.'

She remains still for a moment, then she rises and goes to a bookcase. She creates a gap on a certain shelf and inserts the book – Tolkien to the left of it, then Tokarczuk, then Tóibín, and I realise the whole collection is arranged by author.

I say, 'Are you a librarian?' She frowns at the question, so I add, 'It's just I work in the National Library.'

'I was a school teacher,' and she shakes her head slightly. 'Years ago, though I did volunteer in the library as much as I could.'

I remember something Emma said in the flat. 'Your daughter told me once that she buys more books than she can read. That she just likes to fill the shelves. I can see why now.'

Mrs Harte smiles again. She nudges the books so that the spines align, and goes back to her seat.

We sit for a while in a silence that feels companionable, or at least, not uncomfortable. A long, dark hair snakes over the armrest of the sofa. I pick it up and let it drift to the floor.

'Mrs Harte, I hope you don't mind me saying this, but I don't believe Tom would have harmed Emma. Despite what's been said in the news recently.'

Her eyes seem to focus on the middle distance, but then they fix on me again. 'I don't either.'

'Have you heard anything at all from her? Did she leave a message, or write to you? Do you have the smallest inkling of where she might be?'

Conflicting emotions play on her face. She seems to consider for a long moment what she's about to say. Just as she parts her lips to speak, there are footsteps on the stairs. Floorboards creak in the hallway. The doorknob scrapes and turns, and I look to see who will enter.

It is Emma Harte's sister. She wears black leggings and thick socks and a shapeless woollen jumper. Her face is rounder. Her dark hair is tied back in a ponytail.

She stops when she sees me, glances to her mother. The stillness is broken by the dog, who slithers from the beanbag and trots over with his tail wagging.

She says, 'I was wondering who came to the door.'

'Clara, this is … sorry, I've forgotten your name.'

'James.'

'He's a friend of Emma's.'

I stand and smile sympathetically and think about extending a hand, but she remains by the door.

She says, 'I never heard her mention a James.'

'We met in college,' I say weakly. 'I just came to offer any support I could.'

She regards her mother again more intently. 'We've had so few visitors.'

I say, 'Oh, well, I'm glad—'

'That's how we wanted it.'

The tension in Mrs Harte's demeanour returns. Fidgeting with the tassel of a cushion, she says, 'James asked if we had heard from Emma at all.'

Clara becomes still. 'My sister is missing without a trace.'

Her mother says, 'That's what I was about to tell him.'

'You can't imagine the toll, the stress we have been under. Do you think we're here to provide updates to any stranger who calls to the door?'

Her reaction strike me as overblown, though it's difficult to say what would be natural in this situation. Their defences are raised, and there's nothing I can glean from them now. If they're aware of Emma's whereabouts, then it's because they are protecting her, and they won't tell me. If they're not aware, then me saying that I know she's still alive can only lead to questions, and renewed focus from the police.

I say to Mrs Harte, 'I'm sorry if I have intruded. I will be thinking of you.'

She doesn't meet my eye. With an elbow on an armrest, she covers her brow.

I nod to Clara as I pass, and she follows me into the hall, hovers as I turn the latch to open the door. Before I step out, I look at her, and speak quietly.

'It's very important that I speak with Emma. If you are able to communicate with her in any way, tell her to get in touch with James. Tell her there has been a complication, and that it has put her in jeopardy. That's all.'

A colour has risen to her cheeks. Before she can respond, I slip from the house and walk down the driveway. She is watching from the door as I open and close the gate. I look back at her silhouette in the hall light, and then I turn and hurry along Victoria Avenue.

CHAPTER 15

17 DECEMBER

A burble of water drifts from the bathroom, and occasionally Libby's tuneful humming. In the living room I have the spare Huawei MediaPad on my lap. It has proven handy for keeping certain online research off my personal devices. Now I have a site open called GeoImgr. There are two windows, one an interactive map of the world, the other a dropbox for uploading photographs. I copy in the picture of Sarah in a rainforest with the baby macaque plucking sunglasses from her head. Once it uploads, I pan and scroll through the map, and zoom in to the town of Ubud, in the uplands of Bali, Indonesia. I stick a pin in the map, and the site invites me to *Write EXIF data?* I click the button, download the picture again, now with the correct geo tags, and I save it to a folder on the tablet.

I haven't noticed the water turn off and Libby's approach. She puts her head around the door, bare shoulders above a towel and strands of wet hair. 'James, the toilet is being weird again.'

Too late to hide the device so I just leave it on my lap. I pretend to be exasperated. 'What did you do now?'

'I didn't touch it.'

'It was fine before you showed up.'

'Yeah, well, I guess I have that effect on things.' She nods to the tablet. 'What's that?'

'Christmas present for Ultan. Just setting it up.'

She smiles and says, 'Very generous.' She ducks back out, and from the hallway she says, 'We only have twenty minutes.'

I carefully shut down everything on the tablet, re-box it, and place the box out of sight, and out of reach, on top of the bookcase.

The bathroom is clammy. I keep having to wipe the mirror to shave. Flecks of stubble floating in the froth make me think of the DNA test. I remember how I left the coat in the room in Mountjoy Square, bundled up with others, none of them particularly clean. Anything could have rubbed off. Could they really have picked out some skin cells from my hands? A stray strand of hair? Distracted, I nick the bottom of my neck and draw a drop of blood. I press a square of tissue paper and let it stick, watch the red dot expand, then crumple the paper and drop it in the toilet. The flush works fine, but Libby's right, the cistern is filling with a choked trickle.

By the time I'm out of the shower it's still going. I clear off the toilet rolls and air freshener and lift the back lid. I gingerly prod at the bright orange ball and spindly arms. In the murky water at the bottom of the cistern something seems out of place, or misaligned. I delve into the cold, feel around until my fingers grip a wooden shaft.

It's lodged against a valve, but with a twist it releases, and I draw it out.

Water cascades as I lift out a knife, a stainless steel blade about four inches long with an oddly curved tip, the cherry-wood handle embossed with a Japanese character. I think of the leather roll of knives on the table in re:Thread, the blade missing from the middle pouch. I remember Emma Harte hiding the flash drive here. She must have hidden the knife as well. But why not take it with her? Because she didn't need it anymore? Suddenly what she did that night seemed a lot less spontaneous.

Libby is putting on make-up in the standing mirror in the corner of the bedroom. The door is open, and she sees me come out of the bathroom. I hold the knife behind my back, pretend I'm holding up the towel. I've never seen her in a dress before. Black and closely fitted at the top with a skirt that ends just below the knees. She raises an eyebrow and smiles at me standing in the doorway.

I say, 'I've fixed that now,' and she tuts in appreciation.

'Such a handyman.'

I cock a thumb over my shoulder and say, 'Just have to get something.'

In the kitchen I put the knife in a little-used cupboard. If Libby finds it I can just say it's an elaborate pizza cutter. Back in the bedroom I don some slacks and my best shirt and come to stand next to her, just as she's putting mascara away in her bag. She's slightly shorter in her stockinged feet. She holds my arm and leans her head on my shoulder as we stand side-by-side in the mirror.

'We almost look like real people,' she says.

I smile and look at her and kiss her forehead, then lean down to kiss her lips. She puts her arms around me, kisses my jaw and the side of my neck. She says, 'You can't be walking around in a towel like that.'

We're sidling towards the bed when her phone pings. She draws back and takes a breath. 'That'll be the cab.'

When we step outside we see Eliza Whiteside's car idling in the driveway. Eliza is placing a large suitcase in the boot, while her father waits in the front passenger seat, a tartan blanket pulled up and over his shoulders. She closes the boot, sees Libby and me standing in the reflection, and comes over to us. Quietly she says, 'Sorry again, James. It's a wonder he didn't burn the whole house down. You know, he couldn't even remember turning on the stove.'

Libby looks at me quizzically. I tell her briefly what happened, or at least the story I told Eliza, and she says, 'Oh, that's terrible.'

To Eliza, I say, 'Are you taking him home to Avoca?'

'For a few weeks. After Christmas we'll have to find something more permanent.' Her gaze sweeps up and over the house, and she says to me, 'I'll be in touch about the tenancy,' which sounds ominous.

As she manoeuvres the car from the driveway, Allen looks out at us. I raise my hand in farewell but he doesn't respond. His eyes linger on Libby as the car pulls away.

The cab we ordered is parked on the street, and ten minutes later we're at Colin's place. Before I press the bell, Libby reaches over to grip my arm. She fixes her hair in the sidelight window and smooths the lapel of her jacket.

'Okay,' she says.

'They're going to love you.'

Danni answers the door wielding a spatula. She hurriedly greets Libby and says, 'Bit of an emergency with the dauphinoise,' then she ushers us through the house and into the kitchen/diner extension at the back. The table has been lengthened and set for Mam's birthday lunch. A Johnny Mathis CD is playing. The air is a heady mix of Chanel and white wine and roasting juices. In the corner the birthday girl is sitting in state, next to my Aunt Peggy and Peggy's taciturn husband Gerry. Colin is in the garden having a smoke with cousin Frankie, but they've begun walking towards the sliding doors and file in with loud hellos.

I introduce Libby. Mam briefly puts on glasses to look at her. Colin holds out his hand on his way to the fridge and says, 'Nice to meet you,' and Libby hesitates, and I say, 'You met her already in Fagan's, you dolt.'

'Oh, yeah, that's right.'

At the kitchen island, Danni looks up and says, 'When?'

'Week or so ago. Bumped into Jim looking at the match.'

I kiss Mam's cheek and give her a card with a restaurant voucher. '*The Irish Times* raves about this place,' I say. 'All the ingredients are foraged locally.'

Aunt Peggy says, 'Foraged in Raheny? No thanks.'

Libby has brought Mam a book wrapped in silver paper, a biography of Eleanor of Aquitaine. Mam says it's wonderful and leaves it aside on her seat.

From the fridge Colin calls out my name and asks me to help him fetch booze from the utility room. Libby throws a quick glance that says, 'Don't leave me,' but I squeeze her hand and follow Colin into the small space beside the kitchen. The washer-dryer is humming. Bikes are chained up next to a wine rack. An old fridge stands alone in the corner and Colin opens it up.

He glances over my shoulder while handing me a six-pack and a bottle of prosecco. 'Unwelcome developments.'

The cans are ice cold. I shift them about so they settle on my sleeve. 'Oh?'

'Danni knows about the Delphine situation. At least I think she does. She's been acting weird, dropping strange comments. I think Louise knows as well.'

'But how?'

'That's what I was going to ask. You didn't let anything slip, did you?'

'Of course not.'

'I mean, not many people know about it. Only you and Arthur.'

A gale of laughter from the kitchen and we both look towards the door. Colin takes an ice bag from the freezer, almost a solid block, and bludgeons the counter to break up the cubes.

I say, 'Whatever you can say about Arthur, he prides himself on his discretion. Are you sure this Delphine didn't go behind your back, trying to stir the pot?'

'I broached that, yeah.' He grimaces. 'She didn't take the imputation with good grace.'

'But surely you'd know if Danni had found out? Wouldn't she be on the warpath?'

Another dash and the block disintegrates. He empties the cubes into a steel bucket, takes a Marlborough Sauvignon from the rack and thrusts it into the ice. 'Just be on your toes,' he says.

Frankie has been holding forth in the other room. Older than Colin by a few years, he works in Google Analytics and always gives the vague impression that he's seen your search history. When we come back in, he says, 'Couldn't believe it when you appeared on the front of the papers, Jim. I said, not my quiet-as-a-church-mouse cuz.'

Danni opens the oven door and waves away smoke with her tongs. 'Yeah, thanks again for looking out for Louise like that. God knows what might have happened otherwise.'

'He should have gotten her out of there before it kicked off,' Colin says, handing out IPAs and topping up wine.

Mam says to me, 'It's a terrible business. I've never seen you going to things like that before,' and she casts a sidelong glance at Libby.

'Well, it was meant to be peaceful.'

'What was the ruckus about this time?' asks Frankie. 'Rent hikes? Water charges?'

Libby says, 'It was Emma Harte.'

'Oh, that's right,' he says. 'Ireland's latest hide-and-seek champ.'

She looks at him for a moment and forces a weak smile.

Colin says, 'Jim seems to have that figured out though. You were saying it's the boyfriend.'

'Well, that's the consensus now that he supposedly reappeared and went missing again.'

'It's always the boyfriend,' Frankie says, and he returns Libby's smile. 'You should keep an eye on Jim here.'

She says, 'I have been.'

Mam waves a wine glass. 'I don't like all this crime talk.'

Peggy says, 'I don't remember us ever getting murdered, Betty, when we were young. It's the girls these days, making a holy show of themselves.'

Libby parts her mouth to speak but instead takes a long sip of beer.

'It's just the media, Peg,' I say. 'Every incident is pored over.'

'And still they can't catch anyone.'

Colin cracks a can and says, 'So not all bad. Anyway, don't let Louise hear you go on like this or she'll report you to the thought police.'

I ask, 'Is Lolo here?'

'Out with Specker. She's coming later. Well, she said she would. She's a law unto herself now that she's famous.'

In the kitchen, Danni has plonked a roasting dish with a glistening sirloin on the countertop, and she asks Colin to fetch the thermometer.

Can halfway to his mouth, he pauses and says, 'Of course, dear.' He goes to search in a drawer and hands her something.

She says, 'That's a child's thermometer.'

'It reads temperature, doesn't it?'

'It's two inches long.'

'Well, how am I supposed to find anything in this house when you keep moving things?'

She brushes past him to the same drawer, withdraws the long needle-like meat thermometer, tests the point with her finger and spits the beef. After a moment she says to the room, 'I hope you like it bloody.'

While the meat rests, we take our seats. The boys come in from the living room with some young cousin in tow whose name escapes me. They sit opposite Libby and look at her shyly, but when Ultan asks what her favourite Pokémon is, and she gives some appropriate response, they warm to her. Colin and Danni are plating up, an increase of muttered whispers and clanking cutlery. Just as everyone is served, the front door opens and closes and in walks Lolo with Specker in tow. She has a new hairdo, head shaved on one side, the rest of her hair swept over to cover half her face. She's wearing purple lipstick and a black miniskirt. Specker has made an effort with a white shirt buttoned all the way to his chin.

Colin says, 'Yet again, your instinct for when dinner is ready is unerring.'

Aunt Peggy is looking at Lolo's hair in horror. 'Did the police do that to you?' she asks while Lolo goes to hug her grandmother. She and Specker help themselves and join us to complete the table, with Colin and Danni at either end. Colin lifts his glass for a toast. 'You know what they say about Dublin mammies … that they age terribly but live forever. Well, I for one hope the second part is true. So happy birthday, Mam. Here's to you, and here's to family.'

We all repeat 'To family' and raise our glasses, except for Lolo. Danni looks across the table at Colin and returns her glass to its coaster unsipped.

While the potatoes are passed around, Mam says, 'We won't feel the days slip by till Christmas.'

Frankie asks, 'Any plans this year?'

'No, nothing special.'

He says, 'Colin, will you ever take the family out to lunch on Christmas Day and give poor Danni a break?'

Mam says, 'Oh, I'd hate that.'

Colin says, 'She enjoys the cooking. At least, she says she does.'

Danni tilts her head at him, but her expression doesn't change.

Mam says, 'What about you, Sarah … sorry, Libby, do you go home for Christmas?'

'Yes, back to Mayo every year.'

'How quaint.'

'I've never actually stayed in the city for the holidays.'

'Well, I'm sure we could fit you in. There's always plenty.'

Danni says, 'Well, let's not make plans just—'

Libby says, 'No, it's fine, Danni. In fact, I've roped Jim into coming to meet my folks this year.'

A silence falls over the table, except for Johnny Mathis crooning, *It's not for me to say*. Mam has become still, her fingers resting on the lip of her glass.

Had I agreed to that? I vaguely remember bringing it up when Libby had caught me daydreaming about forensic linguistics. But Mam has an unhealthy fixation with Christmas and the gathering of family, especially since Dad died.

I clear my throat, turn to Libby and speak gently. 'I thought that was going to be Stephen's Day, or the day after.'

'Oh.'¹

'I mean, there's the whole week before New Year.'

'Yeah, of course. I had it in my head …'

'You should come up here for the day.'

'No, my parents are expecting me.'

Mam has relaxed and she says, 'Well, you can't let them down. And it's only one day. God, I don't know why everyone makes such a fuss.'

Libby forces a laugh and looks at her plate, her cheeks a little pinker. She's pretty when she's embarrassed.

Colin says he's going to get more wine and heads towards the island. Uncle Gerry changes the subject by saying, 'This is a gorgeous bit of meat,' and we all murmur in agreement. Mam adds, 'The dauphinoise is a little crisp.'

Danni's eyes slide up to look at her.

Colin returns to top up glasses. Danni holds hers out. As he finishes pouring, she bumps the top of the bottle for more.

The conversation needs a steer, so I ask Frank how work is going.

'Can't complain. Had to troop out to Grange Castle every day during the cold snap to keep an eye on the servers. I mean, they love the cold, but only so much.'

'It was like that in the library. Everyone on call in case of emergencies. Luckily, I wasn't needed.'

'Must have been a bit grim though in your little basement.'

'I had Lib for company the whole time.'

'Ah, very cosy.'

Danni turns to her and says, 'You didn't mind being left on your own for a day?'

Libby is mid-sip and she cocks her head a little. 'Pardon?'

'When Jim had to help Colin clear the drive of the office.' She looks at Colin along the length of the table. 'For the big meeting, remember? The client who was in town for just a few hours. Despite the weather.'

Colin wants to glance at me, but he catches himself. He rotates his glass by the stem. 'I hardly kept Jim a full day.'

'You were gone a full day.'

Lolo has paused her eating to rest her forearms on the corner of the table. She watches the exchange with a half-smile.

I reach for the gravy bowl, make sure my hand is steady as I pour. 'I didn't mind, Danni. I owed him a favour and now we're quits. Anyway, I was back home by lunch hour. Right, Lib?'

Libby's eyes are on me now. I turn to her with the bowl and say, 'More sauce?'

She searches my face, which I keep blank and unblinking. She frowns a little, focuses on me again and shakes her head.

'How did that meeting go after?' I say to Colin, replacing the bowl and wiping a drop from the spout.

He relaxes into his seat. 'Not bad. Succession planning for a drapery business in Castlepollard. Bit dull, but there'll be a nice commission. I might get Arthur involved on the probate side.'

'I'll mention it to him.'

For the remainder of the meal, I catch Libby and Lolo and Danni stealing glances at me. The older folk begin to reminisce about growing up in Drumcondra and birthdays past. Colin joins in happily. He laughs at the anecdotes, nudges the boys to listen and learn something. He keeps filling his own glass, goes to fetch yet another bottle, and he gives my arm a grateful nudge while leaning over to top me up.

A few minutes more and thankfully the food is finished. Danni gets up to clear the plates. Specker says, 'I'll help, Mrs Lyster,' and she says to him, 'You're very good.'

Colin, now in rare, reckless form, says he has a great future as a busboy.

Lolo turns her head to look at her father, then grimaces and rubs the back of her neck. Libby notices and asks how she's feeling after the other night. I fear Lolo will act aloof again, but she regards Libby in a new light, as if recognising a comrade from the front lines. She says, 'I was sore for a day or two, but better now. I'm thinking of setting up a GoFundMe, sue that cop for assault. My dear parents don't think it's worth pursuing.'

'You're blessed you weren't charged,' Colin says. 'So you're going to let the matter drop and concentrate on your exams,' and after a beat he adds, 'love.'

I say to her, 'Have you picked your subjects for the Leaving yet?'

'Not all of them. I like history and English. That's what I'll concentrate on.'

Libby smiles and says, 'James and I could give you grinds. Would you like to study that in college?'

'Not sure what I want to do.'

Colin says, 'Maybe you could become a roadie for Specker here.'

Lolo blinks slowly. 'Actually, I might go and study abroad. Get out of Dublin for a while. I've been looking at Ljubljana University. It's beautiful. There's something about it that really appeals to me.'

Mam says, 'Where's that?'

'Slovenia.'

'Why on earth would you want to go there?'

'Ask Dad.'

Mam turns to Colin, who shrugs and says, 'One of her notions.'

'But Dad, you're such a fan of Slovenian culture and its people.' He glances at her darkly. Mam says, 'Is that in Czechoslovakia?'

'Close,' Lolo says. 'I'm sure you'll get to visit one day, Nanny.'

From the fridge, Danni says, 'Louise,' and mother and daughter lock eyes for several seconds. But there is no ill-feeling in the look, rather an understanding that all of this will be dealt with, but another time.

Danni approaches again bearing a chocolate cake on a platter, with lit novelty candles saying 62 sticking from the top. She sets her lips in a strained smile.

When she's halfway to the table, a sullen Colin says, 'How many times, Danni? Vanilla, not chocolate.'

She stands stock still. Her smile remains, though the flickering candles give it an uncanny edge. Ever so slowly Danni tilts the platter forward. The cake stirs. It inches and slides, and then slumps to the floor. Two wisps of smoke rise from the snuffed-out candles. We all look down, as does Danni, who says, 'Oops.' She leans over to scoop up a morsel, eats it, and then daintily licks the end of each finger, finishing with her thumb. She says brightly, 'Boys, run upstairs and pack a bag. We're going to spend a few nights at my sister's.' With that she turns and glides from the room, letting the platter drop from her hand.

No one at the table moves. Mam's mouth has drooped open. She turns to Colin, who is nodding to himself, the corners of his mouth downturned. The boys slink off to follow their mother. Lolo says, 'I'm done.' She takes Specker by the hand to lead him away, and a moment later the front door clatters. Frankie clears his throat, makes an excuse and ushers his parents and child towards the door. Mam says she'll go with them. Finally, Colin decides he should rouse himself to see them off.

Only Libby and I remain. There's still a half-bottle of Malbec so I go to top her up, but she places her palm flat on the glass. I look down at the cake and wonder if there's any part of it worth salvaging. To break the silence I say, 'I told you I was the normal one.'

She doesn't reply. She lifts her glass and swallows the last of her wine. She lets her gaze drift across the room, the children's artwork on the fridge, the dappled sunlight on chrome surfaces, the half-empty glasses and rumpled cloth napkins on the table, and then finally she looks at me. Her face has an odd expression, frank and appraising and not unfriendly – the kind of look you might give someone you've only just met.

Libby says little in the cab ride home. Back in the flat I light a fire log to cheer the mood. She goes to change out of her dress, comes in to the living room wearing leggings and a hoodie, with a headache tablet fizzing in water, and her empty laptop bag slung on her shoulder. I slump into an armchair and listen to the patter of rain against the window. A flicker of firelight plays on the hearthrug. It's beginning to feel cosy, and so I'm sorry when Libby fetches her computer to power it down and put it away. It means she's heading back to Munster Street.

'You're not staying?'

She's rolling up the charging cable, which she stuffs into the side of the case. 'I can't, I'm way behind on work.'

'The sofa's all yours if you want it. And I promise to be quiet.'

She doesn't respond. She's checking under cushions for her wireless mouse. Finding it, she adds it to the case and closes the Velcro flap. She lets the bag slither to the floor, sits down wearily and takes a long sip of her tonic.

'Well? How about it?'

This time she gives a wan smile, and says, 'The books I need are back home.'

I nod and say, 'Oh, okay,' and wonder if that's the first time she's lied to me. If so, it wasn't bad, though she said the line a tad too quickly.

The lattice of kindling I built on the fire has taken light. It crackles and sparks, and a gust of wind outside sends a small puff of smoke into the room. I like the sweet smell of it and wish I could settle down beside Libby now and just stare at the flames.

I say, 'I'm sorry for the shitshow that is my family.'

Her smile is a little more genuine. 'I liked some of them.'

'Which ones?'

She thinks for a moment. 'Lolo and Specker seem nice. And I feel bad for Danni.'

'You'll like Mam as well the more you know her. She just has some funny ways.'

Libby doesn't look at me. She swirls her glass and takes another sip.

I think of going to sit beside her, but she's still uneasy. 'I'm looking forward to meeting yours. I could do with a dose of normality.'

'The Millers can have their moments too.'

'None like that, I'd say.'

She considers this and concedes. 'No, none like that.'

She hasn't put shoes on at least. She's still wearing the tights from earlier under her leggings.

I get up to place a guard in front of the fire. 'Sorry as well for the Christmas mix-up. I didn't realise you had definite plans in mind.'

'No, that was my fault. I read you wrong. My family is fairly relaxed about Christmas. I keep forgetting it's not like that for everyone.'

'It sounds much better.'

'Yeah, perhaps.'

'Like I said, I could come over to see you in the days following. It would be a relief to get away.'

She draws her legs up and grips her shins. As a gesture it seems defensive.

'Why don't we leave it this year?' she says, and she laughs slightly. 'I'm always doing this, getting ahead of myself. I mean, we've only just started going out. We don't have to be spending Christmases together just yet.'

I feel a familiar prickle in the back of my neck. I rub at it, then laugh as well, and say, 'Maybe you're right.'

Instead of going back to the armchair I sit next to her on the sofa, leaving a space between us. She shifts her legs a little further.

I smooth down a cushion, fiddle with the hem for a moment. 'Not to get all serious, but generally I love how things are going between us. If you want to slow down a bit that's totally fine. But I'm …' I search for a word, but all I can think of is, 'happy.'

Her eyes soften and she tilts her head. She reaches over and I take her hand. A squeeze of my fingers before she withdraws her hand again.

'I really like how things are going as well,' she says. 'I'm so glad that I met you. You're not like any guy I've known before.'

I'm sensing moderation in her praise. Her face looks conflicted for a moment. She says, 'It's just … I'm not sure if—'

'Is it because of what happened today? I mean, you don't ever have to see my family again if you like.'

'No, it's not that.' She qualifies. 'It's not just that.'

'What then?'

I berate myself for asking too quickly. She needs space first, then convincing. I hold up my hands and say, 'Sorry, I didn't mean to press you.'

She glances at me, I think with gratitude, and then looks at the space between us for several seconds.

'James, I don't think you're fully over Sarah.'

I don't respond at first. I let the moment stretch and wait for her eyes to meet mine. When they do, I ask, 'What makes you say that?'

I'm not sure what expression I should have. Sympathetic, abashed, sincere? Perhaps she sees the uncertainty, for she frowns.

She says, 'Lots of little things.'

I nod slowly, as if I'm taking that in. I rest my foot on the coffee-table ledge, nudge the box of photographs that Emma looked through the night she was here. I should have returned those before now.

'You may be right, Libby, and I don't want to downplay how you feel, but honestly I think I am over Sarah. We had been together for a while, I know, but we were drifting apart in the final few months.'

'You were planning to go abroad together.'

'That's the thing. The more I thought about that, the more *we* thought about it, we knew it wasn't what we wanted. I was relieved more than anything when she said she preferred to travel alone. It had run its course. The time had come to end things.'

'Was it her idea or yours?'

'To go abroad?'

'To end things.'

Her gaze has become steady, discerning. Best to be truthful.

'Hers. I was willing to try the long-distance thing for a year, but that's because … you know what I'm like, I tend to put off those kinds of decisions. She didn't want to be tied down. I understood that. I respected it. So we parted ways.'

We remain silent for a minute. The fire burns cheerfully. Water gurgles in the drainpipes outside. I think about reaching out to hold her hand again. Probably too soon.

Instead, I ask, 'How's your head?'

She looks at the glass and drinks the frothy dregs. 'A bit better. It was the Malbec, I think.'

'Col always buys the nice bottles.'

'So do you,' she says, without smiling.

She places the glass on a side table and pushes it away from the edge. A small streak of water is left on the wood.

Libby faces me again. 'Why are you always checking her social media?'

'Sarah's?'

She nods once.

A flat denial is no use. But 'always' isn't right, and deserves some pushback. Anyway, how does she know? Have I been that careless?

'I suppose I'm worried about her. You hear these terrible stories of women travelling alone. Each new post just shows me she's okay.'

I'm sure I've never checked Sarah's feed while Libby is around. Have I been liking posts by accident? Or leaving Instagram open on my laptop? Could Libby have searched my internet history without me knowing?

'Anyway,' I say, 'it's not like I message her, or leave comments.'

I'm explaining too much. I can sense an edge in my voice. I could bring up Paschal, an ex of hers who sometimes stays at her house, is part of the same college society and circle of friends. Though I have a feeling that would not go down well.

I take a breath and speak gently. 'Libby, if you want I'll stop looking altogether. But really, I'm just checking she's safe and well. I mean, I still do care for her. I still consider her a friend.'

She shakes her head. 'I don't want that.'

'Then I'm not sure what the problem is.'

'Do you like Danni?'

The question is unexpected and I pause and frown.

'You mean, do I fancy her?'

'No, do you like her as a person?'

'Of course I do. Danni's great. Lolo takes after her.'

'But you lied to her so easily.'

I feel a wave of irritation at Colin and his ham-fisted attempts at subterfuge, but I stifle it in case Libby thinks it's directed at her. 'You're right,' I say. 'That was bad. I did it for Colin. He's always been getting me to cover for him. Ever since we were kids. I suppose I just do it out of habit. And I was conscious of Mam as well. I mean, if I just flat out contradicted him, how would that have gone down? I could see a blazing row, Mam's day ruined. It was a spur-of-the-moment thing.'

'Well, you delayed the row by about twenty minutes.'

'Yeah, I know.'

'And you roped me into it as well.'

I should feel ashamed about that, and I hope it shows in my face. 'I'm really sorry, Lib. That was just bad luck.'

Her demeanour has relaxed a little. Maybe she just needed to get these things off her chest. I reach out my hand again, and she takes it, keeps hold of it this time. Rubbing her thumb over my knuckles, she says, 'I just want to know that I can trust you.'

'Of course you can,' I say at once, and I shift closer to her. She leans towards me. I put my arm around her shoulder and she rests her head beneath my chin.

I stroke the top of her arm. After a quiet moment I say, 'I'm glad that you were able to talk to me about this stuff. If you're ever worried about anything, just ask me and I'll tell you the truth.'

Am I laying it on too thick? Libby doesn't seem to think so. She snuggles closer. We do watch the flames for a while, though the fire has dwindled and could do with a stoke. I don't want to move Libby just yet. We stay huddled on the sofa as the light fades, and the rain falls softly on the windows.

CHAPTER 16

19 DECEMBER

Another airless room. Fluorescent lights and no windows. Several wooden chairs with orange fabric seats line the walls. Some bare tinsel is strung along the ceiling. I'm sitting in the corner with only one other person present, a middle-aged man reading and re-reading notes. His leg is quivering, bobbing up and down, the motion transmitting itself through the tightly packed chairs so that I can feel a tremor in the armrest. I check my phone. A message from Lolo. Try not to worry.

On the hour, the door opens and a woman's finger beckons the man from the room. He takes a deep breath, tidies his notes, and slowly shuffles out. I'd grown used to the quiver in the armrest and the chair feels odd without it. My mouth is dry. I should have brought water. I say, 'What now?' out loud, just to see if my voice sounds normal.

My phone beeps again, Libby this time. You'll be amazing xx.

Libby had still gone home on Saturday evening, but I was glad we were able to smooth things over. I was also glad to have the flat to myself to get some work done. I respond with an x to her and then open up Instagram. Sarah's latest post shows her on a beach in Sri Lanka, aquamarine sea, listing palm trees, rickety rowboats pulled up on the sand. She's wearing a wide-brimmed sunhat and a summer dress, her fringe partially covering her eyes. Her caption: Missing the xmas rush in Dublin! I double check the geotag. *Unawatuna, Galle District, Sri Lanka.* Her most recent posts are gaining some traction. This one has several 'likes', none from accounts I recognise, and one reply, from her friend Polly. Super jealous!! Can't wait to hear all your adventures when you get home ... and then several love hearts, a coconut emoji, and a plane emoji.

In the waiting room, the radio is being piped in. After an ad break a smooth-voiced presenter introduces the man who just left, a Professor Swailes. They begin to discuss rent pressure zones in Dublin. Swailes sounds less nervous than he looked. The door opens again and in walks Paschal, satchel slung on his shoulder and easy smile. His beard has been neatly trimmed even though no one will see it. There's a young producer at his shoulder, clipboard and headset with a slender microphone. She says, 'You're up after the next break, lads.'

Paschal says, 'Grand, grand,' and he comes to sit beside me. I tap out of Instagram and put my phone away.

She pauses on her way out. 'By any chance, are either of you non-binary?'

We glance at each other. I ask, 'Why?'

'It's just not a great look to have three blokes on discussing feminism.'

Paschal shrugs and says, 'I could be,' and she nods and makes a tick on her clipboard and backs out of the room.

A few days ago the photo that Paschal had taken of me in Libby and Miranda's living room had gone viral. The Twitterverse had truly believed that by their efforts they had unmasked a misogynist cop and forced my release, all in a heady few hours of pile-ons and public shaming. Activists could point to a tangible, feel-good result to their campaigning, and my solemn face and dishevelled hair had come to represent the whole affair.

Even Libby had been swept along when journalists and radio researchers began getting in touch. She said that I just had to go on, and I couldn't think of a reason to say no. Paschal inveigled an invite as well, as spokesperson for DUGES and organiser of the Emma Harte vigil.

In the green room I say, 'I was scared you'd be a no-show.'

'Wouldn't let you go in alone. Nervous?'

'Not really.'

'Nothing to be nervous about,' he says, rubbing his fingers over his knuckles. 'The trick is to just say what you've prepared no matter the question. That's what the politicians do.'

'I haven't prepared anything.'

'Well, let me do the talking.'

He begins to pat a disjointed rhythm on both knees, then says, 'Saw Miranda earlier. She wished you luck.'

'At her place?'

'Yep.'

'Was Libby there?'

He looks at me, his lips pursed. 'She'd already left for college, I think. Why?'

'Just wondering.'

He looks ready to make some comment but gets distracted by the radio. Swailes is wrapping up. The presenter teases the next segment before the commercial break: uproar in Dublin city centre, police brutality, institutional sexism, violence against women, as well as new techniques in poodle-grooming, in just a few.

Paschal bats the side of my knee. 'Get your game face on.'

We're fetched by the producer, who leads us through brightly lit corridors. Swailes passes us coming the other way, a lightness to his step as if he's just been given the all-clear from a biopsy. We reach a door with a green light above it, and the producer leads us in. A darkened booth with a mixing desk, a sound engineer in oversized headphones, a giant window to the studio. We're brought through another door and introduced to the host, Gary O'Reilly, who is leaning back in his chair reading through a script. He glances at us over half-moon spectacles and waves expansively from behind the table.

'Lads, lads, come in, get comfy.'

The table is hexagonal, each side with its own microphone on an adjustable arm. Another man is already seated, and I recognise him – David Flynn, the contrarian newspaper columnist. His curly hair is compressed by the strap of his earphones, and he smiles at us with glistening lips.

'Which one of you is Lyster?' he says.

'That's me.'

'We had a nice exchange on Twitter a few weeks ago. Do you remember?'

'Yeah, vaguely.'

'Fantastic traffic. Great numbers. We should have another back-and-forth after this.'

The producer sits us down. She shows us how the headphones work. I ask if they're necessary, and she says I won't be able to hear the call-ins without them. She gets us to speak into the mic. I almost say, 'What now?' again, but then I just start to count. From beyond the window the engineer gives a thumbs-up. Paschal's voice breaks when he begins to count, but he coughs and continues. Flynn's eyes flick towards him.

The producer says, 'Twenty seconds,' as she pulls closed the heavy studio door and takes her seat at the sound desk.

Flynn clears his throat a few times and swallows. O'Reilly lays out his script sheets on the table in front of him and then he winks at us. 'Piece of piss, lads. Okay, let's do it.'

There's a moment of stillness. Above the table a light turns red, the radio jingle suddenly plays in our ears and Paschal jumps. O'Reilly puts on his voice. 'You're very welcome back to *The Morning Edition* with me, Gary O'Reilly, here on Newstalk FM. Before we move on to the events of last week, a quick look at the headlines. The Central Bank is being urged to regulate the trade of so-called cryptocurrencies after a huge spike in prices. In Bangladesh, a train derailment has led to the deaths of some forty passengers. And gardaí have said that the body of a young man has been discovered in wasteland near Glasnevin Cemetery. As yet, the body has not been identified, but the death is being treated as suspicious. Now, joining me in studio …' and he begins to reel off our names.

I look at the faces of the producer and the engineer, but the headline means nothing to them. I don't know why I thought he wouldn't be found. I don't know why I didn't think of moving him in the meantime. But then again, how could I? It took two people to drag him out there. I've no car, not even a licence to hire a van. I try to think of how we left him. Bedclothes and bin liners. Emma took the knife with her. And the bloody towels. I should clean the floor again. That duvet cover had matching pillow cases. They'll have to go. We'd been wearing marigolds during the clean-up. Had I touched him at all without them? Only to shake his hand maybe.

Beside me, Paschal is exhaling slowly through pursed lips like he's practising Lamaze. O'Reilly says my name, but it's just in introduction. He calls me an archivist activist 'and possible anarchist', before moving on to Paschal. Flynn rubs the top of his lip and blots his fingertip on a piece of paper. O'Reilly wraps up the intros.

'Gentlemen, you're all very welcome.'

'Pleasure, Gary,' says Flynn.

The host glances to me and Paschal, but I don't feel like greeting him again. After a moment, Paschal manages, 'I'm fine, thanks,' which wasn't really in answer to anything, so O'Reilly moves on.

'By now,' he says, 'we're all aware of the events from last week, that shocking image of a policeman pinioning a young girl at a vigil protesting garda incompetence in the search for Emma Harte. The response of the gardaí, as well as the melee that broke out, calls into question the limits of protest, and raises the spectre of institutional misogyny within garda ranks.'

I can feel my phone vibrate. It's on silent, but there's a faint static chirp in the headphones. The producer hears it as well and she glares at us through the window. She'd been pretty adamant about airplane mode. I play dumb.

Flynn says, 'Before we begin, Gary, can I just put on record that these two young men should be in jail right now? It's high time we started backing the blue in this country, because maybe, just maybe, our men and ladies in uniform would have a better chance of finding missing people if they didn't have to babysit a bunch of woke students at the gates of the Dáil.'

While there weren't any bodies it didn't seem so bad. Wickham wasn't dead, he was just missing. The police could root and grub as much as they wanted. Eventually they would have given up. But not anymore. I can feel my own breath become short. The studio suddenly seems too warm, too enclosed. But with a long inhale, the feeling recedes.

O'Reilly says, 'Paschal O'Toole, you were the organiser of the demonstration, and while I'm sure you had the best of intentions, surely it was your responsibility to ensure that protesters remained completely peaceful.'

Paschal has been nodding through the question, and he continues to nod in the silence that follows. His dry lips part and then close again. The moment becomes heavy with anticipation, a slight edge of panic. O'Reilly's eyes widen. This additional layer of stress is too much, so I lean towards my mic and say, 'It wasn't a demonstration, it was a vigil. A completely legitimate one given that the life of a young woman is at stake, which seems to have been forgotten in all this made-up controversy. And it was peaceful, until the police tried to break it up.'

O'Reilly pulls a newspaper from under his script. 'You say peaceful, but here I am looking at an image of you, Mr Lyster – that is you, isn't it? – with a garda officer in a headlock, his cap rolling in a puddle, a blur of people running amok in the background. Just what gave you the right to take the law into your own hands?'

'Sometimes doing what's right and what's legal isn't the same.'

Flynn says, 'Have you ever heard anything more entitled? Let the police go on strike then if you think you know the law better than them. Let's dissolve the thin blue line and see how you and your pink-haired friends hack it against real criminals.'

The earphones are chirping again, this time quite clearly. I hold my hand up to the producer and take out my phone to switch it off. Two missed calls from the 089 number.

The phone blinks off and I leave it aside. I find speaking to be soothing. Maybe it's a kind of disassociation. 'Mr Flynn takes for granted his own entitlement to walk the streets unafraid. Women can't do that, and instead of trying to fix the problem, what does he tell them? Don't go out alone, don't get an Uber, don't go jogging, don't drink this or wear that. If he lived under such restrictions, he'd be calling for revolution in a week.'

'Excuse me, I have three daughters by two different wives. I hardly think of anything except their welfare and safety.'

Paschal finds his voice to say, 'Forty-one per cent of Irish women know someone in their circle who has experienced violence.'

But that turns out to be a bit of a conversation-stopper, so O'Reilly says, 'Let's go to the phones.'

A queue has formed of young people wishing to tell Flynn how he's a sexist, bigoted blowhard from the dark ages, and his grin increases with each call. Carol from Carlow asks me out on a date. I tell her I'm otherwise engaged. Paschal hopefully says, 'I'm single,' but we're already on to the next caller.

Mary from Derry suggests that Flynn could still be redeemed if he would just educate himself, rid himself of these problematic views, and he responds with, 'What is it with your lot and re-education camps? Absolutely chilling.'

The clock is ticking towards ten. O'Reilly says there's time for one more call. 'Sarah, go ahead.'

A voice comes into my ear. 'Am I on?'

'You are indeed, Sarah. What is it you'd like to say?'

'Oh, I'd like to say so much. It's been so interesting listening to these three men speak about women's lives and safety. Especially that guy who tackled the garda. It's James, isn't it? Hello, James.'

Her voice sounds slightly different because of the static on the line, the change in inflection we all have on the telephone. But still, I can tell it's Emma Harte.

I say, 'Hello, Sarah.'

She lets a moment of dead air linger, to the point that O'Reilly touches a headphone. Then she says, 'I just thought it's interesting in all this talk that there's no mention of the man found murdered up in Glasnevin. How is it that the lives of young men can be discarded like that? No vigils, no protests. Just forgotten, like they were worth nothing to begin with.'

Flynn nods expansively and says, 'Absolutely right. And it goes beyond that. What about the bias in family courts, in the health service, in education outcomes?'

O'Reilly leafs back a page in his script and says, 'Sarah, to be fair, there's no indication that this man was murdered. Gardaí have just called it suspicious.'

'Oh, he was murdered all right.'

Paschal clears his throat. 'While it's true that the murder rate in Ireland is higher among men than women, it has to be remembered that men are almost exclusively responsible for those murders. The problem remains one of toxic masculinity.'

A pause on the line, and then: 'Who was that just speaking?'

'That was Paschal,' O'Reilly says, 'activist with DUGES and organiser of the Emma Harte vigil.'

'Paschal, I'm sure she would thank you if she was able. We're so lucky to have guys like you to advocate for us. Guys who understand completely the oppression, even the micro-aggressions, women face, and who can articulate them so well.'

Paschal is touched, oblivious to the sarcasm, or perhaps choosing to ignore it.

'And James, the man of action. Willing to fight a battle that's not his own. To put himself in harm's way despite the consequences. If only feminism had more allies like the two of you, then perhaps the streets would finally be safe for everyone.'

The producer is pointing at her watch. O'Reilly nods and says, 'Sarah, I want to thank you for phoning in. Great to have your perspective in a conversation such as this.'

In a quiet voice, Emma says, 'I'll be in touch again.'

Slightly confused, O'Reilly replies, 'Of course, any time. You have our number.'

'So don't worry.'

He frowns and presses a button to cut her off with a slight shake of his head. 'Now, as it's just about ten o'clock, it's time for news and weather.'

Newstalk stumps up a cab to shuttle me and Paschal home. We say little until we settle into the rear seat and the driver sets off. Paschal runs his fingers through his hair and lets out a long breath. 'Couldn't have gone much better, I think.'

I look across at him. His smile seems to be in earnest.

'Yeah, not too bad.'

'Did you see how I flummoxed Flynn with that forty-one per cent stat? That's what I said about coming prepared.' He takes out his phone to check messages and social media. 'Reviews are in. You're getting some mentions as well, to be fair.'

In the front the driver is singing along to Nat King Cole. Paschal pauses his swiping. 'What about your one at the end? Jesus Christ. Imagine bringing up violence against men in a discussion about Emma Harte.' He shakes his head. 'Some women have a hard time staying on message.'

The driver lowers the volume. 'Come here, are you the lads I was listening to on the radio?'

'The very same,' Paschal says. 'How did we do?'

Rheumy eyes seek us out in the rear-view mirror. 'Well, I think that Flynn fella makes a lot of sense, to be fair. You should be out here when the clubs close. The state of some of the young ones that climb in where you're sitting now. They're lucky I take my marriage vows seriously.'

Lucky them.

He says, 'So what do you think happened to the girl? Mate of mine reckons she was having an affair with that new TD from Galway and was bumped off when it was about to be exposed.'

I say, 'Isn't that TD gay?'

261

'He only says that to get votes. Anyway, it's sticking out a mile it was the boyfriend.'

Paschal pockets his phone and says, 'No, not Wickerman. He's many things but not a killer.'

I crack open a window to let in some air. 'You said you knew him?'

'Used to get some gear from him when I was going through ... my phase. Harmless enough guy.'

'Did you ever meet Emma?'

'Maybe. Wicker had a type. He actually phoned me out of the blue a few weeks ago, after he went AWOL. I answered and there was only silence. May have been a pocket dial.'

I remember Libby's place, me calling the 089 number with Paschal's phone. It rang out, but he or she must have phoned back later just to see who would answer. I think of the two missed calls received in the studio, and I fish out my phone to turn it on.

Cold sunlight is filtering through the trees outside the archbishop's palace. Paschal says, 'James, I meant to tell you, I'm sorry if I've been making things awkward between you and Libby. She's probably spoken about me.'

'Not really.'

'I admit I was a bit jealous when you showed up. But it turns out you're sound. Upshot is, big man, you have my blessing.'

He holds his fist towards me. I gingerly bump his knuckles.

He says, 'You're not going to work?'

'I've a few days' leave to use up before year's end. What about you?'

'If Newstalk are paying I might as well visit the folks in Sutton.'

We're approaching Fagan's. Paschal says he'll be in touch about more DUGES events. 'Have to maintain momentum.' I get out and close the door and the cab sets off through Drumcondra. I call in to Tesco to pick up some essentials and then head home. Once inside I shrug off my coat and throw my keys on the shelf.

A noise makes me pause. Voices at the end of the hall – bright, chatty radio voices. I approach my bedroom and peek inside. The bed is made, the duvet smooth. The clock radio is tuned to Newstalk. I'm sure I left it off earlier, and anyway, it's not a station I like. I click the button and listen to the silence. I call out, 'Libby,' but no one answers.

The bathroom is dark. The extractor fan is whirring. I check the internal stairwell. Doors locked as usual. The living room feels warm, and I put my hand over a radiator. Someone has turned it on low. An odd smell lingers in the air, sweet and slightly smoky, and there's a faint noise, like heavy rain falling in a puddle.

In the kitchen, Arthur is cooking sausages in a pan. He's wearing his office clothes, rumpled shirt and dark slacks. He licks the tips of his thumb and forefinger and turns one sausage over by hand. Two slices of toast pop from the toaster. He looks up and notices me.

'I was famished,' he says.

'What's going on?'

He shakes the pan and then points at the shopping bag. 'I hope you got butter.'

'How did you get in?'

From his pocket he takes a key and holds it so it catches a gleam. 'You gave me the spare, remember? After the last time you got locked out.'

I walk towards him and place the shopping bag on the counter, reach in and take out a tub of Dairygold.

He smiles. 'You're a gentleman.' Then he lowers the edge of the bag to reveal the top of a wine bottle. 'And a scholar. You going to open that?'

'Do you often let yourself in for lunch?'

'Not with the state of your larder. When did you start eating lentils?'

'Libby likes them.'

'Ah, Libby. She certainly converted you to the cause. Heard you on the radio. Almost believed you myself.' He finds a knife in the drawer and tests its edge, quickly butters his toast and scrapes the excess on the tub. 'Want some?'

I shake my head. He takes the bottle of wine and his plate to the table and sits in my seat. The bottle is a screw cap. He opens it and sniffs at the neck.

'What the fuck do you want, Arthur?'

'A glass would be nice.'

I fetch two rinsed mugs from the sink, plonk one on the table and sit across from him. He looks at the 'World's Greatest Uncle' mug and fills it almost to the brim. I'm left to pour for myself.

'I'm disappointed, James.' A slurp of wine. He slices a piece of toast in three and places a sausage on one of the strips. 'If I murdered someone, you'd be the first person I'd tell.'

I look at him lift the sausage and toast strip and begin to chew thoughtfully. I pick up my own wine and take a drink. 'You must have started early today.'

'I mean, it's not like I wouldn't have some knowledge to bring to bear.'

Behind him, propped behind the bin and the brushes, is the basin I used to clean the living room. The fork he's using is like the one I used to scrape blood from gaps in the floorboards. Perhaps it is the one.

'Luckily I haven't murdered anyone.'

'There may be a question of degree all right, if it's voluntary manslaughter, whether joint enterprise plays a role ... exactly the kind of nuance I could have explained to you. I mean, instead of the shite we usually talk about.'

I watch his face closely, but he's inscrutable. With a knuckle he pushes his glasses up the bridge of his nose.

'I'm tired, Arthur. I've had a stressful morning. Will you tell me what you're really on about?'

'Got a call last week from a detective,' he says. 'That night you were in town fighting the power. You were adamant that she call me, which I appreciate, by the way. And it's a good job she did.'

'Shauna Shaw?'

'That's the one.'

'She told me she couldn't reach you,' I say. 'That I didn't need a solicitor because they were releasing me.'

'Well, that first part was a fib. And cops love to let on that people don't need representation. It makes their lives so much easier.'

'Why didn't you tell me any of this?'

'I was waiting for your formal letter of engagement, or at least a quiet word over a pint. If you didn't want to bring it up, wasn't my place to broach it.'

'So why broach it now?'

'Because you're making a balls of absolutely everything.'

He takes another long sip from his mug, manoeuvres the next sausage onto its strip of toast.

'Chances are you're going to be interviewed under caution. Shaw knew that if she brought you in cold you wouldn't say a thing.' He gestures at me with his fork. 'And quite right too. So, to lay the groundwork she disclosed to your legal counsel, i.e. me, a summary of the evidence.'

The untidiness of the cooker is bothering me. I stand up and walk over. 'An interview under caution isn't the same as an arrest.'

'No. Unless you decide to leave halfway through, then it can quickly turn into one.'

I run the pan under the hot tap and leave it in the sink. A squeeze of washing-up liquid on the induction hob foams from the residual heat. I rinse a cloth and begin to clean the grease spatter.

Arthur says, 'I'm glad to hear you say you haven't murdered anyone. That's certainly the line we're going to take.'

'It's the truth.'

'Even so, there are issues that have to be addressed.'

'Such as?'

'The DNA test.'

I wring suds from the cloth and dry my hand on my trousers. The butter has been left open. I close the lid and return the tub to the fridge.

'Colin's off the hook,' says Arthur. 'Cleared. Completely exonerated. Unfortunately, the sample returned is of a close male relative, which means it belongs either to you, your dear deceased father, or one of your nephews aged seven and nine.' He glances up at me. 'My money's on Senan.'

He spots a jar of Ballymaloe relish on the table and scoops out a dollop. 'The detective also spoke to some ACA security guy in Mountjoy Square where the coat was found. She showed him your picture. "That's the cunt," were his exact words. So, you had Emma's coat. You dumped Emma's coat.' He flashes me an admonishing look. 'Why on earth did you put it in there?'

'Seemed like a good idea at the time.'

'They figured out that it wasn't actually her coat as well. Her parents didn't recognise it, nor any of her friends. Threw them off the scent for a while. She was wearing it in that CCTV picture though. The one where you're walking beside her. I copped it was you the minute I saw it. Still don't know why others haven't. And do you think that's the only camera in Dublin? They'll find more, if they haven't already.'

I watch him dab relish along the length of a sausage and say, 'Shaw certainly gave you the lowdown.'

He shrugs. 'I tend to ask the right questions.'

I go back to my seat and take another sip of wine. Not as nice from a mug, for some reason. Arthur puts down his knife and fork and rests his hands on the edge of the table. He looks at me squarely and says, 'James, I'd be willing to represent you, but it's important that you tell me. Did you kill her?'

The lenses of his glasses make his eyes small and penetrating. There's something else about his expression. A tinge of apprehension, of nervousness. Something occurs to me. A conversation we had in Fagan's months or years back. 'Never confess to a lawyer,' he said. 'Only speak in hypotheticals. For if they know you're guilty they're forbidden to lie to a court on your behalf.' Chances are such ethical considerations don't apply in the real world. Especially for Arthur.

'No,' I say. 'I haven't killed anyone.'

He studies my face for another moment, then he picks up the knife and fork again.

'In that case,' he says, 'it might be time to cooperate. Tell them what you know. Let them swab this place from top to bottom if they have to.'

An image comes to mind of hazmat suits in my front room, black lights and cotton pads, brushes and magnetic powders, fibres from the hearthrug, scrapings from the floor, prints from the sofa. It has begun to feel inevitable. No matter what I try, I can't seem to prevent it. And though I've scoured the flat more than once, I just know they'll find something.

Arthur hasn't mentioned Wickham at all. Has he heard about the body found nearby? Would he make the connection if he did? When it comes to it, how long does it take the police to identify a corpse? Emma had removed his wallet, his ID. He couldn't have looked pretty after three weeks in a plastic bag. Not the kind of scenario where you pull back a sheet for his nearest and dearest to cover their mouths and tearfully say, *Yes, that's him.* I remember lifting the corrugated iron, the snowflakes collecting in the folds of the bin liners. I thought the smell would have been worse. It was like when grass is left to rot inside a mower. A slight edge of sweetness. The cold weather must have helped. He'd be identified all right, once the pathologists got at him – dental records, finger prints, that kind of thing. But perhaps that would take days, if not weeks.

Briefly, I think of telling Arthur all about it, but his old advice rings true. I can tell him later if he really needs to know.

I say, 'Out of interest, what if Emma Harte is still alive?'

'No use if there's no proof. They won't take your word for it. And you could still be done even if she's never found. You don't need a body for a murder charge.'

'It's not just that. I spoke to her less than an hour ago.'

He blinks twice in genuine surprise. After a moment, he nudges his plate aside, the last sausage half eaten. He sips his wine, removes his glasses to wipe a lens. When he looks at me again the corner of his mouth turns up. He nods thoughtfully, and says, 'Yes, that should help.'

CHAPTER 17

20 DECEMBER

The archival box of death photography sits on my lap as I take the bus into work. It's another cold, dark morning and all the seats are filled. As my stop approaches I carry the box underarm down the steps, out into Kildare Street, and into the rotunda of the library. In the storage area, I find the bay and the shelf where it belongs and slip it back into place. No one any the wiser. I take down the box beside it to bring to the office for cataloguing. It's heavier than usual. Loose objects slide about inside, so I hold it flat while I'm walking.

For once Bridget is early, and we offer each other a perfunctory good morning. She glances at me while I sit. Ever since the day I spied her with Shauna Shaw I've had the feeling that Bridget's looks and comments towards me have been pointed and knowing. While waiting for my laptop to boot up, I say, 'Bridget, about that email I sent a few weeks ago. I'm sorry if it was … you know, terse. I should have just brought it up instead of writing to you.'

She has half turned in her seat to look at me. She doesn't say anything.

'I mean, if there is some issue outside of work that you're concerned about, you know you can always just mention it to me.'

She waits to see if I've anything more to add, and then says, 'I don't have any issues.'

'Oh. Well, that's good.'

A tilt of her head. 'Is that all?'

'The other day, in the courtyard, I saw you having a smoke with someone.'

'Yeah?'

'She was a policewoman, wasn't she?'

'How do you know?'

'What were you talking about?'

A flicker passes her face. The briefest smile, perhaps. 'Nothing. Just the weather.'

'You don't know why she was here?'

'Something to do with that vigil, I think. I'm not sure.' I hold her eye for a moment, and she says, 'Why do you ask?'

'I was just wondering.'

Helena arrives. She lightly greets us both and thanks me for fixing the flyer. Bridget turns her attention back to her computer, and soon we've settled into the routine of archival description. I open the new box on my desk. A photograph is enclosed in brown card at the bottom, but a few other items rest on top. First is a small cache of letters tied in threadbare pink ribbon. I undo the string and open one, written by a young lady from Mount Merrion to her beau, or her betrothed, or her lover, in Bristol. She only signed off with an initial, L. Her writing is neat, her messages sweet and sentimental, but with each additional letter her hand becomes a little more untidy, until the last is little more than a spidery scrawl. The tenor of her writing remains the same. She loves this man. She longs to see him again, is consumed by thoughts of him. There is nothing in the letters to suggest that he ever wrote back.

In the box there's a small round metal tin that at first feels empty. I unscrew the lid. Inside, a lock of flaxen hair is looped and tied up in itself like the symbol for infinity. I let it slip silently onto my desk and touch the strands with the tip of my finger. Dry and fragile, like a doll's hair. I pick it up to hold close to my nose. Not a hint of perfume.

Next is a heavier object wrapped in brown paper. I unwrap it carefully and come face to face with L, a death mask of pure white alabaster. She looks entirely peaceful. High cheekbones, a narrow mouth, the smallest arch to her nose. The line of a cap goes across her forehead. Peeking underneath is the impression of combed hair. I hold the tress next to the mask and wonder if it was snipped when the cast was made.

Finally, I look at her photograph. She's sitting on a swing beneath the bough of a tree, both hands gripping the ropes. She's wearing a high-waisted gown and on her head a floral wreath. I'm not sure how they managed to keep her upright. Hidden braces, perhaps. Her eyes were closed when the picture was taken, but in the intervening years, someone has painted opened eyes directly onto the albumen, and L stares at me from her perch.

With my phone I take a snap of the picture, email it to myself, open it on my computer and import it to Photoshop. I touch it up and add effects, and then set some white text against the shadow of the tree. '*Memento Mori:* The Unsettling Art of Death Photography, a National Library of Ireland Exhibition'.

I save it to the shared drive, and then pick up my brush to set to work on the letters.

That evening I take the short walk from the library to Trinity. A freezing fog lingers over the campanile. There's a dark gleam on the cobblestones. Lights glow in the windows of the Graduates Memorial Building, where students are gathered in the entrance before a debate.

I follow them up the steps into the foyer. A square oak staircase spirals overhead. Students mill about or stand in small groups. There's a long table with empty glasses and cheap wine and cubes of cheese on toothpicks. I spot Libby and Miranda in a corner and weave my way towards them. As one of the speakers, Miranda is dressed semi-formally in a deep-red skirt, figure-hugging black top and a silver triskelion pendant. She's the first to see me and smiles broadly at my approach.

'The Flynn-slayer returns,' she says. 'That's two rounds now in which you've handed him his arse.'

Libby sees me, stands on tiptoes to kiss my cheek. 'You were great. I had you on earphones in the library.'

I wish Miranda well for the evening and tell her she looks lovely. A slight colour enters her cheeks. She says, 'Ah, thanks. Best foot forward and all that.'

I remember the first few times we met – her general aloofness, the reservation of judgement, her forbearance for Libby's sake. I know she was just being protective, but it had irked me then, and it still irks a little now, as if I should be grateful to have won her over.

'You'll do great,' I say.

We get some wine and chat and watch as the crowd begins to drift into the debating chamber. A bell is rung, and Miranda says she'd better go take her place. The room is double-height, with panelled walls painted red and green, gilt-framed portraits, and throne-like wooden chairs on a small raised dais. A long table is set in front of a lectern, and the speakers for and against the motion are arrayed across from each other, all in evening wear as if they've just sat down to a dinner party.

But the grandeur is rather shabby. The seats for the audience are grey plastic, and there are unused stacks of them listing in a corner. The carpet is threadbare. Under the windows, hulking column radiators make me think of schoolrooms in the Christian Brothers. Behind us is a raised balcony with carved wooden balusters. A crowd has gathered up there as well, leaning their arms on the handrail to look below.

Libby and I find some seats near the front as the room fills up. She's quiet, and her eyes are half closed as if she's drifting off to sleep.

I bump her elbow and say, 'Was it an all-nighter?'

'And an all-dayer. Got the assignment in this afternoon, though. Sorry, it had been stressing me out the last few days.'

'It's fine. I'm glad you got it done.'

'What was the upshot for Colin and Danni?'

'Haven't heard anything. I doubt no news is good news.'

There are a few hushed apologies and the scraping of chair legs, and then Paschal flops into the seat beside me. With a thumb and forefinger he pushes his hair behind his ears and lets out a long exhale.

'Thought I wasn't going to make it. Tutorial ran over.' He leans forward to look past me but only gives Libby a brief hello.

'Was trying to reach you earlier, Jim. I've been thinking of a splash for the newsletter. "Tales from the frontlines", eye-witness narratives from inside the holding cell. We could make it into a series.'

'Yeah, Paschal, I've been thinking of stepping back from this kind of thing. Radio interviews and so on. It may be getting out of hand.'

'How do you mean?'

'I got arrested.'

'But not charged. World of difference.'

'Still, it could look bad from a career point of view.'

He blinks and says, 'Your career as a librarian?'

'Archivist.'

'We've a chance to affect real change here, Jim. Emma Harte has given us that opportunity.'

Wearily I wonder why I'm wasting time arguing, so I say to him, 'I'll think about it,' and he replies with, 'Nice one.'

From one of the throne-like chairs, a willowy guy in a tuxedo calls the room to order. He hurries through preliminaries with some poor jokes that elicit sympathetic laughs, and then introduces the motion: 'That this house embraces the prominence of allies in modern activism.' He calls on Miranda to open the case for the proposition.

Friends of hers whoop and cheer as she makes her way to the lectern with a glass of red in one hand and her notes in the other. She speaks well, has an easy grace and confidence, is funny and self-deprecating. She says that weeks ago, had she learned that she'd been assigned to the proposition of this motion, she would have been aghast. 'After all, what could be more absurd than celebrating the voices of the privileged, of cis white men in particular, in the very movements in which the marginalised are supposed to take centre stage?'

However, in that time she had come across an example of what allyship could truly mean, and what it could achieve. 'It happened in the wake of the tragic disappearance of Emma Harte.' She grips the side of the lectern and looks towards me. 'Be it on social media, or on legacy media, or even in the streets, this person has shown that sometimes the voice of an ally is the one that cuts through. And when that happens, we should not grumble that the spotlight is on the wrong kind of activist. We should embrace the fact that it shines our way at all.' She points and says, 'I am talking of course about James Lyster.'

Necks crane and heads turn. Those who recognise my name begin to clap. The rest join in. Miranda beckons me to stand. I shake my head. Beside me, a smiling Libby gently pushes at my arm. It is Paschal who rises and fairly drags me to my feet. He gestures at me in an exaggerated manner, remains standing as cheers echo in the room, and he resumes his seat a few seconds after I do.

As the noise dies down, Miranda takes a sip of wine and says, 'James didn't know I was going to use him as a prop. He's going to kill me.'

The crowd titters. I smile up at her.

She carries on, reels off her points effectively, the audience now fully relaxed and engaged. I count the number of speakers to estimate how long this is going to take. About halfway through the next speech, the first from the opposition, I feel my phone buzz and I slip it out to hold next to my hip. A text from the 089 number with a picture attached.

Tilting the screen so only I can see, I open it up. It's a high-angle shot of this very room, Miranda at the lectern, rows of seats in a semi-circle. All heads are turned to where Paschal and I are standing. He's pointing to me theatrically. Libby is looking up and smiling.

I glance over my shoulder at the balcony. It's narrow, with only five or six people visible at the front. All of them are focused on the speaker. I pocket my phone and whisper to Libby, 'Just have to find the gents.' Paschal frowns as he shifts his legs to let me out, but then takes the opportunity to sit beside Libby. Several eyes follow me as I skirt along the side of the chamber and out into the foyer. A handful of students are standing around chatting, some by the windows, others on the stairs. I climb past them to the first-floor return, but then it occurs to me that the picture was taken several minutes ago. Whoever sent it would have left the balcony before they did so. I look down the stairs again to the ground floor. One girl stands alone. She's wearing a deep-navy coat, black skirt and tights and ballet flats. Her hood is raised and her head is bowed. One foot is propped against the wall.

Abruptly, she turns and walks away, pulls open the large door, and slips outside. I hurry down the stairs to follow her, hindered for a moment by students on the steps. The night air is freezing cold. Lamps around Front Square cast pools of yellow light in the fog. I look about for her, see her walking past the Old Library towards the Arts Block. I don't want to run in case she hears my steps, so I lengthen my stride and begin to gain on her.

She's approaching the Arts Building tunnel when I get close enough to say, 'Wait.'

She doesn't pause or look back.

I say, 'Wait,' again, and reach forward to take her elbow. Her arm feels slight beneath the thick woollen sleeve.

She startles and turns and pulls her arm free. The movement makes her hood fall. She's wearing white earbuds. Her features are Asian, Japanese or Korean perhaps. She looks scared. Passers-by stop and frown and regard me suspiciously.

I say, 'Oh my God, I'm sorry, I thought you were a friend of mine.'

Cringing slightly, she takes a step and says, 'It's okay.'

I hold up my hands. 'Really, I didn't mean to frighten you.'

She forces a smile. 'It's okay,' and she continues through the pedestrian tunnel towards Nassau Street, glancing at me before she moves out of sight.

Two lads have stopped as if to make sure I don't follow her. I scan Fellows' Square, but everyone else seems lost in their own concerns. Nothing for it: I make my way back to the GMB, to the warmth of the chamber, and to the warm regard of its audience.

Miranda's side carries the motion, and we head across to Doyle's for some celebratory drinks. After the first few rounds, the graduate students can no longer stomach the price of the pints, so Libby suggests we buy some cans and take them back to my place. She asks if that's okay, and after a quick mental scan of the flat and how I left it, I say, 'Of course.' We pile into a taxi. I pay for it on the app. They all offer to reimburse me but I won't hear of it. Miranda oohs when she sees the tidiness of the living room. Paschal heads straight for the armchair and makes himself at home. I have an uncomfortable feeling that the space is being colonised. Something about Paschal's pose reminds me of how

Tom sat with the knife in his neck. I merge an image of the two of them in my mind.

I open the gin and a bottle of wine, put the cans in the fridge, and a frozen pizza in the oven. In the living room I turn on Netflix to play something in the background.

On the TV, Paschal scans the homepage and says, 'It's recommending a lot of cold-case documentaries starring dead women.'

'The algorithm knows me too well,' I say. 'There's *Alias Grace*. Lib and Miranda would like that.'

Libby says, 'Doesn't a girl get murdered in that as well?'

'Yeah, with an axe. But a woman did it, so it doesn't count.'

Miranda says, 'Spoilers.'

'Or maybe she was covering for her boyfriend, I forget. I read the book.' I nod to the shelf where Atwood resides. Like Mrs Harte, I'd once tried to organise the authors alphabetically but gave up after Banville. Miranda goes to peruse the shelves. She spots Austen, Tartt and Winterson and makes approving noises.

In the end I just play some Spotify and we settle down to talk. The conversation is relaxed and happy. Miranda and Paschal have a good-natured argument about which version of *The Handmaid's Tale* is better, the book or the show. The cooker pings and I go to take the pizza out. I use Emma Harte's fabric knife to slice it into quarters. Libby smiles as I hand out food and top up glasses. She's curled up and cosy on the sofa, a plate on her lap, and a beer on the armrest.

It's rare that I have this many people over. It almost feels pleasant. I remember Bridget saying that I relied on a girlfriend for a circle of friends. I look around the room at this particular set and suppose it could be worse.

Paschal has been idly scrolling on his phone. He pauses and says, 'Jesus.'

Libby asks, 'What?'

'The body they found in Glasnevin was Tom Wickham.' He's peering at the screen as he thumbs through an article.

The girls are silent for a moment. Miranda asks, 'What about Emma Harte?'

'She's not mentioned here. Well, her name is mentioned, but there was only one body.'

'Does it say how he died?'

'Stab wound. It says gardaí believe that the murder may have been gang-related.'

Which is the best news I've heard all evening. Libby is looking at me quietly, and I realise I haven't reacted at all. I lean forward and say, 'Are you okay, Paschal?'

He frowns, wondering where the question has come from. 'Why wouldn't I be?'

'You did know him, after all.'

'Barely. I mean, I'm sorry he got stabbed, but I won't be losing much sleep over it.'

But the connection has made him uneasy. He excuses himself to go get some water. Miranda and Libby have become quiet as well. The beers are running low so I offer to fetch some more.

In the kitchen, Paschal is by the sink. His phone is on the counter and he's continuing to scroll. I say to him, 'Do you need a glass?'

He jumps slightly, looks over his shoulder and says, 'Thanks.'

I take one from the cupboard and hand it to him. He checks that it's clean, holds it under the tap and drinks it all at once. Water dribbles between the bristles of his goatee.

I come closer and say, 'Listen, Paschal, I didn't want to mention it out there, but yesterday in the cab, you said Tom Wickham called you.'

He remembers, and I see the realisation play on his face.

'Was it before or after the night Emma Harte disappeared?'

'After. You and I met for the first time at that public search, remember? It was the following week.'

'Do you think it's something you should mention to the guards?'

'No, I really fucking don't. Wicker got himself involved with a bad crowd in Finglas. He thought he could outsmart them, and look how that turned out. I don't want anything to do with it.'

'Then if you haven't already, you should delete the call. Delete the whole contact.'

He nods and swipes through his phone to do just that. 'What was he calling me for anyway? I hadn't spoken to him in years.'

'Maybe he was desperate. Trying anyone he could.'

'Well he could have dragged me right into the shitter.' He takes a breath to calm himself and puts his phone away. He catches my eye again and says, 'Thanks for this, James. I appreciate it.'

'No bother.'

When we go back to the living room, Miranda says, 'What were you two whispering about?'

I say, 'Football,' and she says Paschal hasn't watched a game of football in his life, and he says, 'It's about time I started.'

He lifts his coat from the chair and says he might head. Miranda casts an inquiring look to Libby, who says, 'I'm going to hang on.'

A few minutes after they leave, Libby is dozing on the sofa. The result of cramming for an assignment and an evening of drinks. I kiss her forehead and tell her to head on in, that I'll be along in a while once I've tidied up. She nuzzles close to my face and says, 'I'll probably be asleep,' and I say, 'That's fine.'

I carry glasses and plates to the kitchen, fill the sink and leave them to soak. While I'm rearranging the cushions I see Miranda's triskelion pendant on an armrest. She will be looking for it so I set it aside. I'm putting empty cans in a black plastic bag when there's a tapping on the window.

Scooping up the necklace, I bring it into the hall. I'm half holding it out as I open the front door.

Emma Harte looks at the jewellery. Her eyes move up to meet mine. She smiles and says, 'For me, James? How kind.'

CHAPTER 18

Her hair is cut short and dyed blonde. Her brows are still dark, making her eyes appear larger. She's wearing fingerless gloves, a large scarf over a denim jacket, torn black jeans and Doc Martens. The light from the hall barely reaches her. She looks healthy. Her cheeks a little fuller than I remember. Life on the run must suit her. I should feel angry or frustrated, but something else stirs inside me, and I realise that I'm glad to see her. I take back the pendant and stuff it in my pocket.

She says, 'You wanted me to get in touch.'

'Clara?' I ask, and she nods and says, 'So here I am.'

I glance over my shoulder. At the end of the long corridor my bedroom door is ajar. The lights are off. I step outside and half close the front door. Emma doesn't make space, so I move to the side of her. She looks at me. Her breath coils around her face in tendrils.

'This isn't the best time,' I say.

'It's the only time.'

'My girlfriend is asleep in the bedroom.'

Her eyes widen. 'Sarah?'

I shake my head. 'Someone new.'

'Can I see her?'

'No.' I look up the stairwell. It's pitch black, but for the slight glow of streetlamps. 'We could walk for a bit.'

'James, you don't disappear by taking long public walks.'

'Did you drive here? We could sit in your car.'

'Or we could just forget it.'

'Wait.'

The façade of Whiteside's house looms above us. Dark and quiet and vacant.

'I can bring you upstairs. But you have to be quiet.'

She holds my eye and pretends to button her lip.

I tell her to hang on for a second. 'I'll be back to get you.'

With a light tread I walk down the hall to the bedroom, ease the door open a little so a sliver of light falls on the bed. Libby is curled up beneath the duvet, a mass of hair on the pillow, her face turned away. She's a quiet sleeper in general, but the way the bedclothes rise and fall shows that she's dead to the world.

I'm about to head back when the sound of the front door closing echoes in the room. Emma has come inside, one hand covering her mouth, the other raised in apology. I can't tell if it's genuine. I look again at the bed. Libby hasn't stirred, her breathing as steady as before.

When I go back to Emma, she's gazing in at the living room like someone visiting a childhood home. She takes in the drinks shelf, the armchair, the hearthrug. She points to the black plastic bag on the floor and raises an eyebrow.

I brush her elbow and beckon for her to follow. She glances at the spot on her arm that I touched.

Quietly, I open the door to the internal stairs, use my phone to light the way and begin to climb. Once Emma has followed a few steps, I whisper for her to shut the door again, and she does so. The two of us are now enclosed in a narrow stairwell, almost in darkness except for a sharp, narrow spotlight. I continue upwards and hear the soft clomp of her shoes behind me. I undo the slide-bolt at the top of the stairs, and lead Emma into Whiteside's hall.

The heating has been left off and it's like a fridge. In the sitting room, the Superser is standing beside Whiteside's chair. I shine the torch at the back of it, open the gas nozzle, press down the ignition with a loud clunk. Soon all three panels are burning, providing warmth and enough light to see by. I go to the windows to check that the drapes are closed tight.

Emma is looking around. She says, 'If I'd known you had this gaff to yourself I'd have stayed here.'

'Whiteside, my landlord, only left a few days ago.'

'Pity. What happened to him?'

'He just ... got old. Where have you been staying?'

'Here and there.'

'You've been moving around?'

'No.'

She picks up an empty vial from the little side table and gives it a silent shake.

'Actually,' she says, 'it's not so bad being on the lam these days, once you have a little hideaway, of course. A new phone, a couple of fake accounts and everything gets delivered to your door.'

'Are you not going stir-crazy? Are you not lonely?'

'Turns out what's been holding me back all my life is other people.'

'You're just going to hole up forever?'

She replaces the vial and says, 'Forever's a long time.'

She sits on the floor with her back to the sofa to be nearer the heat. 'Tell me your news,' she says. 'Who's the girl?'

'That's not important.'

'But I've been starved of gossip for weeks. Give me her name at least.'

'You don't need to—'

'It's Libby, right?'

I look at her sharply and she bites her lip.

'I may have been keeping an eye on your Twitter. I thought, either this girl is stalking you or going out with you. She's pretty.'

I sit in Whiteside's armchair. I can feel the slight indentation of his body.

Emma says, 'Where did you meet?'

'On a bus.'

'Ah, a romance for the ages. Does she burn incense?'

'No.'

'A step up from Sarah already.'

'There's something we need to talk about.'

'I've a feeling she's the one, James.'

'It has to do with Tom.'

Her nose wrinkles. She rests her head on a seat cushion.

I say, 'He's been found,' and she blinks slowly and says, 'I know.'

I smooth the linen armrest cover. 'It was better when he was a suspect and not a victim.'

'He was always going to be found.'

'That's not the problem, though. Well, not the main one.' I remind her of the Afghan coat and how she tossed it in bins beside the Tolka House. 'Did you ever go back to retrieve it?'

Frowning, she says, 'No. Why would I? It smelled of clove cigarettes.'

'Someone did. And they got hold of Tom's burner phone.'

'How do you know?'

'They've been calling me with it. Sending pictures. Even following me.'

'Who has?'

'They've never spoken.'

'So just block the number.'

'That's not the issue. The phone ties me to Tom. Without it I could say I never met him. If the guards get hold of it now, I'm the first number they find.'

She considers this for a moment, a flicker of light on her face, and she begins to nod. 'That's a pickle all right.'

It's warm enough now for her to take off her scarf. She folds it up and lays it on the sofa.

She says, 'It sounds personal, whoever's doing it. If they wanted to drop you in the shit they could have turned the phone over. Seems to me that they like having this power over you.'

'Maybe.'

She draws one leg up to hold her knee and begins to look around at Whiteside's ornaments and framed pictures. Everything is cast in a bare red light like a photographic darkroom. She says. 'I'm not sure how you think I can help.'

'You could let it be known that you're still alive. You'd only have to show your face on a security camera for a second.'

'But that would leave us back at square one. Tom is dead. We're alive, therefore we're both prime suspects.'

'At the moment, Tom is dead, you're missing, so I'm the only suspect.'

'I won't let you take the blame, James.'

'How do I know that?'

She holds up her little finger and says, 'Pinkie promise.'

I lean forward and say, 'Remember when Tom was able to track you down here? It was because of the phone. I asked if it had a tracking device, and he said no, it was just a security app.'

Her eyes become still. She says, 'Yeah, I'd seen him use that a couple of times. It's called *Find my device* or something like that. It shows on a map where your phone is at any moment.'

'Could we not do that now?'

'You'd need to log into his account.'

'Do you have his login details?'

'Not off the top of my head. I mean, do you know Libby's logins? Did you know Sarah's?'

'But could you get them?'

She rubs her face. 'Probably, yeah. They might be saved on my computer.'

'If you're able, send them to me.'

'What will you do when you find out who it is?'

'I'll think of something.'

Emma spots the Powers on the sideboard. She pulls herself up and goes over, comes back with the bottle and two tumblers, which she gets me to hold while she pours the measures. I'm about to suggest filling Whiteside's jug with water, but Emma is content to drink hers neat, so I do the same. She takes her tumbler and goes to sit on the sofa.

Holding the glass on the armrest, she says, 'It's nice to be able to chat with someone.'

'Do you talk to Clara?'

'Snatches here and there. We have a system so we don't get caught.'

'What about your mother?'

'She doesn't know.'

I think of Mrs Harte forlorn among her books and records. 'It must be hard for her.'

'James, you keep going on as if this will last forever. It's only been a month.'

'So you're going to come home one day and waltz in like nothing happened?'

'Not exactly. But not far off.'

A siren sounds somewhere in the distance. It swells for a moment and then recedes. Emma doesn't react to the sound. I say to her, 'What are you doing for money?'

From inside her coat she retrieves a small object and shows it to me. It's difficult to see at first, but then I recognise the flash drive with *Ledger* written on the side, the one she'd hidden in the toilet.

I say, 'What's on it?'

'It's a wallet. For cryptocurrency. That's how we were paid by Tom's … associates. Completely untraceable. And you can buy almost anything with Bitcoin these days.'

'Hasn't the price of crypto just spiked?'

'Yes. Yes, it has.'

'How much is on it?'

'More than I need.'

'So you stole it from Tom.'

'No. I stopped him stealing it from me.'

She puts the device back in her coat and buttons the pocket. I take a sip of whiskey and say, 'Well, I'm glad it was all worthwhile.'

'Oh, James, don't pout.' She seems amused for a second, then looks away and allows her eyes to rest on the glowing mesh of the heater. 'You know, you can always come with me if you like.'

The offer hangs in the air between us. There's a low purr from the pilot light, a sudden creak in the rafters. I imagine slipping from Whiteside's front door with Emma, down the steps, and into her car. I imagine Libby awakening to an empty flat. Her meander from room to room, switching on lights and calling my name. I picture the dishes in the sink, the clothes in the dryer, the plastic bag of empty cans on the living-room floor. Everything untouched and abandoned like a ghost ship.

What exactly is keeping me? A dysfunctional family, a monotonous job, a barfly best friend. Why not just toss it all aside and start again? There's Libby, I suppose. I think of her asleep downstairs. I should go back, but just now I don't want to.

Against the dim light of the heater, my whiskey has a lovely amber glow. 'We'd end up killing each other,' I say.

She remains still for a while and then turns to me. Her eyes wander over my face. She says, 'Maybe we could take turns killing each other.'

'Who goes first?'

'Depends on how much of a gentleman you are.'

She smiles and eases her head back on the sofa. The silence feels comfortable, unselfconscious. Her eyes are resting as if she's drifting to sleep.

Quietly, she says, 'Sometimes I miss Tom.'

I don't say anything. Her eyes open, but only to look at the ceiling.

She says, 'I know he was infuriating, and hot-headed. He was going to get us both in serious trouble one day. Still, I'm sorry it ended the way it did. It's not something that's ever mentioned. How you can grieve for a person you've murdered. Sometimes I pretend that we just broke up, so I can feel sad about it without feeling guilty.' She glances at me. 'Does that make sense?'

'Maybe you're grieving for the life you've had to leave behind.'

She thinks about this, then sips the last of her drink and stands up. 'I'd best go.'

Instead of retreating back down the internal stairs, we go to Whiteside's front door. The Chubb is locked, but a set of keys hangs from a hook on the wall. I unlock the door and open it quietly. Before she steps out, Emma stands in front of me.

'I meant it, James. If it comes to it, I won't let you take the blame.' She stands a little on her tiptoes and lifts her chin. Her face comes close, but then she pauses. Her eyes meet mine, and she says, 'Go back to Libby.'

She walks out and down the steps. Her shoes crunch along the gravel drive. She wraps her scarf around her neck as she walks. Above her, the night sky is clear and cold, with a bright smattering of stars unusual in the city lights. She reaches the entrance of the driveway and glances back at me, turns right and walks out of sight. I look at the silent, still scene for a moment, and then close and lock the door.

In the sitting room I return the whiskey and tumblers to the sideboard. I turn off the heater and feel my way back to the internal stairs. When I let myself into my own hallway, I close the connecting door as quietly as I can.

It feels as though I stepped momentarily into a different reality. Now I'm back in my own, and the weight of it bears down on me. I have a fleeting sense that a chance to escape has come and gone, and that there may not be another. In the living room I collect the bag of empty cans by the sofa and take it into the kitchen.

Libby is sitting at the table, wearing a hoodie and leggings and thick socks. Her hair is dishevelled. An empty Solpadeine wrapper lies next to a glass of fizzing water. She squints at me and says, 'Where were you?'

Her tone is not accusing or particularly suspicious, just tired.

I feel a weight in my pocket. From it, I pull the triskelion pendant. It hangs from its cord and rotates slowly, like I'm trying to hypnotise her.

'Miranda left this here. Went to see if I could catch up with them, but there was no sign. Maybe they got a cab.'

Libby looks from me to the pendant. She begins to shake her head, as if disappointed.

'I've given up reminding her not to leave stuff everywhere. I'll bring it home with me tomorrow.'

She lifts her glass to take her medicine. I stand behind the chair, lean down, and kiss the side of her face.

'You're wrecked,' I say. 'Will we go to bed?'

She nods and kisses me back. I take her by the hand and lead her through the flat, switching off lights as I go.

CHAPTER 19

22 DECEMBER

At the gates of the Botanic Gardens a giant Norwegian Spruce is decked in coloured lights and baubles. Libby says it's like putting a stuffed elephant in fancy dress outside of Dublin Zoo. We take a walk through the Christmas market, dozens of stalls erected alongside the glasshouses, the orchid and the succulent houses. Libby buys a few knick-knacks to decorate my place. We get some mulled wine in biodegradable cups, and stroll among the yew and the maples, through the mill field and the vegetable garden. Libby links my arm as we follow the path on which Emma pushed Tom in his wheelbarrow, his legs lolling over the lip. We skirt the high wall to Glasnevin Cemetery, watch our step on the sharp decline to the Tolka. Libby naturally wants to follow the path as it turns right. But I pause to peer through the branches and undergrowth to where the perimeter wall meets the river.

One of the poplar trees in the gardens has tufts of mistletoe growing on its bark, which is rare for Ireland. I had planned to show Libby, but as we draw near, there is a cluster of couples with selfie sticks, so we continue on. We warm up in the palm house, take a turn around the rose garden, and then decide to have a drink in the Gravediggers pub. While Libby's at the bar I check Sarah's Instagram. The latest is the picture of the baby macaque pulling sunglasses from her head. The geotag says *Ubud, Bali*. The caption: **Making new friends! Bucket list ... tick.** A few 'likes' from her usual followers, but there's a response from someone new. The handle is just a string of letters, but the profile pic is Emma Watson as Hermione Granger. It must be a throwaway account belonging to Emma Harte, for her reply says, **This looks familiar!** and then: *DoubtingThomas13 – tweh@!123.* Wickham's login details.

Libby is returning with two pints, so I close everything. Before I put my phone away, a message from Col: **Lolo AWOL. Report sightings.**

Libby asks if all is okay. I tell her what Colin wrote. 'But there's no need to worry. It's not the first time she's done a bunk.'

'Sounds like it'll be a tense Christmas.'

'Yeah. Danni is still away. Col wants me and Mam to come over next week, but she's going to Aunt Peggy's.'

'What are you going to do?'

'Dunno yet.'

Libby holds her glass up to be clinked and then takes a drink. 'If you need a place to escape to, Claremorris is still available.'

'How many siblings do you have again?'

'Five, but they won't all be there.'

'Still, I'd be well outnumbered.'

'Maybe, but you have a way of winning people to your side.'

She says it with a smile, but only a half one.

I've yet to buy a gift for Lolo, so we head to Breen's Bookshop in Phibsborough. Libby enjoys making recommendations, and soon I have a small stack of volumes under my arm: *Hotel du Lac, The Bell Jar, My Cousin Rachel*. I wonder aloud if I should pick up a few for Ultan, and Libby says, 'Didn't you get him that tablet?'

I look to the side and say, 'Oh, yeah.'

We walk back to my place. Clouds are gathering and the wind picks up. A cold rain is falling as we reach the gate, and we hurry over the gravel to the basement steps.

Shauna Shaw is sitting in the stairwell, her collar raised, a vape pen in one hand. She has heard our approach and is looking up at us over her shoulder. Libby stops when she sees her, and offers an uncertain, 'Hello.'

Shaw blows some smoke. She gets up and smiles and cocks her head a little to better see me. 'I was hoping to speak with you, Mr Lyster.'

Libby glances at me. I begin to descend the steps, reaching for my keys. 'Of course, but don't you have my number?'

'I was passing by, so I thought, why not stop in? I hope it's not a bad time.'

'Not at all.'

Libby is behind me now and I can't see her face. She has met Shaw before, right here in fact, but neither has acknowledged the other by name.

I ask, 'Were you waiting long?'

'A few minutes. It was nice until it started raining.' She smiles and says, 'I was determined to get you.'

I open the door and she follows me in, wiping her feet several times on the mat. I take her into the living room, letting my eye rove over everything while I'm still in front of her. Libby comes in as well. She places her bag on the sofa, and says, 'Should I leave you to it?'

I presume the question is directed at me, but Shaw says, 'There's no need. I mean, if James doesn't mind.'

I put Lolo's books on a side table. I turn to them both, and say, 'Will I make tea?'

Shaw asks, 'Any coffee?'

'Only instant.'

'Sure, that's all I drink.'

As I fill the kettle I can hear their voices in the other room. Should I text Arthur? It feels a bit late for that. I set out mugs, sugar bowl and a jug of milk on a tray. I open the drawer to get some spoons and see the re:Thread knife in the cutlery holder. I take it out, look around as to where I might put it, but in the end I hide it beneath the breadknife and the carver.

The kettle clicks. I spoon coffee granules into the mugs, fill them with water and take the tray inside.

Libby is setting baubles on the mantelpiece, including a small wooden reindeer with twigs for antlers, and a Jack Skellington figurine. Shauna Shaw has stepped back to look at the effect, and she says, 'Perfect.'

The detective takes a mug, catching my eye as she does so, and wanders over to look at my books. She goes to the window and seems to check what can be seen from the outside. In the winter sunshine there's a smudge on the glass, a whorl of lines from a thumbprint. She studies it for a moment. When she turns around she does so slowly, as if looking at the whole room in panorama.

I ask her, 'Would you like milk or sugar?'

She answers by taking a sip. 'No, this is gorgeous, thanks.'

She takes a seat on the sofa. Libby fixes her own mug and sits in the armchair. I stay standing by the fireplace.

Shaw seems content with the silence for a while. She blows steam from her coffee and takes another sip, then nods to herself as if she's just decided something. She looks at us both in turn. 'What I'm about to say is quite delicate. It may even be upsetting. But I hope you realise I'm just doing my job.'

Libby's eyes become round with concern. She glances at me and then back to Shaw, who says, 'It relates to the disappearance of Emma Harte.'

She pauses to look at me, as if she thinks I might react to the name.

My voice is steady when I say, 'What about it?'

Shaw puts her mug on the coffee table. She leans forward with her elbows on her knees. 'For reasons that I won't go into, your brother Colin became a person of interest in the investigation. He voluntarily submitted to an interview and to a DNA test, giving us certain information that has proved very useful.'

Libby has become still, her shoulders hunched, both hands holding the mug in her lap.

Shaw says, 'The DNA test has ... not been conclusive,' and here her eyes flick to mine. 'We would like to rule your brother out as a suspect, Mr Lyster. And for that we require your assistance.'

I lean my arm against the mantelpiece, brush against an unexpected bauble, and stand straight again. 'What was he suspected of?'

She says, 'Excuse me?'

'What crime did you think he committed?'

'Specifically?'

'Yes.'

'Well, kidnapping, false imprisonment, murder and concealment of a corpse.'

Libby gasps a little, and Shaw says, 'Admittedly, that represents the very worst-case scenario. But in the force we find it's best to cover the bases.'

Despite the sarcasm of her tone, her face is stony, her eyes sharp and focused.

I say, 'How is it that I can help?'

She brushes some rainwater from her coat. Small droplets land on the floorboards where Tom bled out.

'Naturally,' she says, 'your brother is adamant that he didn't do anything so heinous. And he claims to have an alibi. You, Mr Lyster.'

The night in Fagan's comes back to me, when he came in all flustered. *I told them I was with you,* he'd said, because really he had been with Delphine. It was Arthur who convinced him to take the DNA test. I was dead against.

Is she trying to catch me in a lie? She knows the DNA points to me instead of Colin. If she spoke to Bridget, she knows I was in the Biscuit Factory with the after-work crowd. She has a picture of me walking with Emma Harte on Dorset Street.

I ask, 'What day was that again?'

'The twenty-fifth of November.'

'No, I mean day of the week.'

She arches her brow a little. 'Friday night into Saturday morning.'

Unless, that is, she lied to Arthur. If the DNA test showed nothing, if the figures in the image remain unidentified, then what does she have?

I say, 'It's difficult to remember specific days.'

'Do you and your brother often spend the evening together?'

In my mind I see Bridget and Shaw together in the courtyard, their body language, the light way in which they chatted. Bridget told me they had spoken of nothing important, and suddenly it's clear to me that she was telling the truth. Bridget isn't sly. She isn't vindictive. If a detective had asked questions about me, she would let me know.

'Just wanted to make sure I was getting the days right. Yes, there was a Friday night last month in which Colin came over. Danni and the kids were visiting their grandmother in Sligo. He was at a loose end.'

Both Libby and the detective are looking at me now. Shaw says, 'He stayed the whole evening?'

'I think it was a late one all right. We watched the Friday-night game. We ordered pizza. His marriage is going through a rough patch, and we talked it through.'

Her face is difficult to read. She picks up her coffee again, but seemingly only to warm her hands. She says, 'If it came to it, would you be willing to swear that in an affidavit?'

'Yes.' I take a first sip of my own coffee and go to sit beside her. 'Is there anything else I can help with?'

Shaw gives Libby a long, penetrating look, then stands and says,

'No, that about covers it. As I said, I'm sorry for raising something so delicate. But I had a feeling you could help.' She hands me the mug. 'Your brother has a robust alibi,' she says. 'And now, so do you.'

She wishes us a merry Christmas. I show her to the door. She doesn't look at me as she leaves. I listen to her climb the steps, and to her footsteps walking through the gravel.

Libby is standing in the middle of the living room. She seems smaller than before. She seems uneasy. I go and hug her, and her head rests beneath my chin.

The mantelpiece is in my line of sight. I tell her that I like the ornaments.

She laughs slightly, and says, 'Yeah.'

'I'm glad that's all over.'

She's quiet for a moment, and then says into my chest, 'Was that true? About Colin?'

I draw back a little.

'You mean, whether he was with me that night?'

She nods.

'No. I was out with Helena and Bridget and Douglas. A few others from work. He was with that new woman of his. He didn't want to tell the cops, though, so he asked me ...'

'To cover for him again.'

'I know, but—'

'I understand,' she says. 'What else could you say?' She leans her head against me once more. 'I'm just glad you told me.'

Later, while Libby is in the kitchen on the phone with her mother, I take down the MediaPad tablet from on top of the bookcase. In a browser I search *Find my device* and I'm taken to a webpage linked to my Google account. On the right is a window showing a map of the surrounding streets in Glasnevin, a green phone icon pinned to Whiteside's house in Botanic Road. On the left are details of my own phone, its model, my number, the percentage of battery remaining, and a heading that says, *Last seen: just now*. My phone is beside me on the sofa. I pick it up and check the details. All correct.

There are more options on the computer, such as *Play sound*. I tap on that, and my phone begins to emit a loud chiming noise. I stop it quickly. Next is an option to *Secure device: Lock your phone and sign out of your account. You can also display a message on the lock screen.*

That sounds tempting. When I find the 089 number I could shut it down completely with a parting *Fuck you*. Although, that might tip my hand.

At the moment, my phone details are displayed because I'm signed in to my account. I tap on the J at the top right of the screen. Google pops up with a cheery, *Hi, James!* I sign out. Immediately, I'm invited to sign in again, or *Use a different account.*

I type in 'DoubtingThomas13' and the password 'tweh@!123'. The screen shifts. A progress bar appears. I half expect to be met with an *Invalid username or password* box, but instead the account loads. A large capital T appears, with the new greeting, *Hi, Thomas!*

Now when I return to *Find my device*, Tom's details are displayed. The phone listed on the top left is the 089 number. There's no battery notification. The *Last seen* heading gives a date and time from two nights ago. On the right, the map shows Trinity College, the phone icon pinned precisely to the Graduates Memorial Building.

The *Play sound* and *Secure device* options are missing as well. I tap the help icon, which says that the phone can only be tracked if it's turned on and connected to the internet. Otherwise it will display the last known location. Whoever sent the photo during the debate must have switched the phone off. I'll have to wait for them to turn it on again. Still, I'm pleased with the proof of concept. In the kitchen, I can hear the conversation wrapping up. I turn the tablet off and conceal it above the bookcase once more.

Friday is Libby's last day in Dublin before she travels home to Mayo, so we stay in to prepare our own mini-Christmas meal. The kitchen is warm and softly lit. I play Sufjan Stevens Christmas songs. We make our own cranberry sauce with frozen berries, muscovado sugar and orange juice, and leave it aside to cool. While prepping the veg, Libby searches for a knife. She briefly lifts and examines the re:Thread blade, returns it to the drawer and takes the carver instead. I open a bottle of prosecco and pour two flutes. While the chicken and potatoes roast in the oven, we build a fire, and wrap presents near the hearthrug.

I give her the gift I made for her. From the TARA research archive in Trinity I had downloaded all of Libby's published papers and her BA dissertation. I typeset them in an elegant Caslon font, added a contents and a title page, had them printed on Munken paper in the royal quarto size, and had the whole lot bound in dark-blue cloth by Duffy's bindery. I even had a slipcase made. Pressed in silver foil on the front it simply says, *Libby Miller – Volume I*.

She rubs her fingers over the cloth. She slides the book in and out and thumbs through the pages. Her eyes soften. Kneeling down, she leans over and kisses me.

We set the table with colourful napkins, an ice bucket for the prosecco, the best delph we can muster, a gravy boat and a bowl for the cranberry sauce, a lit candle, our two laden plates, and Jack Skellington standing in the middle.

Libby says she'll have to post a picture, and I say lightly, 'Do you really want to be that person?' and she says, 'Yes, I do.'

She snaps a few until she gets one she likes, adds whatever filters she deems necessary, and opens Twitter on her phone to share it with the world. I go and put the surplus roast potatoes in the oven to keep them warm.

Libby's voice comes to me over my shoulder. 'Sarah's name is trending.'

I look back at her. She's sitting at the table with the phone held in front of her face.

Slightly confused, I say, 'The name Sarah?'

'Your ex-girlfriend. Sarah Sibthorpe, right? Who else could it be?'

Rather than go to her, I slip out my own phone and open the app. Sarah Sibthorpe is the top trending topic in Dublin. I tap on her name and the first post is from @PollyPockets – Sarah's old friend Pauline.

With a picture of Sarah's face she has written: SOS ... FIND MY MISSING FRIEND.

A thread of tweets continues below. Each with a different photograph of Sarah, each with a fervent message from Polly. Sarah Sibthorpe hasn't been seen or heard from since 12th November when she apparently left on a round-the-world trip. A new post, She has recorded her journey every step of the way. Yet she has not returned any messages, and every hotel in which she apparently stayed has no record of her being there. The tweet below shows the original photograph I took of Sarah on Burrow beach, with the wide-brimmed summer hat and the fringe in her eyes. Polly wrote, Sarah's Instagram posts are being doctored. This is a photo she sent to me earlier this summer ... The next post is the picture of Sarah on the Sri Lankan beach. The exact same Sarah, but a different background. And this is what she posted to Instagram only a few days ago!! Something is terribly wrong. SOS! PLEASE FIND MY FRIEND!

I have read all that in an instant. So has Libby. She's still holding the phone, but now the back of her hand rests on the table. She seems scared to look at me.

I say, 'Jesus. Looks like Polly went off the deep end.'

Libby stands and begins walking towards the living room. I say her name. She ignores me. So I follow her. The living room is warm and festive, wrapped presents on the table, a guard in front of the fire. Libby has paused in the middle of the room with her back to me.

I say, 'What's wrong?'

My voice prompts her to move again. Her coat is draped on the sofa, but she has walked past it towards the hall door.

I say, 'Sarah's not missing. I spoke to her a few days ago.'

This causes her to stop. She turns slowly. Her drawn expression makes her face unfamiliar. Is she scared? Or embarrassed from overreacting? Her features settle as she focuses, and I can tell at once that she has seen through the lie.

Quietly, she says, 'I want to go home.'

'But your coat, Lib, your present. What's gotten into you?'

She moves towards the door again. The brass knob scrapes as she turns it, but the bolt doesn't catch, and she twists the knob about uselessly. There's a knack when it goes like this. If she keeps twisting now it will never work. She tries twice more, and then her arm drops to her side and her shoulders hunch. I approach, my footsteps loud on the floorboards, soft on the rug. She moves aside and takes a step back. I reach past her, gently turn the doorknob until I feel it hook on the latch. I twist it and open the door.

I'm in her way now, and she remains still, waiting for me to make room. She doesn't meet my eye. Behind her, firelight glints on the pressed foil of her volume. The wooden reindeer with the antler twigs appears primeval and uncanny. On the sofa, her coat is draped in such a way that the sleeves are outstretched, like someone who has fallen. I look at her face, so pretty in this golden light, and my heart breaks to see her so anxious.

I say to her, 'I've really enjoyed the time we spent together.'

This only seems to make her feel worse. Her lips press together, and she seems on the verge of tears.

I take a step backwards so she can get by. She hesitates, then edges towards the door.

As she passes, I take hold of her arm. 'Libby, wait.'

Instead of yanking her arm away she cringes and tilts her head towards her shoulder. Her expression is pained. Her eyes are closed. When she speaks she just sounds tired. 'Let me go, James.'

'I just want to explain.'

'Please.'

Her phone rings. She startles. The phone is held in the arm that I'm holding. We can both see the name Miranda flash upon the screen. Her thumb moves to dab the green button, and I shake her arm until she drops the phone, apologising as if I've done so by accident. It clatters to the floorboards, where it continues to jingle and buzz.

Libby punches me in the side of the head. She draws her arm back to swing again. I catch it this time. A sharp kick to my thigh. I twist her about and pinion both arms. She tries to wriggle free, she thrashes, she pulls me off-balance, but I'm able to hold tight. Her strength is ebbing already. She fills her lungs to scream, so I clamp my hand over her mouth. My thumb digs between her eye and the bridge of her nose. I can feel her breath run over my wrist. My fingers press into the soft flesh of her cheek.

'For fuck's sake, Libby. I'm not trying to hurt you.'

But I'm already hurting her. I can tell by the way she tries to move her head, the way her voice whimpers against my palm. Why won't she just stay still? I plead with her to stay still.

On the floor, the phone stops ringing, and we're both surprised by the silence. Libby becomes quiet, her energy spent. She's almost a dead weight, as if her legs have gone from under her. But I can feel her breath. I can feel her eye darting.

Everything I do or say will only make this worse. I should just let go. Let go and walk to the kitchen. Don't worry if she attacks me. Don't worry if she collapses. She'll get up again. Just leave her here. Close the door between us. Give her time to find her way out. Worry what to do then.

Should I say that's what I'm about to do, or just do it? Should I let go of her mouth first? What does it matter if she screams? She doesn't seem to have the strength anyway. Her face is lolling forward against my palm.

As I'm about to release my hold completely there's a knock on the front door. Libby's whole body tenses. She finds her feet. Her head jerks. Instinctively, I hold tighter.

She tries to yell, but all that comes out is a hoarse whisper. The knock sounds again, and I say, 'Just wait.'

Is it Miranda come to check on her after she wouldn't answer? Is it Shauna Shaw returned to arrest me at last?

Libby is sobbing now. Frustrated, I say, 'Libby, will you just wait?'

A gentle rapping sounds on the window. The blinds are drawn. I shift her a few feet to the right in case we're visible through a gap. Her feet almost drag along the floor. My clinch is too tight. I loosen it, but at once she begins to squirm again. The side of my hand pushes up against her nose. She aims a backwards kick at my shins. It connects, but it's too weak to hurt.

A voice outside calls, 'Jimmy?'

I stand still and listen. Even Libby seems to quieten.

'Jim, it's Lolo. Are you there?'

I'm aware of Libby's hair brushing against my chin, the smell of shampoo so familiar. I picture Lolo's face, and the sudden revulsion I have for myself is like a wave of sickness. I let go. I push Libby away. She stumbles and falls backwards on her elbows. She scrambles to get away. When she looks at me, all I can see is Sarah, the same frightened, bewildered eyes. I try to go to the sofa, but my legs are leaden and clumsy. Behind me, the living-room door creaks open.

My coat hangs from the back of the armchair, a scarf stuffed in its pocket. I'm about to go into the kitchen when I remember the tablet on the bookcase and its cache of Sarah pictures. I scoop it down. In the hall Libby is struggling with the latch. A clunk as it turns, a gust of cold air, and then high-pitched, frantic voices.

Stepping into the kitchen is like stepping into a dream. The table is perfect. A wisp of steam rises from the gravy boat. The candle shivers. The prosecco sparkles. I hurry to the counter and pull out the top drawer. Among the jumble is the key to the wicket gate in the garden. I'm about to close the drawer when I spot the re:Thread knife. I take that out as well. I don my coat, place the key and the knife in its pockets, and then open the back door.

A glance at the kitchen before I go outside. The door to the living room is ajar, but I hear nothing. All I see is a corner of the fireplace and Lolo's books in their colourful Christmas paper. I leave everything behind, and hurry down the garden path towards the narrow wooden gate.

CHAPTER 20

23 DECEMBER

I'm glad of the rain, of the cold, whistling wind. Nearly everyone on the street has a hood raised. Nearly every face is half-concealed by a scarf. It'll be dark soon, but the paths are busy for a Friday evening so close to Christmas. I turn corners at random and arrive at the main road of Drumcondra. Fagan's looks inviting in the half-light. Briefly I wonder if Arthur is inside. It feels wrong to walk where it's so busy, but it's necessary. First I join the queue of Christmas shoppers by the ATM at AIB. One by one, people fiddle with wallets and purses, they peer at the screen and tentatively push buttons, as if the whole concept is new to them. At one point I see a garda car approach the junction with Botanic Avenue. It stops at the lights, diagonally across from me. I keep my head down, my hands stuffed in my pockets. Did the face of the guard turn towards me? I hunch my shoulders and look at the blank wall of the bank. The lights turn green and the car steals by silently.

I know that using my card will leave a digital marker, but I need the cash. I withdraw the daily limit of €600 and fold a wad of fifties inside my jacket. There's a bus stop next to the bank. The number 16 is approaching, heading to the airport. The driver doesn't glance at me as I pay for a paper ticket. Upstairs, the deck is quarter full. I go to take a seat in the empty back row and fish out my phone. It's been on silent the whole time. Eight missed calls. Six new texts. I don't bother looking. Everyone on the bus faces away from me. I lean forward and place the phone on the floor. With the heel of my shoe I push it into a corner under the seat. Its no-slip case should prevent it from moving about. After Fagan's the first stop is St Patrick's College. I ring the bell, descend the stairs and exit by the middle doors.

The rain is falling as sleet. In the Tesco Metro I fill a shopping bag with granola bars and energy drinks, toilet paper and a bottle of whiskey. At the self-service checkout there's a camera above the screen, its monitor showing a live picture of me scanning my items. A shop worker has to approve the whiskey. The girl who comes over looks barely out of school. She says, 'Show me your face.'

'Why?'

'I have to check that you're over 21.'

For a moment I consider handing the bottle back, but then I turn from the camera and pull the scarf down. She peers at me and seems satisfied.

I need to find shelter for the night. When I was younger, some friends and I would traipse through the grounds of All Hallows College on our way home from school. Back then it was a seminary running short of seminarians, now it's an extension of the DCU campus. It has open parkland, a complex of ecclesiastical buildings, manicured lawns and winding paths. In a corner, sheltered by the high stone wall of Grace Park Road, there's a thick copse of ash trees, and hidden among them, an abandoned maintenance shed – a small concrete hut with a slate roof.

The gates of All Hallows are open. The buildings are used for student accommodation, but this close to Christmas they've emptied out. In the distance I spot a few people hurrying towards the chapel. A strain of choral music drifts from the opened doors. The stained-glass windows are illuminated. I keep close to the perimeter wall, leave the path and enter the trees, and pick my way through the undergrowth. The limbs are bare, but dense enough that soon I lose sight of the houses and the colourful windows of the church. I reach the back wall, about twelve feet high and made from rubble granite. A little to the right stands the hut, much smaller than I remember. The whitewashed concrete has become grey and worn. Slates are missing from the roof. There's no window, and the wooden door has a padlocked bolt.

I shake it a few times. The whole thing seems pretty flimsy. Here and there at the base of the wall are small granite blocks that have fallen out over time. I lift one and heft it. I press the block high against the slats of the door and sweep it down over the bolt and the lock, knocking both from the rotten wood. I wait again in case there's a reaction to the noise. Nothing but the hum of traffic on Grace Park Road.

Inside, the space is empty, except for dirt and leaves heaped in the corners, a stack of green firewood and a broken wooden chair. Cobwebs cling to every surface. Out of the rain and the wind it almost feels warm. I clear some space on the rough concrete floor and sit down, my back to the wall, my legs crossed in front of me, and I close my eyes so I don't have to look at the darkness.

Maybe half an hour passes, maybe more. My jacket is wet, though it's still warmer to sit with it on. I can feel the MediaPad tablet bulky in one pocket. I take it out and power it on, look around the derelict room again with the light from the screen. Only 46% battery remains, and I've no means of charging it. The device connects to the internet, a public hotspot maybe, or Wi-Fi from the student houses. I google *Sarah Sibthorpe* and get several results: her Instagram profile, Polly's recent Twitter thread, and already there's a newspaper headline from the *Examiner*: Concern grows for Dublin woman reported missing. I scroll through the article. Towards the bottom is a picture of me – the one that Paschal took in Libby's house, with my hair dishevelled and my face serious; the one that had the caption, *This is what a feminist looks like.*

Gardaí urgently wish to speak with James Lyster (pictured here), former boyfriend of the missing person.

Libby must have called them up. I can't say I blame her.

I check Twitter. Polly's original post has thousands of retweets, tens of thousands of views. Among the replies are self-proclaimed Photoshop experts pointing out discrepancies in more of Sarah's Instagram – pixelated borders, inconsistent shadow, unrealistic reflections. They're finding stray artefacts and blurring in images I didn't even touch.

My name is trending. The same photograph from the *Examiner* is doing the rounds. The irony is not lost, even for Twitter users, and the memes and comments have begun. I go to the DUGES profile.

Paschal must have deleted the original tweet. Out of curiosity, I sign in. I have thousands of notifications, either posts sent directly to me or those that have tagged my name, mostly mocking, some aggressive.

But there are only three new direct messages. I click on the small envelope icon to open DMs.

All three are from the same account. The profile pic: Emma Watson as Hermione Granger. The first message is just a 'sad face' emoji. The second says, *You okay?* And the third: *That place we talked about. Xmas. Noon* and a bull emoji.

I think about replying, but there's no need. Twitter notes the date and time a message has been received. If Emma checks again, she'll know that I've read it.

Down to 42% battery already. I'm about to close everything when I see an open webpage from earlier. The *Find my device* portal, still logged in to Tom Wickham's burner phone. The map has changed. Instead of Trinity it now shows Dorset Street, the phone icon pinned to the road close to the canal, and the *Last seen* heading says, *Just now.*

The page refreshes and the icon has moved. It's closer to Clonliffe Road. Another refresh and the icon is in Drumcondra, as if it's coming towards me. Whoever has it must be in a car or on a bus. The latter more likely, for the movement has slowed to a walking pace. The icon hovers over the bus stop. It crosses the street and enters one of the buildings. I zoom into the map. It's the Centra supermarket. The little green phone remains pinned there for quite a while. Are they dithering over what to buy? Are they stuck in a queue? It's only when the icon remains for more than ten minutes that I understand.

I put the screen to sleep and place it back in my pocket. My legs ache as I stand. The rain has let up a little but it continues to squall. I close the door to my shelter, wrap the scarf around my face and lift my hood.

No one pays me any heed on the short walk to Drumcondra. Next to the large windows of the Centra is a nondescript door with a few brass nameplates. I go inside. There's a small reception area at the bottom of a staircase unattended. I climb three flights in a narrow stairwell to the top-floor landing and a single white door. Without knocking, I push it open.

Arthur is sitting in his cramped office. Beige walls, grey filing cabinets, a Formica desk. There's a skylight in the slanting ceiling, inky black except for gleaming rivulets of water. He's working at a laptop, a Centra ham and cheese sandwich and a packet of Tayto opened beside him. He looks at me over the rim of his glasses, then leans back in his office chair, making it squeak.

He says, 'This time it might be above my pay grade, James.'

Without speaking, I put the tablet on his desk with the 'Find my device' page showing. He peers at it. In case he's unsure what it means, I tap the *Play sound* option. A loud chiming echoes in one of the desk drawers.

Arthur holds my eye. He opens the drawer and takes out Tom's phone, still with a charger attached. He places the phone next to the tablet. The chimes continue to ring, and he says, 'How do you stop it?'

I dab the screen again, and we regard each other in silence. I sit in the chair opposite him, lower my hood and unwrap my scarf. A little fan heater is blowing under the desk and I appreciate the chance to get dry. I point to the charger in Tom's phone and say, 'I wonder would that work on the tablet?'

Arthur leans forward to check. He transfers the connector from one to the other. It fits, and a little green light appears on the MediaPad.

'Nice one,' I say. 'Can I keep that?'

'Sure.'

He tidies away his sandwich and lifts the half-finished packet of crisps. He's about to dip his hand in, thinks better of it and leaves the bag aside.

'So,' I say. 'Did you have fun?'

He considers this and says, 'Not as much as I'd hoped.'

'You're the one who found the Afghan coat?'

He nods and says, 'I am.'

'So you were watching us. You knew Emma Harte was alive all this time?'

He nods again, and says, 'I did know that.'

'What were you doing around there?'

'I was in your gaff.'

When I frown he says, 'With the spare key, remember? Not the whole night, mind. You were in town so I had a quick recce. On the way back I saw you walking with some mystery girl. I said, I'll hang around and see what happens.'

'But why?'

'On account of what you did to Sarah.'

It happened five days before she was due to leave, a trip she was taking alone, but one we'd planned together. We had researched itineraries, booked flights, and ferries and hotels. We had honed her bucket list. I knew this was something she wanted to do herself. Her self-reliance was something I admired, and envied. Sometimes resented.

To Arthur I say, 'How did you know about that?'

His fingers are laced over his stomach. He says, 'Because you're not half as clever as you think.'

I had told Sarah that I didn't mind waiting for a year. I could book short trips to hook up with her, in Wellington, or Kyoto, or São Paulo. We were both happy. We were both looking ahead. Until the day she came to the flat.

'All those times we had a few pints, James. I mean the three of us. On a random weekday night or a Sunday afternoon. Didn't you think that she might consider me a friend as well?'

Sarah had been in a strange humour. Ill at ease, when usually she was so relaxed. I thought it was nerves with D-Day approaching. But then she sat me down. She held my hand. She said it was unfair to leave me on my own in Dublin when I should be free to find someone new. I told her that it was just for a year, but she shook her head. She didn't know if it would be a year, or two, or three. She wanted to see where the world took her, without anything tying her down back home.

'By the way, I knew she was going to break up with you,' says Arthur. 'She told me beforehand.'

When I tried to convince her again, she stopped me. There was something more. She said she no longer loved me. At least not in that way. She had almost waited to tell me until after she'd left. But I deserved to hear it from her directly.

Arthur reaches under the desk with his foot and flicks a switch to turn the heater off. He says, 'We were due to meet before she left. Just a coffee. For farewells and bon voyage. She was a no-show. Fair enough, these things happen. But she didn't reply to messages either. Messages weren't even getting through.'

I had tried to make my heart go cold. I had shrugged and told her it was fine. I wished her safe travels. But that was the thing about Sarah. She could always see through me, and her pity made me seethe. Still holding my hand, she stood and drew me up. She hugged me, and whispered in my ear that she hoped we could be friends. I put my face into her neck. I wrapped my arms around her.

'And then your silly little pictures began. She never told you, James. But she had changed her plans. The first few stages anyway. And do you know why? So that you wouldn't know where she was. So that you wouldn't be able to follow her. She had no intention of travelling through France or Italy, and yet there she was clutching her ticket for Charles de Gaulle. There was the view from her hostel overlooking Montmartre. I rang them. Not only was she not there, they said she had cancelled her booking weeks ago.'

I didn't want to let her go. When she began to disengage, I held her tighter. She said my name. I just wanted to keep her there, just for a few more moments, to give her time to reconsider. She was pushing gently at my arms.

'No one else knew her original plans,' Arthur says. 'No one else had access to her accounts. Only you had the know-how to fake the photographs.'

'Polly saw through those.'

He shifts in his chair and says, 'I may have planted the seed there. She spotted me in the street one day, asked if I'd heard from Sarah. We embarked on a fruitful correspondence. Each of us sharing our concerns. Polly was very suggestible. I think in the end she believed she'd uncovered it all by herself.'

The more Sarah pushed, the tighter my grip became. She said my name again, an edge of panic this time, and I realised then something had sundered between us. There was no going back. I can't remember how long I held her. A few seconds maybe. No more than ten. When I released my hold I shoved her away.

'Why didn't you just go to the police?'

Arthur raises an eyebrow. 'The guards? Imagine trying to convince a desk sergeant that this person who posted a picture is in fact missing. I needed more. I went to your place and found nothing. And then you gave me something better.'

I didn't push her that hard. Just enough to get her away. She stumbled backwards. Her heel caught a corner of the rug and she toppled with her hands held out behind her. She couldn't stop her head from cracking against the coffee table, with a sound like hurleys clashing.

I cover my eyes and squeeze the bridge of my nose. 'Did Shauna Shaw ring you that night?'

'She did. And she had fuck-all. The DNA was a dud. The security picture inconclusive.'

'What about the ACA guy?'

'Went down and spoke to him myself. That's what I mean about the guards. Useless.'

At first, Sarah pushed herself onto her elbows as if she wasn't hurt. But I remember the look she gave me. One of shock and fear and betrayal. Something bad happened then. Something ruptured inside her. Her eyes rolled backwards. A trickle of blood from a nostril ran between her lips. She slumped, with her head drooping to the side. After that, she didn't move again.

'I was trying to convince you to cooperate,' Arthur says. 'Or I was hoping the cops would just show up with warrants and forensic kits. But you always managed to wriggle free. Typical of the Lysters. Nothing ever seems to stick.'

I wait for him to look at me again. 'Are you going to call the police now?'

'No. Let's see how you get on by yourself. I'm going to Fagan's for a drink.'

Her eyes were glassy. No pulse. No breath. I probably could have explained it away. But it would have always hung over me. The doubts. The suspicions. And she was due to leave anyway. No one would wonder if she set off without fanfare. That's what she was like. Not on speaking terms with her father. Old friends had drifted away. All I had to do was maintain the charade.

'I'm sorry I can't join you.'

He nods, and for a moment it seems like he's sorry as well.

'Could you not have just asked me about it?' I say.

'I probably could have, yeah.'

'What was all this, Arthur? Some chip on the shoulder? Some slight from our childhoods?'

Shaking his head, he laughs and says, 'There you are. It's all about you again.'

A gust causes the skylight to rattle. Rain drums against the glass. Arthur looks up and says, 'I'm glad I'm not out in that.'

'It was an accident.'

His eyes come down to meet mine.

'Sarah, I mean. It was just an accident.'

He says, 'You've been accident-prone lately.'

Which is true enough. I stand and pluck the charger from the tablet. Arthur shifts to the side and takes the plug from a socket. I wind the wire carefully around the prongs, and I thank him.

I put my scarf back on. 'If you're talking to Shauna Shaw, tell her to go back to where they found Wickham. Tell her to widen the search, closer to the cemetery wall.'

I'd bought a large suitcase in expectation of long-haul trips. Sarah fitted into it easily enough. From jogging I knew of the waste ground behind Addison Park, had explored it once or twice. I waited until it was late, but not too late. I put on some good clothes, and dragged Sarah in the suitcase through the streets of Glasnevin. Not many people were about, but none paid the slightest bit of notice. I was just back from the airport, or on the way. All perfectly natural. I can remember the sound of the small plastic wheels on the pavement.

Arthur leans back in his chair again, both hands gripping the plastic armrests. He says, 'I'll tell them.'

Should I be angry? If he'd kept his foot off the scale I might have made it through. Though to be honest, it always seemed to be on the verge of unravelling. The way he's sitting, I can see the face of the boy I once knew. The brash junior freshman with the world at his feet. I look around at the poky office he's in now, and I just feel sorry for him.

I say, 'Goodbye, Arthur.' As I'm about to walk through the door, something occurs to me. 'By the way, did you tell Danni that Colin was having an affair?'

He purses his lips and shakes his head. 'I'd say he managed to fuck that one up all by himself.'

CHAPTER 21

The first evening in the shelter I sweep the floor as best I can. I ration myself to 10% of the tablet's battery life, but only to use as a nightlight. I leave it on its home screen with the brightness at minimum, the soft glow enough for me to see the corners of the hut. There are leaks in the ceiling, but the water collects against one wall only, and the rest of the floor is dry. I sit cross-legged and set out two granola bars, a Lucozade orange, and the Powers Gold Label. Every hour on the hour, I pour myself a capful, and sip slowly, concentrating on the taste, and the warm feeling in my throat. It's not the worst evening I've ever had.

The same cannot be said of the morning. I wake with a start in pitch blackness, a deep cold seeping through my entire body, and my head pounding. I pull the door ajar. No hint of light outside. The rain continues to fall. The keening wind is eerie and unsettling. I think of the chapel, and wonder briefly if the doors would remain unlocked all night. Surely not. Not these days. Besides, the risk of being seen would be too great. Nothing for it,

I hunker down into a ball with my coat pulled tight, and pray for sleep to come.

During the day, I sit in the doorway and watch raindrops trickle and slide among the branches. I'm building a tolerance to the whiskey; at least it seems to make my head feel better. Occasionally I jump when a car horn sounds from over the wall, or if there's a sudden shout or barked laugh. I imagine I'm a sentinel, posted to guard this small clearing, and I let the gentle patter of the drizzle soothe me.

In the late afternoon I hear footsteps. Twigs snap. There's a heavy rustling in the dead leaves. Out of a thicket a Labrador ambles into the clearing and pads over to where I'm sitting. He's wearing a dog harness with the lead unhooked. His golden coat is matted with the rain. He wags his tail when he sees me, tries to squeeze by to investigate the shelter but I stop him. I try to whoosh him away, but he remains sniffing about the hut.

A high-pitched whistle sounds nearby. The dog's head cocks but he doesn't leave. I hear footsteps approach once more. To get up now and close the door would cause a racket, so I reach for the Powers and offer it to the dog. He sniffs at the neck of the bottle, recoils and snuffles, and saunters off to find his master. I wait for the noise to die completely, and then take a swig.

As night falls, strains of choral music drift from outside. The Christmas Eve service in the chapel. I venture to the treeline. The stained-glass windows are beautiful in the darkness. I wish I could slip inside and sit in a pew, just rest and listen without anyone bothering me. I wander closer. 'O Holy Night' is being sung. To the side of the chapel is a large and elaborate Christmas manger. Mary and Joseph kneel next to an empty crib, surrounded by figurines of cows and sheep and a donkey. The ground is sprinkled with real straw, and to add some texture, someone has draped a throw blanket with arabesque patterns over the background. I look around. I see no one. *Fall on your knees* echoes in the night air. I reach in and take hold of the blanket, slide it out carefully, so as not to dislodge the figures. It's dusty, with stray pieces of straw clinging to its edges, but it's dry. I take it back to the shelter. When I wrap myself up I feel warm for the first time since leaving the flat, and I fall into a peaceful sleep.

Christmas morning dawns, foggy and still. The grey buildings of All Hallows are insubstantial. The tops of the trees are lost in the murk. I slosh about the remnants of the Powers and leave the bottle propped against the wall for someone else to find. Beneath my coat I keep the blanket wrapped around me. I place the broken bolt and padlock next to the door, hesitate, and then wedge a twenty-euro note in the door jamb. The paths of the campus are completely clear. I raise my hood and pass through the gates, out into the city.

Despite the early hour, most houses have their lights on. In sitting-room windows I see families in pyjamas and dressing gowns, kids running amok, grown-ups lounging on sofas. The early-morning walkers who pass me by are more cheerful than usual, offering good mornings and Christmas wishes. I'm wary as I get near Whiteside's house, as if a guard might be posted at the gates. They probably don't do that, especially on Christmas Day, but I remain on the other side of the road, keeping my eyes peeled for anyone who might be observing.

The house looks the same as always. A little dark and forlorn. I wonder if my flat has been left untouched, if the roast dinner sits congealing on the table. Who would clean it anyway? The cops? Colin? Whiteside's daughter? I approach the house, treading quietly over the gravel, and look down the basement steps. Two lines of blue-and-white police tape are crossed over the door. They say, 'Crime Scene – No Entry'.

In Griffith Avenue, I'm half-expecting Colin's house to be empty as well, so I'm surprised when I see both his and Danni's cars in the driveway. Mam's silver Accord is parked on the footpath outside. The gates are shut. All the blinds are pulled, but there are lights in the front room. Perhaps they banded together, put differences aside to support each other, and Mam in particular, until they can make sense of what has happened. I wish I could knock on the door, and tell them it was all a mistake. I wish I could change into clean clothes and play video games with the boys, talk about the books I got for Lolo, have a Christmas-morning beer, help Danni with the dinner, help Colin with the dishes, let Mam win at Trivial Pursuit. From my wallet I take my driver's licence. I place it on the gatepost and then turn and walk away.

The fog has begun to lift. I pass the Jewish cemetery in Ballybough, make my way through Fairview Park and on to Clontarf Strand. Across the bay, smoke rises from the factories on East Wall. Strange yellow clouds gather behind the Poolbeg chimney stacks. I stick to the coast road and continue on. The North Bull Wall is a mile long, a tide-breaker extending straight into the bay. For a while it skirts Bull Island and Dollymount Strand, but after that it's a narrow path surrounded by nothing but water.

Overhead, seagulls wheel and cry. The sea is pale, shimmering white on the horizon, mingling with the denser white of the clouds. At the end of the wall stands a statue of the Virgin Mary, raised some seventy feet in the air upon three stilt-like stone pillars. Perched on a green orb, she faces Dublin with her arms outstretched, an elaborate halo of stars around her head. The Star of the Sea.

Beneath the statue, two benches face each other. Emma Harte is sitting on the right. She's wearing dark glasses. Her hood is raised and her hands are stuffed in her pockets. I sit on the bench opposite. For a while, neither of us speaks. We look at the city and the curve of the bay, the low Wicklow hills and the vast expanse of water surrounding us.

Emma pulls her coat tighter. She turns to me and says, 'What shall we do now?'

ACKNOWLEDGEMENTS

My deepest thanks to John Givens and his writers' workshop for all the support while I was writing this book. I'm hugely grateful to all the other brilliant writers in the group, especially Caroline Madden, Serena Molloy, Maura O'Brien, Antain Mac Lochlainn, Ian Flitcroft, Juliana Adelman and Mary Barnecutt.

My wonderful agent Paul Feldstein has been tireless in promoting the book, and I'm so thrilled to have signed with him. Massive thanks as well to Ciara Doorley in Hachette Books Ireland who has been a joy to work with from the start. Thanks as well to everyone who has worked on the editing, design and promotion of the book, particularly Stephen Riordan, Joanna Smyth and Elaine Egan.

Last year I had the huge honour to be chosen for Dublin City Council's One Dublin One Book. Not only did I have the most amazing time, but the experience gave my writing a massive boost, and I'm so grateful to everyone in the Dublin UNESCO City of Literature office, particularly Jackie Lynam, Anne-Marie Kelly, Chris Nugent and Adrienne Delaney. It was also incredible to receive such great support from Dublin City and Wexford Libraries staff, and I wish to thank everyone who was involved in the campaign.

As ever, my biggest thanks go to my parents, siblings and extended family for their constant support, especially to Conor and Kasia who were there for feedback, chats and cups of ginger tea as the book finally got over the finishing line.

Lastly, my sincere thanks to you, the reader, for picking up *Emma, Disappeared*. I really hope you enjoyed it.